Nicholas Murray is a scruffy bearded fib scribbler, who can be found scurrying hither and thither around Edinburgh, Scotland.

The Stone Curse marks his debut into the published world, to the relief of his beleaguered family and friends, who up until now have had to deal with his unfiltered creative musings alone.

Now, at last, they share that burden with you...

For Lilly, Jack and Oscar

Nicholas Murray

The Stone Curse

AUSTIN MACAULEY PUBLISHERS™

LONDON • CAMBRIDGE • NEW YORK • SHARJAH

A CIP catalogue record for this title is available from the British Library.

ISBN 9781786299086 (Paperback)
ISBN 9781786299093 (Hardback)
ISBN 9781786299109 (E-Book)

www.austinmacauley.com

First Published (2017)
Austin Macauley Publishers™ Ltd.
25 Canada Square
Canary Wharf
London
E14 5LQ

Acknowledgements

This book would never have existed if not for the love and support of my family; Mum and Allan, Dad and Gail, this book wouldn't be here without you all cheering from the sidelines, and supporting every endeavour I've busied myself with over the years.

And Lara, who has had the tiresome task of listening to me go on and on about *The Stone Curse* since its inception, your honesty, patience and faith gave me the confidence to see this challenge through.

But more than anyone, I am indebted to the little folk in my family. Jack, Lilly, and Oscar; without your love, cheer, and collective craziness, I would never have been inspired to sit down and write this book in the first place.

Chapter One
A Kingly Affair

His Royal Highness, King Mallon, the Ruler of Vhirmaa and Lord of the Dales, was about to celebrate his fifty-second birthday. Of course, when it is said that *he* was about to celebrate his fifty-second birthday, it was actually his loyal subjects who were about to celebrate it. In fact, for such a grand affair (and there really was no affair grander than the good King's birthday celebrations) the King himself did little to nothing to add to the festivities. That's not to say he was begrudging of the whole do, quite the opposite in fact. King Mallon was known all over Vhirmaa as being a king of high spirits, and loved nothing more than swigging a few ales, singing a few songs, and having a rare old knees-up; indeed, especially when the knees-up in question endeavoured to stroke his ego, as any good birthday party could, would and should. But beyond gorging himself in his birthday indulgences, the organisation of entertainment, food and drink, parades and celebrations would all come from the people he led as King. As would the laughs and the cheers, as is the wont of any natural born Vhirmean.

Vhirmaa, as it was called in the Old Tongue, was a country that lived in long lasting peace. It had been centuries since the known wars, and even longer since the fabled ones. Much of its peace came from its position in the world, both figuratively and geographically. On a map, Vhirmaa was protected by impenetrable borders. To the north the lands turned frosty and mountainous, and beyond that lay the Frozen Seas. To the west there was the Redding Sea, a great ocean whose storms threatened perilous with the winds that blew from the southern continent. The east of Vhirmaa was protected by a long stretch of mountains known as the Dividing Ridge, the other side of which lay the burning desert of Adhera. And to the south there were the dense forest kingdoms of Thalan. In short, it was surrounded by terrains difficult to traverse, and as such, no other country had ever dared to attack Vhirmaa.

Even if they could, no country would want to. Vhirmaa was known all over the world as being a welcoming, kind and noble country. Its citizens were renowned for their cheerful dispositions, their generous nature, and their ability to throw a party. All these traits were traced back to the Kings and Queens who have sat on the Vhirmean throne. King Mallon was no exception, and saw these characteristics that defined his nation were upheld.

King Mallon was, to say the least, a well-loved king,

and his birthday was a highlight in everybody's year. They would pay tribute in any way they could: bringing gifts ranging from modest to lavish, baking cakes and pies the size of which would intimidate even the most gluttonous of men, singing songs and acting out plays, telling tales of the good King's heroic and noble deeds, praising his name and raising glasses to many more happy years of his ruling. To call the whole affair a birthday *party* would do it a gross disservice. The King's Birthday Festival was more fitting, and it was a festival one did not want to miss, and very few ever did. People from all over Vhirmaa, and even further afield, would travel to the capital city of Honeydale, by sea or by land, to pay tribute to the good King Mallon.

It was by sea in fact that young Oscar Grubb was making his way to Vhirmaa. Oscar was born and raised in one of the many fishing villages on the eastern coasts of the Western Isles, and had sailed across the Redding Sea for the first time to witness the splendour of the King's Birthday Festival. That being said, Oscar was no stranger to the ocean: growing up in a fishing village, after all, meant that even a chap at the youthful age of eleven-years-old was already an experienced sea-wary sailor. The voyage to Vhirmaa, however, was far longer and tougher than any fishing expedition he had ever been on, or so he had always been told, and thus had never been permitted to attend the Festival with his father or his two older cousins, Borris and Norris. That was until this year, and much to Oscar's disappointment, their voyage had been largely uneventful.

Oscar was such a boy who longed for adventure. His

face was always buried in books telling tales of heroic knights and swashbuckling pirates. He daydreamed of slaying dragons, battling dastardly foes and saving princesses from the clutches of doom. Forever tucked into his belt was a wooden sword he had received on his last birthday, and when he wasn't reading adventure stories, he was acting them out, and in the process, becoming quite the little swordsman.

In his village, there was an old swordmaster named Sebastian who claimed to have fought a dozen battles. Oscar never really believed him; however, he did enjoy his stories, even if they were works of fiction. Sebastian also took Oscar under his wing, and started teaching him how to wield a blade, much to the dismay of Oscar's parents.

These lessons were essential in Oscar's mind, though. As were the stories he read. They were more than just the whimsical fantasies of a young lad. In fact, Oscar was quite a serious little fellow, and all these things that could be mistaken for youthful enthusiasms were actually feeding a raw ambition he had growing inside him. Every book he devoured, every lesson he attended, were all building towards an inevitability in Oscar's mind. He just could not imagine himself growing into adulthood without having a few adventurous tales of his own to tell.

This heroic ambition had always been stifled, or at least attempted to be stifled, by his father, Iva D. Grubb, or Old Sea Grubb as he was affectionately known. Old Grubb tried to convince his son to live a simpler, humbler life as a fisherman. 'No good can come of chasing danger,' he would always say, 'Adventure and torture end with the same word; *"Your".*'

Old Sea Grubb was famous for his almost-but-not-quite-right sayings. 'You don't need a map to get unlost in life, just follow the lines of your hands. After all, map spelled backwards is "Palm",' was another good one. Quips that rode the line between sage-like and drivel, admittedly leaning more towards drivel. Old Grubb's heart was in the right place, even if his brain wasn't. Still, try as he might, he could never quell the flame for adventure that burned so brightly in Oscar.

Not even Borris and Norris, Oscar's cousins, could deter the young fellow from dreaming of such an adventurous life with their constant teasing and jeering of the characters in his books. None of this phased him, as even though his cousins were a good decade or more his senior, they were operating on a combined mental capacity equivalent to that of a catfish.

Speaking of catfish, the one bit of excitement that did occur on their trip across the ocean was the catching of their gift for the King: a giant leopard-skin catfish! Giant is no exaggeration either; the catfish was so big that it didn't even fit on their boat, and they had to tow it along on a specially built raft. It had been quite the battle catching it, the weight of it alone nearly causing the boat to capsize when reeling it in, and it took four attempts with the harpoon to spear the beast in the first place! Still, it was a pretty standard job for a catch as big as this, and so one afternoon's moderate excitement in almost a fortnight's sailing did little to satisfy Oscar. Thoughts of this fabled festival, however, kept him plenty giddy, pouring over maps and geography books, endeavouring to learn all he could about Honeydale.

Honeydale's proper name, as it was written on old maps, was Hylkoven, roughly translated from the Old Tongue as "City on a Hill", or "Hill Town." This was because, unsurprisingly, it sat upon a hill. The King's palace sat on the peak, and the rest of the city webbed down from there, consuming the hill in its entirety. The city's humble roots were in bee farming and honey production, and as such it was not long before Hylkoven became Honeydale, and it has been that way ever since.

He studied the history of Honeydale for almost the entire day, from waking till sleep. It was his first instinct when he awoke, and usually he was left in peace to do so, with the odd fishing lesson from his Father thrown in for good measure too. On this morning, though, he had been awoken especially early, with his Father calling him to breakfast.

He climbed out of his little straw bed, pulled on his clothes and exited the far too little cabin that had housed himself and his cousins for the past two weeks. He stepped out onto the deck, where his cousins were already sitting at a small round table, shivering in the morning sea fog. Old Grubb was frying eggs over by a small stove, but turned to beckon Oscar to his place at the table. Oscar sat down between Borris and Norris, both of whom were barely awake. For the sons of fishermen, they weren't very responsive to early mornings. They sat in silence until finally Old Grubb threw eggs, bacon and sausages onto their plates.

'Eat up,' he ordered, 'we'll be in Honeydale soon.

By the time we deliver this fish and get things sorted, we won't be eating again till dinner, so fill yourselves up now.'

He tossed the frying pan to one side, and had started eating before his bottom touched the stool he was to sit on. It was rather a chilly morning, Oscar thought to himself, far too chilly to be sitting outside. He thought better of mentioning anything though, as his father would sooner dip him in the ice cool sea than pander to any bellyaching about chilliness. He wondered, though, how Old Grubb wasn't feeling the effects of the cold himself. Granted, he was a big burly man, with a belly that was sure to keep his body warm and a long bushy moustache that acted as a natural balaclava, but the man wore a kilt every day of his life; how his knees didn't chatter like a ringing alarm clock perplexed young Oscar. But, again, he knew better than to say anything.

'Where's Ma?' Oscar asked.

'Giving your sister breakfast inside. It's far too nippy out here for a baby,' his father informed him.

It was unusual for Oscar's mother to accompany Old Sea Grubb and her nephews on these voyages. She had, of course, been to the festival but not since before Oscar was born. She didn't much care really; she was much happier staying at home with her children, but this was Oscar's first trip to Vhirmaa. She couldn't let her little boy cross the Redding Sea without her, and so it came to be that Tryca Grubb was on her way to King Mallon's Birthday Festival also.

It wasn't long until they had finished their breakfast. Oscar stood up and stretched, while his cousins had a belching competition and his father washed the dishes in the sea. They were soon joined by Oscar's mother and baby sister, Amber, who was barely a year and a half old.

'Iva,' Tryca groaned disappointedly. 'Don't wash the dishes in the ocean. They'll never lose the taste of salt.'

'Exactly! We can save money on seasoning!'

Old Grubb chuckled as his good lady wife rolled her eyes. She walked over to him and kissed him on the cheek.

'Not much longer now, m'dear,' Old Grubb continued. 'Boys! Get your things together, we'll be docking in Hylkoven soon.'

Oscar liked that his father called Honeydale by its proper name. Old Grubb was a proper sea hardy fisherman, right down to his bones. He learned all he knew about the world from old maps and sea charts, much like Oscar and his books. They didn't see eye to eye on many things; one was fiery while the other was cool, but in this regard, they were identical. Not that he'd ever admit it, but Old Grubb liked that they shared this quality.

Oscar did as instructed and arranged the things he was taking ashore: namely, a satchel that kept his rolled-up jacket, a randomly picked adventure book, and a half eaten apple. And, of course, his trusty wooden sword was tucked safely in his belt.

He left his cousins bickering over a certain woollen jumper they both claimed to be theirs, and returned to the deck. His mother was singing to little Amber. It was a song he was very familiar with, *The Calming Wave*, as

Tryca had sang it to him when he was a baby too. All wives of fishermen would sing *The Calming Wave* to their sons, as superstition dictated that this was what gifted them with sea faring legs and prevented them from ever feeling sea sick.

'Oscar!' Old Grubb called, peering over the ship's wheel. 'Come here a minute, would you?'

Oscar climbed the steps and joined his father at the rear of the ship. His mother's voice flowed with the waves, and there was a gentleness in the breeze. Old Grubb put his arm around his son.

'Oscar, m'boy, this is a special occasion. You're coming to the end of your longest voyage yet. You've crossed the Redding Sea and will experience things at the festival, the likes of which you've never imagined. You're also nearing the end of another long voyage: childhood, and…'

Old Grubb fell silent, shuffling his feet. He opened his mouth a few times, struggling to find his voice. At last, he cleared his throat. Here it comes, Oscar thought.

'A feather will blow in the direction of the wind, whimsical and free of cares. But a chicken has to decide its own path.'

Brilliant, Oscar thought. Another humdinger.

'What I'm trying to say, son,' he continued, 'is that it's time to start thinking about where you want to find yourself when you become a man. A man needs a trade, m'boy. To earn a living. So, to help you along…'

Old Grubb held out a long leather pouch, presenting it as if from nowhere. He handed it to Oscar. It was light and rather beautiful, embroidered with colourful fish.

This was his mother's handy work; he could tell straight away. He opened it and pulled out a short, stout rod and handle. He twisted the handle and the rod shot forward, extending with a snap. A reel kept a thin line tight against the rod. It was made of pale wood, and was clearly handmade by a master craftsman.

'A rod of my own design,' Old Grubb said without a trace of modesty. 'Quite a clever little gizmo too. If you pull this trigger here, the line is reeled in automatically. No whizzing and wheezing for you, m'boy. Effortless!'

'It's great, Pa, thank you,' Oscar said, with as much enthusiasm as he could muster, but his lack of interest was telling.

'I know you've never shown much interest in fishing, son. But it's an honest living, and good work too. The Grubbs have been fishermen for generations, and so when we get home, you'll begin your fishing apprenticeship.'

Oscar looked at the rod in his hands. He didn't consider even for a second arguing with his father. He had known that one day he would have to take the apprenticeship, and that that one day was very soon. For some reason, one of his father's old sayings popped into his head. "A fisherman doesn't cast his line in the ocean expecting to catch Leviathan. He does it to appease the Leviathan at home." Oscar always viewed this particular musing as the phrase of someone who had settled in life, taken the safer options. He translated it to mean, "I know being a fisherman isn't the most glamorous job in the world, but I've got a wife and kids at home that want feeding." His mother actually took umbrage with Old

Grubb after he delivered this snippet of wisdom, unhappy with being compared to a mythical sea serpent.

Oscar took umbrage with it for another reason. It was clear, from that one sentence, that he didn't have what it took to be a fisherman. He was different. If he cast his line in the ocean, he not only expected to catch Leviathan: he needed to.

Still, not wanting to hurt his father's feelings, and forcing himself to embrace the inevitable, he put the rod back in its pouch and attached it to his belt.

'Really Pa, I love it. Thank you.'

Old Grubb was about to add something when he was suddenly cut short by the sound of a bell. It was a deep, bellowing ring, although still quite faint and in the distance. Old Grubb took charge of the ship's wheel once more and ordered his nephews to lower the sail, as they would be coming into dock soon. Oscar's face lit up; finally, the big city! Old Grubb sighed as he noticed Oscar's sudden surge of genuine enthusiasm.

'You might want to head up front, Oscar!' he told him, 'I don't think you'll want to miss this.'

Oscar ran up to the other end of the deck and climbed up onto the top of the harpoon cannon that speared out the front of the ship. Slowly the fog started to disappear and silhouettes of something vast began to form behind the mist. Oscar could barely contain himself; it was like opening a parcel with no idea what to expect. Never before had his eyes seen anything even remotely resembling a city, never mind the capital city of Vhirmaa. The boat seemed to be moving so slowly, and the fog seemed to be never ending, until finally,

19

there it was.

The Port of Hylkoven.

Their little fishing boat, although big for a fishing boat, a ship essentially, seemed positively feeble beside the huge merchant ships, elegant private vessels of noble men and women, and the sheer vastness of the arks that brought thousands of people from all over the world to this very port on this day. Looking onto the harbour, Oscar could see a market was going on, selling all kinds of fishing and sailing goods, as well as strange and exotic fish, the likes of which Oscar had never seen. The port alone could be called a city all unto itself, so large it was.

It was admittedly dwarfed, however, by the enormity of the walls of Honeydale behind it. The towers loomed over the harbour with intimidation, yet offered a warm welcome, the crescent moon shape of the port seemingly beckoning all would be visitors in. The morning sun had now all but burned away the fog, and the warm magnolia walls of Hylkoven seemed to glow in a fashion befitting the name Honeydale.

Oscar had never seen anything like it, and no description in any book or song or bard's tale could ever do it justice. Old Grubb and Tryca shared a tearful smile; they couldn't have hoped for a better reaction. Even Borris and Norris, who had been to four previous Birthday Festivals, seemed a little awestruck, pointing and cooing at all the ships and their varying sizes.

Finally, Old Grubb docked their boat and paid the docking fee to the harbour master. Oscar helped his mother and sister alight the ship, while Borris and Norris carried on with round two of their belching match. Old Grubb returned before long, a posse of around a dozen men behind him.

'Boys!' he called down, 'It's time to unload this fish. Get up here and give us a hand.'

And so they did, although Oscar and his cousins' contributions to this task were pretty minimal, Oscar himself taking on a more supervisory role as the dozen or so men hauled the catfish up from the raft and onto a giant cart. The harbour master patted Old Grubb on the back.

'Quite an impressive catch there, Grubb,' he began, 'and quite an impressive crew as well, I see.'

'Only the best for His Majesty,' Old Grubb gloated.

'Well he does love his seafood, does our King.'

The harbour master and Old Grubb marvelled at the catfish for a moment longer, before finally climbing onto the front of the cart. Tryca, carrying Amber, followed, as did Oscar, who sat on his father's knee to make room for everyone. Borris and Norris were relegated to sitting on the back of the cart beside the catfish. Pulling the cart were two enormous bulls. These were no ordinary bulls, however; these were bulls raised on the grasses of Vhirmaa, the docile Grazers of the Dales, and were three times the size of any normal bull.

The cart trudged along for a time until it got to the harbour gate. The harbour master hopped off the cart, being quite a spry chap for an old sea beard, and said his goodbyes. Old Grubb nodded and beckoned the bulls to carry on. They turned away from the harbour and before long entered the labyrinth of Honeydale.

Oscar was in constant marvel at the things he saw. Decorations of all colours, shapes and sizes were being assembled and hung across the streets. Large banners draping over their heads formed multi-coloured tunnels, and the streets were paved with chalk drawings of the King and his kin, beautiful patterns that guided you to heart of the city, the Royal Square.

As their cart went along this path, turning up and down narrow little streets that seemed to offer some new sight for Oscar to behold, they passed pubs and inns, all full of people singing favoured songs of their King. One inn even had a makeshift stage outside, crafted out of some wine crates, where a play detailing one of the King's many heroic acts was being performed by a local drama club, much to the cheers of the ale soaked audience.

After what seemed to Oscar far too short a time, the cart stopped outside one of these very inns.

'Right, this is where you get off,' Old Grubb informed his wife and son, who looked back at him wearing an expression of such devastation. 'Now don't worry, there'll be plenty of time for celebrating later. The festival goes on for days, you know.'

'But...' Oscar began.

'When I get back from delivering this fish to the Palace cook, I promise we will go out and experience all there is to be experienced, okay? You're not going to miss a thing.'

'Can't I come to the palace too? I want to see the palace!'

'And you will Oscar, I promise you, but if we don't

get this room by ten o'clock, Mrs Gallow will give it away.'

'Mrs Gallow?'

'Yes, she runs this inn. I've stayed in the same room every year ever since the first time I came here with your mother.'

'And she's got a temper for things like being late,' Tryca added with a cruel grin.

'She's got a temper for pretty much everything, m'love.' Old Grubb shuddered.

Oscar wasn't following their exchange; instead he hopped off the cart and pouted on the street.

'We'll be back before you know it!' Old Grubb called to his family as the cart pulled away. Borris and Norris, still sitting on the back of the cart, started making all manners of unsightly faces at Oscar before the cart stopped suddenly and both their heads clattered together, causing them to fall in a heap by the mouth of the catfish. Old Grubb turned to Oscar and winked. Oscar smiled back at his father, pulled his satchel over his shoulder, and followed his mother into the inn, affectionately called "Mrs Gallow's Inn".

Oscar stood in what he assumed was the foyer of the inn, although it was so busy that he couldn't tell exactly where in the inn he was. It could've been the kitchen for all he knew. People of all shapes and sizes were bickering and laughing, or haggling and bartering for rooms. One chap, whose bright coloured clothing and long nose made him look like a parrot, had in fact paid for a room and was now offering the key to the highest bidder. He'd even climbed up on some other fellows' suitcase, waving the key about in a teasing fashion. Suddenly the room was in an uproar; that is to say, an even bigger uproar than it already was, with people emptying their coin purses and waving jewellery around in hope of adequate payment. The parrot chap was in his element, until one voice boomed over everyone else's, silencing the rabble almost instantly.

'Oi!' the voice screeched out, a woman's voice Oscar thought. 'There'll be no auctioning of rooms going on here! Every bloomin' year you're at it. I've had enough!'

Oscar looked around to see where the voice was coming from, but couldn't find it's quite terrifying source.

'Alvin!' it cried out again. 'Alvin! Get this toe-rag out of here!'

'Right-oh,' a calmer voice replied, followed by thudding footsteps coming from the back of the room. From out of the crowd, a tall, broad, bearded man emerged, who reached across with his huge arm (his only arm, I might add, his right one missing altogether), picked up the would-be auctioneer and tossed him over Oscar's head, out the door and onto the street.

Oscar stared up at who he assumed was Alvin. Such strength for one man, with one arm no less. Yet, for as intimidating a presence as he was, there was something quite relaxed and docile about his nature. Sure, he had just picked up and thrown a man out the door as though he weighed nothing at all, but he didn't seem angry or even remotely annoyed whilst doing it. No, those emotions seemed to be reserved for this elusive woman with the screeching voice, who was still hollering and screaming at the anxious crowd.

Alvin looked down at Oscar and then to Tryca and Amber. Suddenly, a smile almost as broad as his shoulders crossed his face.

'Tryca!' he chirped. 'You made it! Old Grubb said you might be coming this year, and here you are! This must be little Amber!'

He tapped Amber on the head with one of his giant fingers and smooshed her cheeks together affectionately. At last, his gaze fell back to Oscar, who suddenly felt quite nervous at the prospect of being the next guest to be shown the door.

'Hello young sir,' said Alvin, still beaming his welcoming smile.

'H-h-hello, my name is Oscar.'

'Oh, I've heard a ton about you, Young Grubb. Your father has been itching to get you out here for years. Enjoy your trip across the Redding Sea then?'

'I did, thank you!'

'Alvin!' The screeching voice returned with a vengeance. 'Who are you blathering to?'

'Sweetheart!' Alvin bellowed. 'Look who I've found! It's the Grubbs!'

Suddenly the crowd began to part once again, this time accompanied with groans and exclamations of pain as they were knocked out of the way. At last, a tiny woman emerged and peered up over her glasses at her new guests.

'Old Grubb not here yet? I need to give him a scolding for almost being late!'

'Now, now dearest,' Alvin reasoned. 'Almost being late isn't actually being late.'

'Don't argue with me, Alvin! It's your softness that's made him tardy in the first place.'

'He's a grown man, love. I doubt I've had any influence on him.'

'Don't get brave just because there are all these people around!'

'Nice to see you again, Joselin,' Tryca politely interjected.

'Oh, Tryca, you too,' the tiny tyrant replied, calming suddenly. 'And look at baby Amber, she's as cute as a button. And this must be Oscar. Oh, such a strapping young lad.'

Oscar shuffled embarrassingly on his feet. Alvin chuckled and ruffled his hair.

'Right, well, let's not leave you standing in the lobby,' he said. 'I'll show you to your room.'

'*I'll* show them,' Joselin cut in, her cold tone returning. 'I need you to stand watch here and make sure that colourful idiot doesn't come back in and start his old tricks.'

'Whatever you say, dearest.'

Joselin started fighting her way through the crowd once more, Oscar following cautiously. He couldn't believe just how small this Mrs Gallow was. She was shorter than him, and he was just a child!

After much clambering over luggage and under people's legs, they climbed up the stairs and into a much quieter hallway. Joselin led Oscar and his mother to a door and opened it for them. They entered a quaint little room with three small beds and one large. There was a little balcony looking out onto the street, which Oscar needed little encouragement to go out on to. Joselin offered her good hostess musings, pointing things out like the bathroom and sweets in a jar in a cupboard under there and over where that is and next to that thing and... Oscar had long since stopped listening, leaving Mrs Gallow and his mother to chatter about the ins and outs of the inn. He fiddled with the lock on the glass doors and stepped out onto the balcony. Joselin and Tryca made their goodbyes, and he shouted through one of his own, out of forced politeness.

Oscar watched the busy street below him, with so many people doing so many things. He couldn't wait to get out and experience it all for himself. There was a stall he had noticed on a street not far from the inn that involved some sort of memory game, maybe he could win a prize? And there was a food merchant he saw who had bowls full of exotic spices from the far reaches of the globe, maybe he could try some? Or there was a bard in a pub he heard proclaiming he could sing any song requested, maybe he'd know a song or two about a knight in some heroic battle?

Oscar's head swelled with possibilities. There was no telling what adventures he'd get into at this festival: he'd never been out of his home town before so what exactly the possibilities were, he had no idea. Vexed that he had all this energy but had to wait for who knows how long on his father returning, he sat on the balcony for the rest of the morning, watching the entertainment the street had to offer.

Chapter Two

Of Ancient Times and Tomes

Far from the balcony Oscar was occupying, but not too far from where Old Grubb was delivering the giant catfish, there was a secret library, hidden away within the walls of Hylkoven Palace. Not to be confused with the Royal Library, which was open to guests of His Royal Highness and scholars the world over. No, this was a library known only to a select few. It was the holder of many forgotten books, secret books and books even the most well versed enthusiast wouldn't know ever existed. One such book was a relic of days long forgotten, of an ancient age rarely spoken of anymore. It was a book from the Time of Mages.

Very little was known from that time. In fact, no one actually knew exactly when that *time* was. What little that was known, however, was that the world was once divided into three ruling nations, each nation ruled by one of three magical powers. One nation was ruled by the Dawn Mages, who used healing and protective magic. Another was ruled by the Dusk Mages, who drew upon elemental magic, often with destructive properties. And finally, there were the Twilight Mages, who favoured both healing and destructive magic, serving often as mediators to the nations of more opposing ideologies.

Peace lasted thousands of years, the three nations utilizing one another's unique styles of magic to build a prosperous world for everyone to live in. That was until the Magus Wars began.

No one knew exactly how they started, or who instigated the conflict, but the three great nations were thrown into the depths of war and all but destroyed every living thing on the planet. What mortal men remained rallied together and outlawed magic outright, and the even fewer mages that were left went into hiding, turning their backs on the powers that nearly wiped the world from existence. As the following centuries passed, this dark time was soon forgotten and magic was only ever referenced again as being an extinct phenomenon.

This secret book in this most secret of libraries was one of the last known relics of that forgotten age, proof that magic and the Time of Mages were more than just myth. Again, it was a very privileged few who knew of the book. King Mallon knew of it, as did his father, and all before him who sat upon the throne as ruler. At his discretion, he informed only his most trusted and chiefest of advisers and scholars of the tome's existence. A privileged few indeed, but there was one other who knew. One who wasn't meant to know.

That *one* was a young girl named Lilly Rachert, who was currently racing through the streets of Honeydale, eyes darting between the street name signs and a small scrap of paper in her hand. On the paper was a scribbled map with rushed details on Lilly's destination. What was her destination? A sewer, of all things. A sewer that ran under the entire city, including the palace. More importantly, however, it ran directly beneath the secret library.

Why would a little girl of almost ten years old, whose wavy blond hair and butter-wouldn't-melt smile would have you believe she cared more for dolls, ponies, kittens and all things fluffy and pink, be interested in ancient books in hidden libraries? Furthermore, why would she want to trudge through a damp, smelly and altogether unpleasant sewer to get there? Lilly had her reasons, and to back those up she had a steely determination, unwavering and unrelenting.

That isn't to say that Lilly, although more than eager to wade through sewer muck to sneak into a dusty old room, was a stranger to the fluffy, pink, cutesy indulgences that other little girls love so dearly. Indeed, that steely determination of Lilly's could easily be distracted, if only for a moment, by a big-eyed, button-nosed kitten, or an elegantly crafted doll of a princess, clad in a hand sewn dress of pink, gold and glitter.

For now, though, Lilly was entirely focused on the task at hand: sneaking into the palace. For one reason or another, Lilly had always been fascinated by magic. Despite most children being taught that magic had long been extinct, and that it was possibly never anything more than myth, Lilly's ideas moved in the opposite direction.

Her obsession began with her grandfather, Dysan. He was an unusual old hermit, who had raised Lilly since she was a baby in a shack in the woods south of Vhirmaa. They never sought the influence of the outside world, and Lilly's learned grandfather was wise enough, and experienced enough, to teach her the ways of things and how the world works. Every now and then, though, he would tell her strange stories, describe a world completely alien to her. A world of magic and mages. He presented them as fiction, as bedtime stories to fill her head with wonder. But Lilly wasn't convinced that they were. Especially when his stories invaded her dreams.

One dream, in fact. A recurring dream of a room she had never been in, with a woman she did not know, and a bright light enveloping all. Vague images that would come to her in the night, with increasing regularity.

When asked, Lilly's grandfather dismissed these dreams with a grunt or a sigh, a gesture befitting his usual mysterious manner. This only confirmed it for Lilly: Dysan's stories *were* real. The truth surrounding the mages was out there somewhere, and Lilly would stop at nothing to unearth it.

And so it came to be that Lilly, on the birthday of His Royal Highness, King Mallon, was doing all but partaking in the festivities, and at last was standing in a dark alleyway on one of the few quiet avenues in the city. She scoured the alley, scrutinising every inch of the pavement. At last she found it: a small vent, barely the size of Lilly herself, exposing nothing but darkness. The time had come. She took a deep breath and calmed herself as she prepared to pass the point of no return.

It was no coincidence that Lilly's intended royal break-in happened on the day of the Good King's birthday celebrations. Indeed, any burglar or ne'er-do-well who fancied a bit of high treason knew the King's birthday would grant them a palace filled with precious little guards and plenty of unwatched treasures. It was common knowledge that the King, along with most other people in the city, gathered in the Royal Square for the Grande Show, just as everyone knew how loved the King was and no one would dream of stealing from him. Not that Lilly was planning on stealing anything. She just wanted to read a book; she had no intention of actually taking it. Well, no strong intentions anyway. Should the need arise, however, she may feel compelled to borrow it for a time. This is what she had told herself whilst planning this scheme.

The days of planning had been and gone, though, and Lilly now stood at the entrance to the labyrinth that was the city sewer. The entrance (one of several that is) was hidden away down a narrow staircase in this secluded alley. This gave Lilly ample time to prepare before entering. Opening her backpack, she pulled out a wooden clothes peg. She placed the peg on her nose and pulled her leather boots as far up her legs as she could. Taking a deep breath and closing her eyes for a moment, she considered the insanity of what she was about to do. The consequences of her actions would result in punishments unimaginable in their severity, and no amount of puppy-dog-eyes, cute smiles or any other tried and true charms in every little girl's repertoire, could bail her out of them. Not one to negotiate with doubt, Lilly entered the sewer before reason had a chance to change her mind.

It wasn't long before the smell, which was so pungent that it was like walking into a wall of odour, very nearly made poor Lilly turn back. It had rendered the clothes peg on her nose virtually useless, but if the smell was so awful with it on, she dreaded to think what it would be like with it off. After fighting the urge to vomit, she composed herself and trudged on into the bowels of the sewer. Lilly thought this at the time, and the pun was not lost on her, nor was it appreciated. A foul mood in a foul place makes it difficult for word play to receive their desired response.

That being said, comparatively, the rest of the sewer wasn't nearly as horrid as the smell. On the contrary, the dim lighting from the candles that seemed to glow eternally in the pale blue, stoned tunnels that webbed their way under the city gave it an otherworldly, almost tranquil aesthetic. It was so quiet and detached from the hustle and bustle of the streets above, one could imagine escaping down into this quiet haven for some peace and calm. Of course, should one do that, then that one should be one without a nose, or at least lacking the capacity to smell.

Lilly carefully trod across the cracked, paved walkways, taking left and right turns, seemingly at random. Faintly, her mumbled trail of mental breadcrumbs echoed throughout the tunnels. She appeared to have some vague knowledge of her route, and indeed this operation was not being executed on a whim. Lilly had been plotting this for months, and was now relying on her memory to keep her right. And right it kept her, as it wasn't too long before she was standing before a locked gate, sealing a dark staircase ascending into the palace. The gates bars were thin, almost fragile looking. Lilly ran her fingers along the centre bar. As delicate as they seemed, she could sense an undeniable force within them, a strength that would repel any attempt to bend or break them. After a moment, her finger found its target: a small groove, no bigger than her thumbnail, halfway down the centre. Lilly pulled her bag from her shoulders and rummaged around inside. Eventually, she unearthed a small leather pouch and carefully poured its contents into her hand. From her clasped grip, an auburn light shone through her fingers. Slowly, she brought her hand closer to the groove in the gate. The bars started to tremble and ring, performing a resisting melody. Suddenly, without her say-so, the light shot up from Lilly's hand and dimmed to a gentler glow, revealing its source to be a small unusual gem. It glided from Lilly's palm to the gate and slotted itself into the groove on the bar. The ringing from the other bars increased in volume and vigour, before finally shattering and turning to specks of silver dust on the floor. The gem too dissolved into nothingness, its glow quickly fading with it. Lilly took only a second to refasten her backpack and throw it on once more, before ascending the spiralling staircase up and into the shadows.

The stairs seemed to go on for an eternity. Lilly's poor little legs were aching something awful by the time she reached the top of them, and found themselves exhausted at the foot of an enormous door. A faded brass handle beckoned Lilly to venture to the other side. It was ice cold to the touch and wore a thick layer of dust; it had been a long time since anyone had been on this side of this particular door. After turning the handle, Lilly took a step back as it began to shudder. From somewhere behind the walls, old wheels were turning, yawning off the years of lying dormant. The door slowly slid open, leaving a cloud of dust in its wake. Lilly coughed and waved her hand as she stepped through the dusty fog. She could hardly believe it. She had finally reached her destination, her goal, her quest's end.

Lilly was standing in the palace's Secret Library.

Initially, Lilly was surprised at how small it was. In her daydreams, she had envisioned a massive hall, filled with bookcases fifty-feet high, stacked with more books than any one person could ever read in an entire lifetime. Instead, she found that the room was quite modest in size, and save for a few tatty old shelves, all the books were stacked seemingly at random on the floor. Everything about the room was uneven, from the crooked piles of texts to the off-centre paintings on the walls. Dust had descended upon the library like a white sheet, and had gone undisturbed for what seemed like centuries.

Still, it was *the* Secret Library, and Lilly was standing right in the middle of it. She allowed herself only a few more minutes to marvel at the room, and also at herself - she was really quite proud - before rummaging through every book that her hand fell upon. Each book was a priceless volume of forgotten tales, filled from cover to cover with untold secrets and answers to age old mysteries. None of this interested Lilly, at least not at this moment. However, she couldn't ignore all these books entirely. After all, she didn't know what this ancient book on the Time of Mages looked like. She had to at least open the cover of every book, scrutinising the titles. The enormity of this task was hanging over Lilly's well aware head.

She was thankful then that it wasn't too long before her eyes fell upon an unusual wooden chest, tucked behind a small cabinet that had greyed with age. She dusted off the lid of the chest and admired the elaborate jewel encrusted emblem that was miraculously dust free. It was shaped like a peacock's feather and made of emeralds, rubies and sapphires. She gently brushed the emblem with the tips of her fingers before springing the lock and opening the lid.

Within, she found it was rather bare apart from an old, thick, leather bound book, which bore a collage of green, blue and yellow stones in the shape of teardrops on the cover. The colours of the stones resembled the emblem on the chest, but divided into three shards. Lilly carefully lifted it out of the chest and sat down on the floor. Placing the book on her lap, her hands trembled as they parted the cover from the pages it protected, the top few of which seemed to dance and wave at Lilly, inviting her to indulge in the secrets they contained.

And indulge Lilly did. Or she attempted to, at least.

From the first few words it was clear that this book was written in a language she had never seen or heard before. Each page was more vexing to her than the last, but that didn't stop her eyes examining every detail they could as her thumbs quickly rummaged from chapter to chapter. She did recognise the odd symbol here and there, markings that felt somehow familiar. Decoding this ancient language would be a lengthy task, however, and time was fast pressing on. Already she could hear the cheers from the streets outside, signalling the King's departure from the palace to make his way to the Royal Square for the Grande Show. She needed to uncover the secrets of this book, otherwise all her planning and indeed breaking into the palace, which was no small feat at all, would have been for nothing. So, Lilly adjusted her position on the floor, and continued to scour this most secret of books, in this most secret of libraries, for the most secret of secrets.

Chapter Three
The Grande Show

Oscar had been wandering around experiencing the delights of the festival for a few hours by the time the sun started to set over the looming towers of Honeydale. After sitting on the balcony at the inn for what seemed like an age, his father and cousins had returned to collect him and his mother and sister, and they promptly left to take in what festivities the streets had to offer before taking their places in the Royal Square for the Grande Show.

'What is the Grande Show, exactly?' Oscar had asked Old Grubb, in between pestering him for any and all souvenirs his young, curious eyes caught a glimpse of.

'The Grande Show,' Old Grubb began to explain, drawing out the word 'Grande' to make it sound just that, 'is the main feature of the festival, the centrepiece of the whole affair.'

'Yes, but what exactly *is* it?' Oscar queried further, unsatisfied with his father's vague response.

'Well, last year, The Grande Show was a magnificent production of the King's most favourite play, and the year before that it was an opera performed by the finest musicians and artists in all of Vhirmaa.'

'Wow...' Oscar pondered this for a moment. The only "production" he had ever seen was the less than spectacular puppet show on the pier of his village, with tatty old rotten puppets and an even tattier but not so rotten puppeteer.

'And this year,' Old Grubb continued, 'I hear that we are to be treated to a magic show by the Great Maju!'

'But... but magic doesn't exist anymore, does it? I thought all the mages were extinct?' Oscar wore an expression of utter confusion.

'They are Oscar,' his father warily began to explain: this had been his umpteenth explanation of a random subject in under an hour, and Oscar's ever-hungry curiosity could be rather tiresome, 'but mages and magicians are completely different things. Mages and magic *are* extinct, but illusion and enchantment are as present as they ever were.'

Oscar began to get worried. The lyrical way in which his father was talking suggested he was about to conjure up yet another of his famous sayings.

'A writer knows they aren't creating a real, physical world with their words, but it is making their worlds believable to the reader that inspires them to put pen to paper every day.'

Not his worst effort, to be fair, but Oscar was

puzzled as to what its relevance was.

'You know that magic doesn't exist,' Tryca interjected, always good at interpreting her husband, 'but making you believe it does, if only for a moment, is the role of the magician.'

Oscar thought he understood, but his good-intentioned-but-found-wanting father often left him doubting with all his twisty-turny riddle speak. Still, he had grasped the fundamentals, thanks to his more reasoned mother. Magic had long been extinct, but magicians could use tricks to make you think it was real once again. In one short second, Oscar had made it clearer in his mind than his father ever could. If only Old Grubb had the capacity to explain things as simply as that, Oscar thought.

As they continued to walk through the bustling streets, Old Grubb told his nephews and Oscar stories of this Great Maju. He was the finest magician in the entire world, and his feats of conjuring were admired from town to town and city to city. King Mallon was a great admirer of tricks and illusions, and had long sought to have the Great Maju as the main feature in the Grande Show. It was difficult for Old Grubb to describe the Great Maju's act to Oscar, as he was famous for never doing the same performance twice, so what tricks he would do were impossible to anticipate. All Old Grubb could say was 'Expect the unexpected,' which seemed to impress both Borris and Norris, but not his son, who had always regarded that phrase as little more than a fancy way of saying 'I don't know.'

What Old Grubb did know was that they were

running late, and that if they didn't get to the Royal Square soon, they would lose their seats.

'Have you got our tickets?' Oscar asked his father, for the seventh time since leaving the inn.

'No, Mr and Mrs Gallow have them. Every year I sit in the same seats with Mr and Mrs Gallow, and every year they arrange the tickets for me. But Mrs Gallow is an impatient woman, so if we don't hurry she'll sell them.'

Oscar was beginning to notice a pattern. It seemed his father relied quite heavily on Mr and Mrs Gallow to get anything done over here, which was odd for Oscar, to see the usually "in charge" Old Sea Grubb rely on one of the oddest couples he had ever met. A country fish out of water, perhaps.

'The first time I came here,' Old Grubb continued, 'I was so overwhelmed by the size of Honeydale, I fainted smack bang in the middle of the doll market on Old Trinket Ally, round the corner from Mr and Mrs Gallow's Inn. Your mother was so worried, she latched onto the first man she could find who she thought would be strong enough to lift me.'

'Mr Gallow carried your father back to their inn,' added Tryca. 'Mrs Gallow was kind enough to put us up for the rest of our visit to the city, free of charge, on the condition that we always stayed at their inn whenever we returned to the city. They're kind people, even if Mrs Gallow has a bit of a bark sometimes. Both of them are very kind.'

Old Grubb gave Tryca a nostalgic smile, as Oscar studied the image in his head of his rather enormous father being carried by an even more enormous Alvin Gallow. Borris and Norris, meanwhile, tried to imagine their uncle being so out of control and muddled that he would faint. In the middle of a doll market of all places! It seemed the burly Old Sea Grubb had changed over the years, yet he would never admit as much.

After a short while musing on their guardian's past life, Oscar and his cousins found themselves being ushered by, well, ushers of sorts: snooty men in large, gold buttoned jackets and plump, feathery matching caps. 'This way, that way, tickets please!' they ordered, thrusting people in all directions, supposedly guiding them to their seats. In actuality, they were doing little more than confusing the situation further.

But wait! thought Oscar. *Seats? What seats?!* Indeed, they were far from the Royal Square, and still just standing in a shabby old street. This was the norm, a regular occurrence every year since the Royal Birthday Celebrations began. So many people would turn up for the Grande Show that the queues would start from countless streets away, winding and webbing their way through the city. Frankly, it was chaos, and despite the better efforts of the ushers over the years to bring some sort of organisation and strategy to this ordeal, the whole shambolic affair tested their patience time and time again, until now they were so jaded that their aim wasn't to get you to a seat per se, but to get you out of their faces. A justified attitude to have perhaps for such a thankless job, but their snooty attitudes did not wash well with many a ticket holder. Not least of all, Mrs Joselin Gallow.

'Here's your ruddy tickets!' Mrs Gallow squawked, waving them in a young usher's face and taking the Grubb's by surprise.

'Mrs Gallow!' Old Grubb bellowed, 'Thank goodness we found you in time!'

'I think you'll find we found you,' Mrs Gallow replied in a matter-of-fact tone, which matched the matter-of-fact expression her face was wearing as she snatched the tickets back from the usher. She began leading the way through the maddening crowd, whilst giving Old Grubb a thorough dressing down.

'Honestly Iva, for as long as you've been coming to Honeydale now, you still bumble about like a big galoot!'

Borris and Norris sniggered at their uncle being chastised by such an impish little woman.

'And speaking of galoots,' she continued. 'Hello boys, how are you?'

'Fine, thank you Mrs Gallow,' the boys politely replied in unison. Mrs Gallow rolled her eyes and leaned in to Oscar's ear.

'Are you sure you're related to these halfwits?'

'He takes after his mother's side,' Tryca quipped, causing the tiny tyrant to cackle.

'Joselin!' Mr Gallow barked from amidst the crowd, rather bravely Oscar thought, until he fell into the glare of his good lady wife.

'I mean, dearest Joselin,' he whimpered on, 'we're almost there.'

Pushing through the last of the flock, they all found themselves standing on the western edge of the Royal

43

Square, which was like everything else in Honeydale: gigantic beyond belief. There was no time for being awestruck, however, as Oscar quickly found himself being yanked up onto his father's shoulders. Old Grubb began to ascend a long, narrow staircase, so steep that it was essentially a ladder. It led up to the back row of the western block of seats, and bled people into the rows and aisles, like a tunnel opening up into an ant colony.

On arriving at the top, Oscar could finally see the Royal Square in its entirety. Vast blocks of seats bordered the square, where thousands of people hurried and scurried about in an attempt to get the best view. The northern block stopped short compared to the others to make room for the balcony that hung above it, reaching out from an old cathedral. This was the Royal Box, where the King, his wife and son, and established guests would sit for the Grande Show. In the middle of the Square was a large, raised, circular stage, and surrounding that was the orchestra, who tinkered and tuned their instruments in preparation.

'Here we are!' Mrs Gallow announced, planting herself down in a chair, but not before staring down someone who had made the honest mistake of arriving before her and taken her seat.

Tryca fussed over Oscar, making sure he had enough snacks and juice and could see the stage okay. Borris and Norris were stuffing sweets up their nostrils, much to the embarrassment of Old Grubb, who did his best to calm them.

Eventually though, before the boredom of sitting and waiting could get its hooks into everyone, a loud, sharp

44

fanfare was let loose from a band of trumpeters standing at the front of the Royal Box, their melody prancing around the arena, signalling the King's arrival. All in attendance, including Oscar, who was just mimicking his father's actions, stood to attention and faced the Royal Box. From a wide door at the balcony's rear, King Mallon walked towards his almost throne-like chair at the front of the balcony, waving and smiling at the thousands who had come to celebrate his birthday with him. Everyone cheered and sang praise for the good King, who was quickly followed by his wife, Queen Lunath, and their son, Prince Cedric.

Oscar marvelled at the Royal Family. They beamed with such electrifying energy that spread like wildfire throughout the entire crowd; the delicate wave from the graceful Queen met a roaring cheer in response, the boisterous grinning of young Cedric beckoned motherly 'Awww's' and 'Isn't he a cheeky one?', and the sheer presence of the King commanded respect and love, which he received in spades. Yes, the crowd were going crazy for their beloved Royal Family, but were silenced by another crying fanfare which signalled the King and his kin taking their seats.

As the crowd also sat down, Oscar squinted to see who else sat in the Royal Box. There was a small gathering of noble men and women, all of whom were unrecognisable to most people and immaculately dressed and well groomed. Some were adorned with medals and wore decorated swords on their hips: clearly high ranking military officials. Oscar scrutinised these people of import through a pair of small, brass binoculars that were tethered to the back of the chair in front of him. Every chair had a pair of these binoculars, but most people were now using them to look at the stage. Oscar, realising this, turned his attention to the stage also, and waited for the Grande Show to commence. And commence it did, with a startling explosive crash from the gargantuan symbols in the orchestra.

—

This crash echoed all through the city and found its way to the ears of Lilly, who had nodded off and been sleeping face first in the very book she was supposed to be deciphering. She woke up with a start and looked around her, fearing the crash had been that of guards barging into the library to arrest her. Relieved when she heard the orchestra following the crash and reassured that it was just the Grande Show, she was suddenly struck with blind panic, as she didn't know if this orchestral explosion signified the beginning or the end of the show. She feared she had slept through whole thing. A key point in her plan of breaking into the palace was to *not* fall asleep and, what's more, she had endeavoured to acquire the information she sought from the book and be making her escape by the time the show had ended.

Her head had become so flustered trying to decrypt this strange writing that she rested her eyes for a moment to reboot her brain. However, a moment turned into several and now she feared she had wasted her one chance to read this book. Now faced with a dilemma, Lilly considered for the first time actually taking the book. Her intention had never been to steal it, she wasn't a thief after all, but if the music booming from the

Grande Show signified its end, the palace would soon be packed with people for the Royal Feast, and she could hardly hide in the secret library for the rest of the festival. Lilly's poor head started to get flustered again. *Oh, what to do?!* she dramatically thought to herself.

Luckily, as fate would have it, her decision would be made for her. Suddenly, as if from nowhere, whispered voices emerged from the other end of the room. Ducking behind a large stack of dusty old maps, Lilly saw two dark figures emerge from a secret door disguised as an empty bookcase. Lilly grew concerned, not because she was in very real danger of being quite literally caught red handed - the book was still in her hand, and the leather was sort of reddish - but because something seemed off about these two figures. They were dressed head to toe in thin, black robes and light faded armour. Their whispered voices didn't speak any real words, but instead offered occasional grunts and groans as way of communication. They moved with the shadows, and what little light there was seemed to dim further as they drew near. Their footsteps were silent, despite the uneasiness of their movement. There was something very off indeed about these two, Lilly thought, and she was positive they were not with the Palace Guard.

The two suspicious characters started tossing books and scrolls and pretty much anything they could get their hands on, scanning and hunting the room for something. It didn't take much for Lilly to conclude that this was most likely the book that she had sought herself. Because of this, her mind was now made up: she would take the book, if only to protect its secrets from these would-be burglars. Clearly, they were dangerous and had no right to be in the palace's secret library. Not that Lilly did either, mind you, but she didn't allow that obvious truth to slow her down, as she had already crept over to the secret door by the time her shadowy visitors had reached the chest that once contained the book.

Distraught that the book was missing, the larger of the two uninvited guests let out a long, ferocious snarl. This startled Lilly, who let out a gasp that just inched its way louder than a whisper. The smaller of the darkened duo turned suddenly, and his black eyes met Lilly's pale blues. She didn't grant herself a further moment's hesitation, and ran from the room and into a long corridor, brightly lit and regally decorated. Now she would have to navigate her way out of the palace, which is no small task considering palaces tend to be on the large side, and few were larger than Honeydale Palace. Not to mention she would be fleeing blind; she had never planned on leaving through the palace itself, but instead by sneaking back out the way she came in. She didn't have the foggiest idea about the layout of this place.

Not slowing down for an instant, however, Lilly let her instinct take the lead as she ran down one identical corridor after another. She didn't look behind her at any point, although she could hear the raspy calls of her pursuers not far behind her. On the last corner she turned in this labyrinth, she found herself running towards two men clad in dark blue and grey uniforms, carrying short, elaborately crafted spears.

The Palace Guard!

They saw Lilly running towards them instantly - they're no fools in the Palace Guard - but were more alarmed at the two shady characters hot on her trail. They readied their spears and charged at Lilly and her chasers, commanding all three of them to halt and surrender. Lilly quickly ducked down a small corridor that snaked off halfway between her and the guards. This corridor had one exit, through a large wooden door. She turned briefly before she went through it and saw the guards and the shadowy foes clash, the latter pair drawing thin, black, needle-like swords from what seemed like thin air. As exciting as Lilly thought this little bout would be, she went through the door in the interest of escape and found herself running into the kitchen.

"Kitchen" might be too modest a word to describe the room she fled into. It was more like a massive hall, littered with worktops and stoves and cupboards, and to each worktop, stove and cupboard were a series of sweating and bickering cooks. In the middle of this kitchen was a long, wooden table that stretched the length of the hall, and on it were ingredients of all varieties: herbs, spices, vegetables, fish, meat, seasonings, vinegars, milks, creams, cooking wines, oils and butters. In the middle of this vast array of culinary treats was the biggest catfish Lilly had ever seen. She was frustrated that she couldn't stop and marvel at all the weird and wonderful things she was encountering, but while the guards were occupied with the other two intruders at the moment, they would soon be hot on her heels and more than likely with more guards. Lilly dashed under the long table and bolted along to the other side of the kitchen, where another door was patiently waiting on her dramatically bursting through it. A few of the cooks noticed this odd tiny person darting about under the furniture, but before they could quiz her on who she was or what she was doing, she was out the other end and, as anticipated, burst through the door with dramatic gusto.

Lilly now found herself at the bottom of some stone steps leading up to a courtyard. Phase one of her impromptu escape plan was complete - getting out of the palace. She was still on the palace grounds though, and the guards, now aware of her presence, would not stop their search at the gates. If she was to be truly safe, she had to get out of the city altogether.

A quick assessment of the courtyard concluded that there were a great many more guards on patrol outside than there were in the halls of the palace. Avoiding them would prove to be difficult and time consuming, and time was not a luxury Lilly had at the moment. With this in mind, Lilly instead opted to dive head-first into a giant hedge that bordered the courtyard. The hedge was so thick, however, that it was pretty much only her head that broke through, the rest of her dangling in mid-air like a worm on a hook. Perhaps this wasn't her best plan, but Lilly, nothing if not determined, rammed her hands into the hedge, clasped onto as many wiring branches as she could, and pulled the rest of her body through. This exhausted young Lilly, but the middle of a hedge was hardly the most comfortable place to get some respite, nor was it the best time for such a thing, given the situation. Taking only a moment to get her strength back, she began to flap her arms and legs in an almost swimming motion, and for all intents and purposes, *swam* out of the hedge and onto the grassy hill that held aloft the palace grounds.

Picking herself up, Lilly made haste down a winding dirt path that led into the city streets. Her rustling in the hedge had caught the attention of more guards, who made known their presence by shouting after her. The chase, it seemed, was destined to continue as she sped into the city.

She met with both good and bad luck as she hastened onto the cobbled streets; on the one hand, the streets were all but deserted with the Grande Show in full swing, but on the other, many of them were blocked off or, worse yet, being watched by patrolling guards. This meant that Lilly was limited to pretty much one path: a path that was leading her right to the Royal Square. Though this was not ideal, to turn back and find an alternate route would be to surrender one's self to the Palace Guard, have the book confiscated and the secrets within forever lost to her. Not to mention she would probably spend the rest of her life in a prison cell.

Following this route, it wasn't long before Lilly found herself at the back of the eastern stand of the Royal Square. *How on earth am I supposed to get around this nonsense?* she wondered, shaking her head. And then, as if answering her own question, a thought occurred. Beneath the square was a narrow tunnel that led to a chamber beneath the stage where behind-the-scenes trickery could unfold. She could pass under the square and come out right on the other end, make for the gate and escape the city at last!

Lilly surveyed her surroundings for a moment, until she finally noticed a trap door further along the stand. Lilly wasn't certain, but she reckoned this was the entrance to the tunnel and before she could allow a cautious thought to arise, she was forcing it open and descending into the dark.

The trapdoor closed behind Lilly with a loud thud that echoed along the dark tunnel, and the faint flames of the dimming torches flickered and frenzied in the brief breeze that shot in with the trap door's opening. Although she had spent the best part of her day in a sewer and sneaking around a heavily guarded palace, this was the first point in her adventure that Lilly had felt uneasy. Slowly, she crept down the tunnel, a growing weariness swelling in her belly. A moment or two slugged by when, finally, she found herself standing in a large, circular room full of boxes, ropes, fireworks, tricks and all manners of illusionist wonders. All these things would usually excite Lilly, and it would take a very brave person indeed to try and stop her from setting off a firework. This was not the case at this moment, however, as Lilly was preoccupied with something else.

In the middle of the room was a large column that supported the vast stage overhead. Bound to this column was a slender, pale looking man with a fantastic mane of orange hair and exotic make up dancing patterns on his face. Lilly approached cautiously, until at last this tied up individual caught sight of her and began coughing and spluttering muffled words of help through an old manky rag that had been used to gag him. Lilly decided to help this man, and quickly she started untying the rope that bound him to the column. When his hands were finally free, he pulled the gag out of his mouth and spat a series of dusty cloth balls onto the floor. Lilly took a step back and grimaced at this. When the newly freed man came to his senses, he looked at Lilly desperately.

'Quickly, you must help!' The man screeched in a bizarre accent. 'The King, he is in great danger!'

'Danger?' Lilly queried, 'What do you mean? What kind of danger?'

'Something evil and wicked is about to happen, we must do something! I was attacked by a gaggle of shadowy villains. And the one up there, he is an imposter!'

'An imposter? Wait, I don't understand. Who exactly are you?'

'I am the Great Maju!'

And at that, Lilly was shaken by the eruption of screams from the crowd above. These blood-curdling screams startled the Great Maju, who stumbled backwards into a lever. Suddenly, the ground beneath Lilly's feet began to shudder, gears went into motion and before she could do anything about it, she found herself ascending on a rising platform towards a trapdoor that had sprung open on the stage above her. The Great Maju was beside himself; he had just sent this young girl, his saviour, to her apparent demise. Wrought with grief and self-pity, the not-so-Great Maju shuffled out of the room and down the tunnel in an attempt to escape.

—

A mere minute or two earlier, Oscar was dangling on the edge of his seat, marvelling at the supposed Great Maju's show. The man on stage was clad entirely in black, a hood hiding his face completely as though his head was constantly bowed. He had appeared on the stage with a thunderous flash, two cauldrons either side of him. One cauldron oozed silky, white smoke; the other, a thick cloud of black. The fake Great Maju raised his hands, and as he did, the smoke rose above him and began forming shapes, and soon the shapes formed images: images of people, warriors holding out long staffs and draped in robes foreign to young Oscar's eyes. A voice hissed around the arena. The voice of the not actual Great Maju.

'Once there were two great powers in this land,
Powers that could crush the mightiest mountains into
*   sand.*
They shared their world with kinds lesser than them,
Fed, clothed and housed, when they should have been
*   condemned.'*

The impostering Great Maju raised his arms once more and from them, blood-red smoke poured into the sky, merging with the white and black to create new, more terrifying images. Images of suffering, and of fear. Images of death.

'A third power emerged who preached the truth to
*   their kin,*
That to be anything less than powerful was to live a

life of sin.
But the Dawn and Dusk powers said all life is worth
  fighting for,
And so, the Twilight obliged them, and thus began The
  Magus Wars.'

At that, the white, black and red smokes spiralled and formed into a chaotic ball, frantically pulsating, and with the utterance of "Magus Wars", exploded into a blinding purple light that illuminated the entire city. Oscar, along with everyone else, shielded his eyes. When, at last, the light dimmed, Oscar thought his eyesight must have been somehow impaired, as he was now gazing upon the most spectacular sight he had ever seen.

A dragon hovered above the stage; long, violet scaled, and fiery breathed, its glowing eyes were fixed upon the Royal Box. Everyone in attendance gasped. Some younger children cried and begged their mothers to take them away. But for everyone else, Oscar included, this was the greatest illusion there had ever been. With the false Great Maju's final verse, however, they would soon learn this was no illusion at all.

'The Wars were devastating, and brought the world to
  its knees,
Mortals were spared while mages died, the fall of
  Gods for the lives of fleas.
When the powers were at their weakest, mankind
  made its stand,
And purged the last of the mages, forced to die or

leave their land.

This tale is one of blasphemy, the wrong race died that day,
But not all the mages were lost, and their revenge begins today!"

Right on cue, the dragon opened its enormous jaws and emitted an inferno of purple fire that engulfed the Royal Box, sweeping over the panicking Royal Family and company cowering within. The flames quickly flickered away to reveal no scorch marks or any hint of burning at all, but that the Royal Family and all the other guests sitting there had been turned into stone!

The crowd exploded into panic. Agonising screams wailed through the city. People were frantically clambering over one another trying to escape while the dragon swooped over their heads, reigning down balls of purple flames, each person touched by the fire turning instantly into stone. The cloaked man scored the pandemonium before him with manic laughter.

Old Grubb picked up Oscar and led his family, along with Mr and Mrs Gallow, to the bottom of the stand in an attempt to flee onto the street. Oscar couldn't take his eyes off the villain responsible for this, who had now allowed his head to rise and reveal his face to be hidden behind a white, ghoul-like mask.

This fiend's evil laughter was suddenly halted by something unexpected. From a trapdoor to the right of him, a small girl popped up from beneath the stage. She looked around, puzzled and then quickly terrified as she witnessed this almighty dragon causing all kinds of destruction. Her eyes met with the cold glare of the tall cloaked man standing beside her, piercing through at her from behind the haunting mask disguising his face. He raised his hand and cast a red thunderbolt from his fingertips to right where this young girl was standing. She was quick though, and dove off the stage, missing the bolt of lightning and landing in a heap on the ground.

When Old Grubb and company had at last made it to the bottom of the stand and were close to the cobbled streets once more, Oscar could see the girl clamber to her feet and dart off into the city as well, the hooded sorcerer watching her go.

Old Grubb did not hesitate or stop to look behind him at any point as he dashed down the street. Nor did anyone for that matter; everyone focused on getting out of the city alive, as if the dragon's devastation would go no further than the city walls. Oscar held on to his father for dear life, but as he was not burdened with running himself, he could keep his eyes fixed on the path behind them. His mother kept up with the pace, her hand on Old Grubb's shoulder. She held Amber tight against her chest, the poor child crying with overwhelmed terror. Tryca met her son's eyes and he could see she was scared. Scared not for herself, but for her children.

Oscar's gaze was forced from his mother to the sky, as the dragon suddenly landed on the rooftops of the houses at the end of the street and let out a bone-rattling roar. Astride the dragon's back was the one responsible for all this panic, the wicked sorcerer who had summoned the creature. At his command, the dragon let out a long wave of glowing, violet fire that swept the entire street and turned almost everyone on it into frozen statues of grey stone. All but Oscar and his family, as Mrs Gallow saw the fire coming and warned them all to duck down a small side street that was little more than an alley.

They never stopped running, doing their best to block out the horror around them. They ran through alleys, even open buildings, following Mrs Gallow's expert knowledge of the city's shortcuts. All the while, the dragon was still blasting people at random and circling the city like a vulture awaiting its meal. It was on this street that Oscar again saw the girl that had appeared on the stage, a girl he would soon learn was named Lilly.

Lilly had dodged the thunderbolt and made haste under the western stand and into the streets behind. Small as she was, she was able to dodge and duck her way in and out of the panicking crowd, making her an all-round more efficient escapee than the people surrounding her. She could hear the roars and flaming attacks of the vicious dragon, and it didn't sound far away at all. The Western Gate was her and pretty much everyone else's goal. From there they would be in the open fields, the dales of Vhirmaa, where they could all split up and not be trapped like rats in a maze.

She was on the western streets of the city when a blast of purple fire shot past and exploded in front of her. She was knocked back off her feet, the eruption turning an unfortunate group of men, women and children into solid stone. Before Lilly could find her feet once more, a large hand fell upon her shoulder. Clutching the scruff of her coat, it hauled her up and cradled her under the large arm of a moustachioed, kilt-clad man.

'C'mon missy, this is no place to be sitting about!' Old Grubb warned her, and with the dragon in close pursuit, fled down the street.

With no short amount of quickstepping and ducking, Old Grubb, with both Oscar and Lilly under his arms, Borris and Norris tripping over one another, his wife and infant daughter close to his back, and the Gallows racing forward, had been lucky to avoid the petrifying power of the dragon's fire. Finally, they emerged from an alleyway onto the long street leading towards the Western Gate. Oscar could see that some people had made it out already, and were running off in all directions over the grassy fields.

As they drew close to the gate, the dragon let out its most ferocious roar yet and gave up the chase, shooting straight up into the sky instead, spearing itself high above the city. It spread its wings as wide as it could and took a long, deep breath, its chest ballooning and filling with terrible fire. Its master, still saddled on its back, stopped his maniacal laughter for a moment to cry forth an order to his winged minion in a tongue unrecognisable to all. The dragon opened its jaws once more and a bright light of pure purple formed in its mouth. As it exhaled, the light spread out over the city, creating a dome that would encapsulate the city of Hylkoven from wall to wall.

The purple wall of this falling dome fell into Old Grubb's view, and he could see that no amount of luck would permit him to leave the city. He was too big and too slow. He made a quick estimation in his head, shaking both Oscar and Lilly in each arm, as if to weigh them. As a matter of fact, that's exactly what he was doing.

The dome had almost touched the ground and would soon imprison everyone still inside the city. In a last-ditch effort, Old Grubb leapt forward and tossed both Oscar and Lilly far out in front of him, his strong arms managing to sling them quite a distance. A distance so far, in fact, that they shot out of the Western Gate and landed on the road outside, a mere moment before the edge of the dome touched the ground. As it did, it shone so brightly that the few lucky ones who had escaped the city had to turn away, before it exploded with a shockwave that wiped all across the surrounding fields, knocking all off their feet with incredible force. All cries of fear and terror were transformed into an unsettling silence.

Oscar and Lilly both peered up to see what devastation remained, and indeed, they could not believe their eyes. All of Honeydale, the buildings, the palace, the people, everything within the walls of the city, had been turned to stone. Lilly looked to the sky and saw the dragon flying away, heading east and into the night.

'I don't... I don't believe it,' a voice whispered from behind.

Oscar and Lilly turned to see a steward, the same steward that Mrs Gallow had given a scolding to earlier, slowly walking to the gate.

'My family... my friends... what has happened to

them?!'

The steward ran past Lilly and Oscar, about to re-enter the city. Suddenly, another voice bellowed out from behind.

'No! Stop!' the voice called out. It was the voice of a guard who wore an expression of uncertainty and dread, holding out his hand to gesture to the steward not to take another step. But it was too late. The steward ran over the threshold of the gate, but had only taken a few steps within the city before succumbing to the spell that had befallen the rest of Honeydale, and turned into stone.

Oscar took a step forward and peered in through the gate. A tear trickled down his cheek as he saw what had become of his family. His mother and father, his sister, his cousins, even Mr and Mrs Gallow, all stood motionless, grotesque statues of stone. Their skin, their clothes, all the same shade of dull grey. No sign of life behind their eyes, their expressions frozen terrified. Oscar couldn't force his eyes away from them, even though his heart was agonisingly heavy in his chest. Lilly noticed Oscar's tears, and slowly she stepped beside him.

'That man,' she said, softly, 'the one who helped me, what was his name?'

'Old Grubb,' Oscar replied. 'He was my father.'

With that Oscar began to weep. Unsure of what to do, Lilly hugged Oscar.

'It's okay,' she said, 'Everything will be okay.'

Oscar took these words as little more than feeble attempts of comfort; in fact, he barely heard them, his head clogged with emotion. He felt so lost and alone at that moment, and Lilly could sense it. She wasn't sure where her next words came from, or if she really meant them, but her mouth opened once more and she whispered in Oscar's ear.

'We can fix this.'

These words found their way inside Oscar and hid behind a wall of grief that had suddenly been constructed within him, consuming every feeling, every emotion. He was numb to absolutely everything. But those words... They were hidden for now, but they were in there, brewing in the core of his being.

He returned Lilly's hug and for a moment, as brief as it was, he didn't feel so alone.

Chapter Four

The Hospitality of
Roark Stoneheart

An hour or so had passed since Oscar had wept at the gates of Honeydale, and he wasn't alone. The few dozen people who had managed to flee all escaped leaving loved ones behind. About six or seven City Guards had managed to flee also, and dutifully they had rallied the survivors together and set up a few campfires along the road on the cusp of the valley that crept down from Honeydale.

One of the guards who had escaped was in fact their captain, Pah'lin. Not to be confused with the Palace Guards, who were a little softer and did little more than walk about the Palace a bit, the City Guards essentially policed Hylkoven, carrying out the laws of the King and kept the peace within the walls. Captain Pah'lin took the events of that night as a personal failure. It was his job and the job of his men to keep the city safe. But they didn't. They couldn't. What kind of foe was that? They had never encountered the like. No one had. Dragons were the stuff of legends, and the sorcerer... Pah'lin couldn't fathom what power coursed through him. He couldn't dwell on his pain or guilt just yet, however. He was forever bound by duty and it was his honour to wear the uniform and call himself Captain of the City Guard, so he had to be strong for the fortunate souls who had escaped untouched by the dreaded dragon's flames.

Pah'lin walked towards one of the huddles of people, shivering and crying around the camp fire. He noticed a young boy and an even younger girl sitting alone, away from the group, on a rock facing the city. Oscar and Lilly had been there since the campfires had been set up, choosing to be by themselves. Lilly felt somewhat responsible for Oscar. Perhaps if Old Grubb hadn't stopped to pick her up, they would've had enough time to escape together. Lilly burdened herself with these thoughts, and many others, as she took Oscar by the hand and led him away from the gatherings of people in the camps. Each one of them had cause for grieving, and Lilly thought the least she could do was try and distract poor Oscar from his. She even thought about showing him the bizarre book she had stolen from the secret library, but then she reasoned that perhaps a book written in a dead language that cryptically told unheard stories about magic was perhaps not the best source of comfort. Magic had been the cause of his grief that night, the cause of everyone's grief. She had always wanted to witness magic, to experience its power, but never could she have imagined the horror of what had happened. Even she could not hide the feeling of hate she felt towards magic at this moment, a feeling shared across the camp. So in lieu of showing him the book, she instead decided to introduce herself, and in a quiet whimper Oscar returned the courtesy. Apart from their names though, neither of them offered another word, and sat in reflective silence on the edge of camp.

Pah'lin approached them hesitantly, and cleared his throat before speaking.

'How are we feeling, little ones?' he asked, bowing his head.

He received no reply, at least not from Oscar. Lilly stirred for a moment, but how they were feeling seemed painfully obvious. And indeed it was, even to Pah'lin.

'Sorry,' he continued. 'Silly question. Would you not be better sitting with the rest of the group? You'd be warmer by the fire.'

'We're fine,' Lilly finally replied, coldly.

'I see. And what about you, lad?' Pah'lin turned his attention to Oscar, who was quite obviously far from fine.

'I said we're fine,' Lilly growled.

'Listen, I know you probably just want to be left alone with your thoughts right now, and I can't blame you, but at sunrise we'll be moving on from here and I'd like to know you two have some place to go when we do.'

'We can take care of ourselves,' said Lilly, unconvincingly though, as she didn't know Oscar at all or if he could fend for himself. Lilly was buried in uncertainty, and Pah'lin sensed this immediately.

'Your families, they were in the city?'

Silence. No answer from either child. Pah'lin thought for a moment.

'Where will you go?' muttered Oscar, at last breaking his silence.

'I'm sorry?'

'You said you'll be moving on in the morning. Where will you go?'

'My main priority is to get these people out of the dales and into some kind of shelter, a nearby town or-'

'No,' Oscar interrupted, 'That's not your main priority.'

Pah'lin and Lilly looked at Oscar with concerned puzzlement.

'Your main priority,' he continued, 'is to save the city, to help the people inside. Your main priority is to slay the dragon.'

Lilly shuddered at this; there was a cold determination in Oscar's voice. He had struck a chord with the captain though, as all Pah'lin had thought about since the dragon and its summoner attacked was how to kill it, save the city, and reverse the spell it was under.

'You're right, little one,' Pah'lin replied. 'I won't lie. I do intend to do all that. Myself and two of my men will be heading east after that foul creature, and we will do all we can to undo the wickedness that has fallen upon Honeydale. But first, my main concern is what to do with you two.'

'Us two?' asked Lilly.

'Yes. The dales are no place for two young children to be wandering around on their own, and I couldn't head off in all good conscience leaving you to fend for yourselves.'

'Sending us off with a bunch of strangers doesn't seem all that wise, either,' Lilly argued, raising her eyebrow in a *got-you-there* fashion.

'Perhaps not, but some of my men will be there to keep you safe.'

'Your men?' Oscar queried.

'Yes. I am Pah'lin, Captain of the City Guards, and I assure you, you will be safe with my men. Safer certainly than sitting in a field where many wild things walk.'

'You're not wrong there, Captain,' a voice said, coming from the shadows of the fields.

A stout silhouette rustled through the long grass, until at last there emerged a short, broad shouldered man with lots of hair on his face but precious little on his head, leaving a dome like crown that shone in the moonlight. It was a dwarf, hard faced and horny skinned. He nodded at Pah'lin in a knowing manner.

'And the darker the night,' the old man continued, 'the wilder they are. So, what in the blazes are you doing out here wetting your bottoms in the dew?'

'Roark!' Pah'lin called out, 'Roark Stoneheart! You saw what happened, surely?'

'Yes, I saw what that monstrous wyrm did.'

'That wyrm was no ordinary dragon, Stoneheart. His flames turned all they touched into stone, and he answered to a master, who summoned him out of nothing more than smoke and light. What kind of beast is this?!'

'Why do you ask me?' Roark gave a slight grin as he

asked this.

'Why? Because you are Roark Stoneheart, the Beast Soul! You know everything there is to know about the creatures of this world!'

'A creature with the power to turn people into stone and can be summoned out of thin air is no creature of this world, old friend.'

Pah'lin seemed disheartened by this: he was hoping Roark would have some clue to defeating this beast.

'Creatures that are of this world, however, are wolves, putridons, and even gnolls. All of which roam these fields, and none of which will be far from this camp, so I'd suggest you move.'

'Where would you have us go, exactly?' snarled Pah'lin, who didn't like the second-guessing of the patronising dwarf. 'These people are tired, lost and without homes or even families.'

'And like I said,' began Roark, not fazed by Pah'lin's tone, 'they'll be without lives as well before the sun rises, if you don't move them along. My home isn't far from here. I have a barn, not much too look at, but you could fit all these folks in there. They won't be comfortable but they'll be safe for the night.'

Pah'lin pondered this only for a moment before nodding in agreement. He called his men to attention and gradually they assembled the groups together, ready to march on. Lilly and Oscar even agreed to go with them to Roark Stoneheart's home, Lilly less hesitant than before; Roark's mentioning of those horrid monsters made her less eager to be alone. The putridons especially, as they were particularly foul. A horrid blob of toxic ooze, they slugged along emitting the most rancid odour imaginable, and had to do little more than breathe on you to inflict you with a highly potent poison. Lilly had encountered one before and had no desire to do so again. And so, taking Oscar by the hand, she walked not far from Roark and Pah'lin's side, who were leading the party along a dirt road towards a gathering of tall trees.

Roark's eyes kept meeting Oscar's, who had been staring at him intently since they set off.

'Something I can help you with, young sir?' Roark asked.

'Are you some kind of... adventurer?' asked Oscar, who, despite being a melting pot of the worst emotions, couldn't contain his default curiosity for all things adventurous.

'What makes you say that?'

'Well, Captain Pah'lin called you the Beast Soul, and said you knew all about the monsters of the world.'

'Ah, so you think I got that title from encountering beasts on a great many daring adventure, eh? Well I'm sorry to disappoint you, my young friend, but I am little more than a fisherman.'

'A fisherman...' Oscar was deflated. He thought perhaps at last he had met the kind of adventurer he had read about in his books. Alas, it was just another fisherman, and fishermen were people Oscar knew an abundance of.

'Disappointed, eh? Well I'm sorry, little man. In fact, I can't even claim to be a fisherman anymore, I've been retired so long. The name's Roark Stoneheart. I've been many a thing in my life, from carpenter, to merchant, hunter to fisherman, but I'm afraid to say I've never been an adventurer. I've always had an interest in critters and monsters though, ever since I was a young dwarfling. So, I've watched them, read about them, to the point where I know a lot about them. I'm not sure where the title Beast Soul came from, mind you.'

'I know,' Pah'lin cut in. 'I was just a boy at the time, but I remember it clear as day. I was at the market on Hylkoven harbour, when suddenly the fishermen were calling from their boats, rushing back to the docks. Something was out there, something that had spooked them all. They were right to be spooked too, because suddenly the entire harbour was drenched from a tidal wave that came from this enormous beast emerging from beneath the surface of the sea.'

'What was it?' Oscar asked.

'It was a long necked, scaly skinned, hideous serpent of the sea, with fangs as big as houses and a screeching wail that shattered all the windows in Honeydale. I thought it was Leviathan itself!'

'Not Leviathan,' Roark interjected. 'Just an overgrown hydran viper.'

'Oh, *just* an overgrown hydran viper,' Pah'lin mocked. 'This thing was terrifying; it's yellow eyes were fixed on the harbour. All the fishermen returned to shore as quickly as they could, but one boat remained out there, standing as one small barrier between the viper and the harbour.'

'Pah'lin,' interjected Roark once again, 'You are overdramatising this story a little.'

'Do you mind? Your modesty is not helping, Stoneheart.'

'So, what did you do?' Oscar piped up, annoyed by the interruptions. 'How did you slay the viper?'

'Slay it?!' Roark roared, almost offended by the thought of it. 'Oh no lad, I didn't slay anything. Despite their vicious appearance, hydran vipers do in fact only eat fish. The poor thing had been attracted to the harbour by all the fish from the market. Now, I dare say it would've made a fine mess of the harbour trying to get the fish, and injure, or worse, a great many people in the process. Nevertheless, they only eat fish, and its intent was not to harm anyone, nor was it my intent to harm the viper. Being a fisherman, and a damn fine one at that, I had on my boat a most impressive haul, ton upon ton of fish. So, I tied the net holding the fish to the hauling rig and catapulted my entire day's catch at the viper's gaping jaws. My aim was good and it devoured the lot, after much chomping and drooling. The beast now fed, it turned tail and swam back into the depths of its home.'

'And that was it? It never came back?' asked Lilly, who was quite pleased the creature hadn't been harmed.

'On the contrary,' Pah'lin rushed in, determined to finish the story he began, 'it came back all the time! And Roark here was charged with feeding the beast, which he did gladly. After a while it stopped visiting as often, before eventually stopping altogether. That was how he got the title of Beast Soul.'

Oscar and Lilly were both very impressed by this yarn. Even Roark, who tried to do his best to be humble about the whole thing, quite liked hearing this tale told so heroically.

By the story's end, the group had just about reached their destination. In a small gathering of cluttered trees, there was a shabby little hut with a dim light coming from the window, and beside it a large but even shabbier barn. Roark wasn't lying when he said it wasn't much to look at. Quickly, Pah'lin started guiding people towards the barn. Roark offered to bring food out to them and took the liberty of ordering Pah'lin's men to take out blankets and make beds for everyone. Oscar and Lilly stood outside the hut, unsure of their surroundings.

'Children,' Roark called, 'perhaps you can help me make some sandwiches for everyone?'

Wanting to do their part, Oscar and Lilly obliged and headed into the hut. Lilly, still feeling protective over Oscar, thought this could be a good distraction, but wasn't naive enough to think that he'd already forgotten his recent tragedy. Oscar himself thought something similar; however, there were decisions beginning to form in his mind, decisions that meant making some sandwiches was one small step towards a much bigger plan.

The interior of Roark's hut left about as much to be desired as the exterior. Rickety, gnarled chairs sat facing an unkempt stone fireplace. In one corner, there was a table which sat awkwardly against the wall on account of it missing one of its legs, and in the other corner was a thin, uneven bed with a lumpy straw mattress and a sheet covered in holes. Roark led Oscar and Lilly to what you might call the kitchen, but only if you were feeling very generous. It would be more accurate to say that Roark led Oscar and Lilly to a wall, where a cupboard and a basin had been affectionately thrown against it. Opening said cupboard, Roark handed Lilly and Oscar loaves of bread, cheese and some indescribable meat. Together they started making sandwiches and throwing them in a dusty basket for one of Pah'lin's guards to take out to the barn. Roark, meanwhile, was at the fireplace heating up a pot of stew that had long since seen better days. After a while they had whipped up an adequate spread, and the people in the barn had sandwiches and stew and slept on makeshift beds.

Lilly and Oscar had opted to stay in the hut with Pah'lin and Grubb, along with an old woman whose back was too sore to be sleeping on the floor of a barn. Roark and Pah'lin had whispered discussions while the old woman slept in the bed, which Lilly couldn't imagine was much more comfortable than the barn floor.

Lilly wasn't tired at all, and all she really wanted to do was look at her prize from the secret library. She wondered if Pah'lin would arrest her for taking it, but then what would he do with her? The prisons of Honeydale were very much off limits at the moment, and he had said he was going to chase down the dragon and the one who controlled it. Would he take his prisoner with him? Even if he didn't arrest her, would he confiscate it? Would he even know what it is, or that it was taken from the palace? Probably not. But there were too many risks, chiefest of which was Roark, who seemed like a worldly man who would perhaps recognise it. Again, not very likely. But risky, and Lilly had come too far to take risks. She decided she would wait until everyone was asleep, sneak out of the hut and leave. Oscar, who was now sleeping on a tatty old rug in front of the fire, would be safe with Pah'lin and Roark, so there was no need for Lilly to stick around. With this in mind, Lilly lay down next to Oscar and pretended to fall asleep.

—

Lilly focused her ears so she could hear everyone's heavy breathing and snoring, making sure they were all asleep. Slowly, she got up off the floor and pulled her bag onto her back and crept across the hut towards the door. She turned the handle and opened it just a little, her considerable lack of size allowing her to slip out without forcing the door to creak open widely. At last she was outside. The cool night air was silent, the wind barely made a sound. She tiptoed away from the hut and began creeping towards the edge of this cluttering of trees. She didn't get far, however, before the quiet wind brought with it a most abrasive stench.

Lilly turned to find the source of this awful smell. There it was - odour incarnate. A big fat horrid putridon. It slugged its way towards Lilly, belching and making all manners of unpleasant noises, its murky green skin bubbling and spitting as it got ever closer to her. Lilly rummaged around in her inside coat pocket and pulled out a small dagger, but such a weapon would be useless against this hideous blob, as getting too close would mean risking being poisoned. Despite their sluggish demeanour, putridons were quite quick when need be, and although Lilly could run faster, her legs would get tired long before the putridon would give up the chase.

She held the dagger in front of her, hoping to threaten the slug away, but putridons were too stupid to notice such a thing as a threat, and so it continued to slime its way towards her.

Suddenly, hurried footsteps rustled through the woods, followed swiftly by the sound of something cutting through the wind with great speed and force. Lilly quickly saw that it was a wooden sword, and it had been swung downwards upon the putridon's head. The nasty creature groaned and hissed in pain and dizziness as the sword struck its globular head again and again. Angered, the putridon swung out with its slimy claws and tried to scratch its attacker, but missed its target. Putridons are no great fighters, true, but again they are highly toxic, and at last it belched a vile cloud of green gas that wafted out in front of it, causing the swordsman to hop backwards.

'Are you all right?' the swordsman asked Lilly, who was in some state of disbelief. This swordsman was none other than Oscar. The putridon came to its senses and spat in fury at Oscar, who had positioned himself in front of Lilly.

'Oscar! I thought you were sleeping...' Lilly gasped.

'My entire family, my entire life, was taken from me tonight,' replied Oscar coolly. 'Did you really think I'd be able to quiet my mind long enough to sleep?'

Lilly nodded, embarrassed. Still, she was glad he wasn't asleep as the putridon growled menacingly at her.

'Um, can you... can you kill that thing... with *that* sword?' she cautiously asked Oscar.

'I have no idea,' he replied, 'I've never fought one

before.'

'You cannot,' announced Roark, appearing from behind a tree and shooting Oscar and Lilly disapproving look.

'You as well?!' Lilly yelled, once again pleased that he wasn't asleep, but at the same time disappointed that her brilliant plan had proven to be not-so-brilliant. Roark's sudden arrival startled the globular menace that was this particular putridon, which made the dwarf grin ever so slightly.

'I do apologise, Lilly,' he smirked, 'but I sleep so lightly that I'm barely asleep at all. And Oscar, as skilled as you are, swords, wooden or otherwise, will do you no good in a fight with a putridon. Neither would spears, nor arrows or bolts. Putridons are perhaps some of the foulest creatures imaginable, and particularly hard to stop once they've began their attack. They are a mass of ooze and have little by way of internal organs, meaning stabbing them has about as much impact as slicing butter.'

'So, what do we do?!' yelled Oscar, not taking his eyes off the putridon.

'Well, they do have one fatal weakness,' the smug Roark explained, 'and it just so happens I had some of it in the kitchen.'

'The kitchen?' asked Lilly.

'Yes...' Roark said under his breath, as he rummaged in his pocket.

At last he pulled out a small vial of clear liquid, broke the seal and started splashing it on the putridon. This strange potion caused the monster's skin to burn, making it wail in agony. Distressed, the putridon cowered away and slimed off into the bushes. Roark looked very pleased with himself indeed, and cockily walked over to Lilly and Oscar.

'What was that?' Lilly eagerly asked, 'Some kind of potion?'

'Sort of,' replied Roark. 'It goes especially well on chips.'

'Chips?' asked Oscar, raising an eyebrow.

'Yes. It's vinegar, young ones. By far the greatest condiment.'

Oscar and Lilly giggled at this. Roark was certainly an unusual dwarf, but definitely worthy of the name Beast Soul.

'Now,' he carried on, 'what are you two doing out here? Apart from starting fights with undesirable creatures, that is.'

'It was my fault, Mr Stoneheart,' Lilly said, bowing her head. 'I snuck out and fell into the path of that putridon. Oscar came to my rescue.'

'This much I gathered, but why did you sneak off?'

Lilly hesitated. Both Roark's and Oscar's gazes were piercing, and made her feel uneasy. Could she risk the truth, she wondered? Could she tell them about breaking into the palace, uncovering a secret library and taking some ancient book from it? She quickly determined this was a bad idea, especially with the Captain of the City Guard so close by. However, she was aware that she couldn't in fact read the book, and that the worldly Beast Soul could perhaps help with that problem. Before her hesitant pause became suspiciously too long, she decided to tell a few half-truths.

'I was... collecting something,' she began. 'A book. In Honeydale. That's why I was there.'

She turned and saw Oscar's puzzled expression. *What on earth was she babbling about?* he thought. Lilly pulled her bag from her shoulders and took out the book in question. Roark stepped closer.

'May I?' he asked, holding out his hand. Lilly hesitated again, before finally handing the book to him.

'So, I was collecting this book, like I said,' continued Lilly, 'from a special library. But it's old, the book. So old, in fact, that I can't read it, and so I need to find someone who can.'

'That doesn't explain why you tried to sneak away in the middle of the night,' Oscar said, his tone full of suspicion.

'Yes, it does...' Roark mumbled, flicking through the pages. 'This book isn't just old. It's ancient. And by special library, I presume you mean the Secret Library?'

Lilly was speechless. Not only did he know about the Secret Library, but he had thwarted yet another of Lilly's plans to be sneaky!

'The Secret Library?' Oscar asked.

'Yes,' continued Roark. 'I have no idea why it's called that, though. Most people from these parts have heard of it, although no one knows exactly where it is, beyond that it's hidden somewhere within the palace. Nor does anyone know exactly what's inside it. So how is it that you, a little girl, came to find it?'

'Well...' Lilly muttered. Another sneaky ploy was forming in her head, but she quickly dismissed it. She had not been on good form thus far, and Roark would undoubtedly see through any lie she offered. Instead, she relented to tell the truth. Well, most of it, anyway. She explained her fascination with magic, for one reason or another, and that she had heard about the Secret Library from her grandfather, and of the book that stood as the sole known relic of the Time of Mages. She endeavoured to find it, and ultimately did. It was indeed the truth, but a truth that omitted several details.

'So, you're a thief,' Oscar said sternly.

'I am not!' Lilly grunted. 'It wasn't my intention to take the book. I just wanted to look at it, to read it for myself. But I wasn't the only one looking for the book. Two others showed up. They were strange looking, as if they were formed by the shadows they moved in. When they saw I had it, they chased me. Then the Palace Guards chased me. All the way to the Royal Square.'

'I saw you!' Oscar cried out. 'On the stage! Next to that man!'

Lilly nodded.

'Perhaps it was better that you took the book than your pursuers. I doubt their presence and the appearance of Honeydale's villain is coincidence.'

'Wait a minute...' Oscar interrupted, holding up his hand. 'If this book was written back in the Time of Mages, and is some ancient magical relic, couldn't there be a clue in there to reversing the spell on Honeydale?'

'I suppose there could be,' Roark nodded, handing the book back to Lilly.

'But we won't know until I find someone who can read it,' she lamented.

'Perhaps Pah'lin knows someone who could read it?' Oscar asked.

'Pah'lin is a fool,' grumbled Roark. 'A brave fool, and a noble one to be sure, but a fool nonetheless. Attempting to slay that dragon with swords and arrows would be even more futile than using them to fight that putridon. In spite of my council, Pah'lin still plans on attacking the dragon head on.'

'But if he saw the book, maybe he'd think differently,' argued Oscar.

'If Pah'lin learned of this book, he would take it from me. He would see me as little more than a child and a thief, and any hope I have of discovering the secrets of this book for myself would be gone.'

'And are you more than just a child?' quizzed Roark, with a wry grin.

'I may be a child, Mr Stoneheart, but it was I, not Pah'lin, not you, nor anyone else who found this book.'

'Indeed. Also, I fear Captain Pah'lin would not heed the advice of seeking to translate this book. He is a man of action, and rarely do men of action take time for reason. Learning what these pages conceal would seem to be a waste of time and energy when he could be smiting the dragon with his sword. Like I said, the man's a fool.'

'I can't say I would disagree with him,' admitted Oscar, knowing this was an unpopular answer, and unhappy that he was siding himself with what Roark would call a fool. 'I would rather hunt down the dragon with Pah'lin, destroying it and its master... However, I know Pah'lin would not permit me to go with him and his company, and would instead force me to stay behind, seeing me too as only a child.'

'I see,' Roark smirked, 'And are you too more than a child?'

'I don't know what I am. I've spent all my life reading about other people's adventures, hoping that one day I'd be given the chance to be a hero as well. Now that my own adventure is upon me, I can't say I like it very much. But I can't let Lilly go off on her own. If the secret to saving my family is indeed hidden somewhere in that book, then we must find someone who can unearth it. Both of us.'

Lilly and Oscar shared a faint smile.

'Oh?' Roark grinned. 'And where will you go, exactly?'

Lilly and Oscar's smiles disappeared. Roark giggled under his breath. These two little children had surprised the Beast Soul. They had something about them, something Roark had found in many children but very few adults; they were unaware of their own limitations, and as such were unbounded by them. A naive courage burned within both Lilly and Oscar. They might not know what must be done exactly, but knew that one way or another something had to be done, and that they would do all they could to see that it was. This moved Roark, who glanced around to make sure Pah'lin hadn't woken up and ventured out to find them.

'Well then, it would seem there can be no stopping either of you. However, it would be highly irresponsible of me to let you both go wandering off in the middle of the night without direction. There is more than one

81

putridon in Vhirmaa along with a great many more dangerous creatures than them, so I would suggest waiting till morning before setting off. I'll tell Pah'lin I have decided to keep you both here to help me with chores and what not until something more permanent can be arranged. He'll be too eager to move on to argue with me. Once he and everyone else leaves, I'll see you onto the path for the Golden Forest.'

'The Golden Forest?' asked Lilly, surprised by Roark's keenness to help them.

'It's not far from here, about half a day's walk. I'm not sure if they still exist, but there was once a community of quite peculiar creatures who lived in the Golden Forest known as the Seedlings.'

'Seedlings... Are they monsters?' asked Oscar.

'No, no! Seedlings are bizarre little critters, fairies of one sort or another. They generally stay hidden from most. Timid little things, they are. They do, however, glow with enchantment and are sure to know a thing or two about magic. It's not much but it's something to go on.'

'Do you think these Seedlings could read the book?' asked Lilly.

'Possibly, but like I said they generally keep themselves to themselves and hide from most folk. Your best bet would be to try and find Jackary Stiltz, a hermit who lives in the Golden Forest. He's an alchemist and quite an unusual young chap. He's not much older than either of you, appearance-wise anyway. I have to admit I've only met him once or twice. He is, however, the only human the Seedlings feel comfortable revealing themselves to.'

'Apart from you,' Oscar said knowingly. 'You've seen them, of course?'

'Me? No, no, I'm afraid not. Jackary's told me about them, though. They sound most curious.'

'So, you're sending us into some woods to find a crazy potion maker who claims to see fairies,' Lilly said dryly. 'That doesn't seem very responsible of you.'

'No more questions for tonight,' Roark replied sternly. 'It'll be sunrise soon, and we must get back to the hut before Pah'lin awakens. Some rest wouldn't go amiss either.'

Roark led Oscar and Lilly through the trees and back to his hut. Creeping in, they saw that Pah'lin had not stirred at all, and would awaken with no knowledge of what had happened outside. Lilly and Oscar took their place on the floor, wrapping themselves in the rug. Roark sat on one of the rickety chairs and grumbled something about the old woman who had taken his bed and was snoring bloody murder in the corner. Lilly noticed the sky had already begun to turn auburn with the dawning day, and so closed her eyes in an attempt to get even the tiniest amount of sleep.

—

Lilly's eyes hadn't been closed for long when she was awoken by the sound of people moving around. She sat up to see Pah'lin talking to Roark, whose eyes were wandering over to herself and Oscar, who was still asleep on the floor. She peered out the window and saw Pah'lin's men coordinating the crowd from the barn, getting them ready to move on. Lilly wondered where they might move on to. The nearest sizeable town to Hylkoven was some way away, and she couldn't imagine Pah'lin would lead them in the direction of the dragon.

Wearily, Oscar sat up rubbing his eyes. Pah'lin, seeing that both children were now awake, walked over and knelt down beside them.

'I've been speaking with Roark,' he began, 'and he has agreed to take care of you for the time being, until this whole business with Honeydale is sorted.'

Pah'lin went on to reassure them that he would soon have everything back to normal, and that Roark was a good man. He lied to the children about making things right, about saving Oscar's family. He had no idea if he could do anything at all, and this uncertainty was painted all over his forced smile.

Both Lilly and Oscar nodded and smiled in agreement though while Roark giggled at Pah'lin's expense, who was unaware of the children's plan to set off immediately after he did.

After they had packed up what supplies Roark had been kind enough to offer them for the road, the still distraught group of Vhirmeans were led off by four of Pah'lin's men, while he himself remained behind with two others.

'Where will they go?' asked Roark.

'There's a village about a two-day's hike southwest of here,' Pah'lin replied. 'From there they can move on, or settle. At the very least they won't be stranded in the wilderness.'

'And you? You still intend to go after that sorcerer

and the dragon?'

'Yes, Roark, I do. I know you think it folly, but I must do something. I don't possess the power of magic, true, but I must do something.'

'And good luck to you, old friend.' Roark smiled at Pah'lin with a strange sense of pride. Although he had offered Pah'lin words advising him not to pursue this quest, he was glad he hadn't heeded them. Pah'lin was a noble man with an unwavering sense of duty, and if a dragon's spell could be undone on nobility alone, he would be the hero of Hylkoven for sure. Alas, this was not possible, which was why as soon as Pah'lin and his men had set off on their quest, Roark began preparing Lilly and Oscar for theirs.

He packed their bags with some bread and hard cheese, then dusted off two small flasks and filled them with water from the well at the side of his hut. He then pulled out an old chest from under his bed and rummaged around inside.

'If you're to be running off and chasing adventure,' Roark began, 'then you'll need more than a wooden sword to defend you.'

With that, he revealed two short swords, not much bigger than daggers, and handed one to Oscar and Lilly both.

'You're giving us swords, now?' Lilly scoffed. 'You're really not responsible at all, are you?'

'I suppose not,' laughed the dwarf, 'but I can tell that if I tried to insist you stayed, you'd just run off anyway, and run off ill prepared at that!'

'And like Pah'lin said,' began Oscar, who was rather

expertly swinging his sword around, 'we must do something.'

'Quite right,' Roark nodded. 'And since you are in possession of the one thing that might be of any use, how could I possibly stand in your way?'

'But Mr Stoneheart,' mumbled Lilly, a serious quiver in her voice, 'what if these Seedlings can't read the book? What if no one can?'

'Then we must put our faith in the will of Pah'lin and men of his ilk. But I have never known there to be a book written that cannot be read. If the Seedlings can't read it, then there will be someone else who can.'

After finally persuading Oscar to sheathe his new sword, they left the home of Roark Stoneheart and made for the eastern opening in the trees. Roark escorted them for a time across the fields until they happened upon a path of light brown dirt. He stopped and examined Lilly and Oscar one last time, convincing himself once more that letting them go off on their own was a good idea.

'All right, some words of warning,' Roark began, clearing his throat. 'Do not, under any circumstances, stray from this path. The Golden Forest lies just beyond that hill over there, and it shouldn't take you more than a couple of hours to reach it. Try and avoid any interactions with monsters, if you can. Oscar, I know how eager you are to try out that sword of yours, but the less opportunities you have to use it, the better. Most importantly, however: whatever happens, you must stick together. Never leave each other's side. Understood?'

Lilly and Oscar dutifully nodded.

'Why don't you come with us?' Oscar asked, a

question that he was puzzled had not been answered yet.

'An old dwarf like me? Oh no. I told you before, I'm a retired fisherman, not an adventurer. The Beast Soul they call me, not the Brave Soul.'

'Well, fisherman,' Lilly smiled, 'thank you for helping us.'

'Not at all, little one. Although, if you do happen to find the secret to saving Honeydale within these pages, I think it will be I, along with everyone else in the Vhirmaa, who will be thanking you.'

'We'd best be off then,' Oscar concluded, keen to set off while the daylight favoured them.

'Indeed, you best. Seek out Jackary Stiltz, tell him I sent you, and tell him what happened at Honeydale. Good luck!'

Oscar and Lilly set off down the dirt path that rose up onto a small hill, hiding the Golden Forest behind it. Roark watched them walk on for a while before heading back towards his hut. Lilly, used to travelling alone, was not at all concerned about what unknown adventures lay ahead of them. Oscar, on the other hand, had always relied on his father to keep him right, and was disappointed that Roark Stoneheart had chosen not to go with them to the Golden Forest. Adventure flowed naturally within Oscar, it was something he had always longed for, but now it was a struggle for him to come to grips with it. It was overwhelming for him to find that here he was, embarking on a quest at long last. The unknown loomed over him like a black cloud, and with all that had happened, there wasn't an ounce of enjoyment to be found.

Still, for better or worse, he was on an adventure and had a mission to pursue. He would endure whatever hardships and tests that came along. He would not falter on the path to his goal. This, he thought to himself as he walked down the path to the Golden Forest, was a vow he was determined not to break.

Chapter Five
The Treachery of
Gombaroth

The walk to the Golden Forest was silent for the most part, both Lilly and Oscar burdening themselves with weighty thoughts. In her short sleep, Lilly had her familiar dream once again. The same woman, distressed and face wet with tears, calling out in a language she had never heard before. The room is large but bare, and out of a window behind the crying woman Lilly could see the skies burning red with fire and war. The dream ends with a flash of brilliant white light that hurts Lilly's eyes and forces her awake.

This same dream had been with her since she was a baby, but it had been coming to her almost every night now for nearly a year. Since the day her grandfather died.

Sensing Lilly was falling under the weight of her own mind, and to distract himself from his own, Oscar decided he should get to know his travelling companion a little better.

'So, where are you from?' he asked, realising he didn't even know the most basic of things about Lilly.

'I come from the woodlands in the south, just north of Thalan,' Lilly replied, being purposefully non-specific.

'Thalan? The forests down there are dense they say, maddeningly twisted.'

'Pretty much. It's quite beautiful, actually. Although my grandfather doesn't let me venture too far into the woods of Thalan itself. I mean, he didn't...'

'Oh, I'm sorry...'

Oscar bowed his head, thoughts of his own family's fate consuming him.

'He died about a year ago. His name was Dysan. He wasn't my real grandfather, but he was the closest thing to a family I've ever known. He found me abandoned when I was just a baby. He took me in and raised me. He was very smart, and kind too. He used to tell me stories about magic. I suppose that's what started my fascination.'

'He sounds like a great man.'

'He was, for what I knew about him. He didn't like to share much about himself, and could go days without saying a word. When he did speak though, it was always fascinating. Not just his stories about mages, but everything and anything. He was very well travelled, and had seen many things in his time. He had an answer for everything, there was no end to his knowledge. As he got older, he got sick, and before he died he told me about the Secret Library and the book. He had pages of notes on where to find it, how to enter unseen. I think he had planned on going after it himself, but couldn't in the end...'

'So, you were fulfilling his dying wish?'

'In a way…'

They continued on in an uneasy silence. Lilly never gave much thought to her unknown family as Dysan was all she had ever needed, and given the tragedy that had befallen Oscar's family, she thought to herself that perhaps it was a blessing she didn't have one. Losing her grandfather was not easy, but his death was due to old age, just a final stage of life. He had prepared her for the inevitable and stressed the importance of the quest she must go on once he was gone. Lilly never felt lost, even after losing him. Oscar's family, on the other hand, was taken from him. The only thing driving him right now was the possibility of saving them, and if he could not... Lilly shook her head, in an attempt to wipe that thought away.

They both endeavoured to chat about less serious things for a time, as the afternoon sun took its place in the sky. It was a hot summer day in Vhirmaa, and sweat was forming on the brows of the young duo as they ascended the somewhat steeper-than-it-seemed hill the path had led them to. After much huffing and puffing, they at last reached the top of this bothersome mound.

They marvelled for a second at the astounding view the hill had been concealing: mountains bordered the horizon, wisps of snow on their peaks teasing respite from the unrelenting sun. Shimmering lakes of the bluest water offering cool refreshment separated the acres of grassy fields, the emerald blades of which danced to and fro in the warm breeze. And at the foot of the hill sat an auburn forest of yellow and brown, leaves forever sun kissed in an autumn glow. There could be no mistake: this was the Golden Forest. Its warm mesh of colours beckoned to Lilly and Oscar, who had taken a moment to sit on a nearby rock and drink from their flasks. After a short rest, they got up once more and began the walk downhill, following the path to the entrance of the forest.

The second their little feet stepped through the arched opening of the Golden Forest, Oscar and Lilly were immediately seduced by its otherworldly aura. A scent of warm honey blew through the trees, filling them both with a tingling feeling inside. Oscar even let out a slight giggle, as though the air was tickling him. The flowers that grew within the Golden Forest were unlike anything either of them had ever seen; bizarre collages of blues, reds and greens. One particular flower was so enormous that when the wind blew by it, it let out a deep baritone howl. In fact, it resembled some kind of brass instrument far more than it did a flower. From tree to tree, birds sang light melodies to each other, while grumpy fat toads croaked in the shade. This whimsical realm had charmed Lilly and Oscar, both of whom stopped every two minutes to examine a new flower, or talk to a doe eyed critter.

They rested after a while and made themselves some sandwiches with the bread and cheese Roark had given them. Both the cheese and bread were preposterously hard, however, and finding a decent bite was proving quite a challenge.

'I don't wish to sound ungrateful,' Oscar began, 'but old Stoneheart might as well have given us no food at all. This is impossible!'

'I agree,' confirmed Lilly, who feared chipping a tooth on her rock-like sandwich. Barely a moment later, her eyes fell upon a solution. Not far from where they were sitting, a bush of purple plums playfully swayed in the breeze, as if waving Lilly over.

'Over there!' she exclaimed, jumping to her feet and running over to the bush. 'Plums!'

'Wait!' warned Oscar, who hurried to catch up with Lilly. 'They might be poisonous!'

'Poisonous? Really?' Lilly replied, with mocked concern. 'They're plums, Oscar! Juicy, plump plums!'

'This one isn't too juicy,' Oscar said, picking one of them from the bush. Indeed, it was quite rotten, and the whole thing turned to ashy clumps in his hand. He grimaced as it slopped to the ground.

'Hey, you're right,' Lilly said slowly, examining the other plums. 'They all are!'

Lilly picked one, and like the other had done in Oscar's hand, the plum crumbled in hers. All the plums on the bush were rotten, and in fact, the entire bush seemed to have withered a great deal in the short time they had been standing there.

'There's something not right here,' Oscar cautiously muttered.

They looked around them and found that a flower not far from the plum bush had all but wilted. And another exactly the same, right next to it. Concern grew in Oscar and Lilly. It quickly became apparent that the deeper into the forest they were going, the greyer and sicker it was becoming. Something was most certainly not right, and although they contemplated turning back for a brief moment, Lilly and Oscar marched further into the Golden Forest to find out what that something was.

The air grew thick and long gone was the scent of warm honey. The gold and brown leaves that flourished in the trees had fallen to the ground as crisp, blackened shells. Oscar looked behind to see that the path they had walked down, which had been every bit as golden as the forest's name suggested, had too turned grey and lifeless. Whatever was happening to the forest was spreading rapidly throughout it. Lilly noticed that the birds had stopped singing, and indeed there were no birds to be seen at all. Or toads. Or rabbits. Or any little critters. All at once, Lilly and Oscar seemed to be very much alone. Oscar wasn't too sure though.

His eye had caught a glimpse of something dashing by a nearby tree, but had disappeared by the time he turned to see what it was. His ears pricked up when he thought he heard a hushed voice coming from a brittle black bush, but then found silence when he went to examine it. Oscar allowed his hand to rest on the helm of his sword as uneasiness grew inside him.

They soon found themselves in a small opening, standing upon dead grass. Oscar and Lilly looked at each other, hoping the other would decide on which direction to go, when suddenly they were startled by a voice from behind them.

'Have you seen any Dancing Beetles?' the voice said.

Oscar and Lilly spun around, drawing their swords as they did. Before them stood a boy, a few years older than themselves. He wore a long green overcoat that cloaked his unkempt shirt, tatty trousers and worn boots. He had a satchel over one shoulder that was stuffed with mushrooms, weeds, and all other manners of forestry forages. He didn't seem fazed by the swords waving in his face. His wide eyes darted hurriedly between both Lilly and Oscar, patiently awaiting an answer to his question.

'Well?' he asked. 'Have you seen any?'

'Dancing... beetles?' Oscar quizzed.

'I didn't know beetles could dance,' Lilly added.

'No, no,' the boy shook his head. 'A Dancing Beetle is a weed. I need to find one!'

'Who are you? And what's going on here?' Oscar quizzed further.

'The forest is sick! It's dying! It's cursed!' the boy hectically cried. 'This is why I need to find a Dancing Beetle! I need to make a potion!'

'A potion?' Lilly asked knowingly. 'Does that mean you're an alchemist?'

'Yes, yes!' the boy replied, no longer paying attention to Oscar or Lilly. He was looking under bushes and logs for this weed of his.

'You're Jackary Stiltz!' Oscar announced, sheathing his sword once more.

'You know my name? How curious…'

'Yes!' Oscar replied enthusiastically. 'Roark Stoneheart sent us here to find you. He said you can show us to the Seedlings so that we might learn more about magic.'

'Roark Stoneheart? Seedlings? Magic?'

'Yes, we need help translating a book,' Lilly answered.

'Now is not the time for books!'

Jackary spun on his heel and dove into some bushes behind Lilly and Oscar. He pulled them apart before sighing in a pleased tone. Before him was a glowing, blue weed that twisted and turned out of the ground. It was a Dancing Beetle. Jackary took out a small knife and started carefully digging around the roots of the weed.

'Please, Jackary,' Lilly pleaded.

'I said, now is not the time! I have to save the forest!'

'What exactly is happening to it?' asked Oscar.

'It has been cursed! Gombaroth is sucking all the life out of it!'

'What's a Gombaroth?'

'Gombaroth is a nasty old toadstool that has been a part of these woods for as long as there has been a Golden Forest. He has forever been jealous of the Guardian of the Forest, the one that breathes life into this place. Jealous of her power. I'm not sure how, but he has managed to find a way to make himself stronger by making the forest weaker!'

'Guardian of the Forest?' asked Oscar, puzzled.

'Power?' asked Lilly, even more puzzled.

'Yes, yes, yes!' Jackary barked, growing impatient.

He gently pulled the Dancing Beetle from the earth and placed it carefully in his satchel.

'Like I said, now is not the time for books or

questions. Now is the time for saving the forest!'

'Right!' Oscar said loudly, stepping towards Jackary. 'We will help you stop this Gombaroth. If we can, we will help you save the forest.'

'Yes,' Lilly agreed, standing next to him, 'and then you'll help us, right?'

Jackary nodded enthusiastically. Oscar and Lilly looked at each other, nodded, took a deep breath and readied themselves to spring into motion. Jackary giggled slightly; he found this all rather exciting.

'Wonderful!' he exclaimed. 'To action!'

Lilly and Oscar took only one dashing step forward before they were stopped immediately in their tracks. To action, it seemed, meant sitting down, as that is exactly what Jackary did. He began pulling out various mushrooms and weeds and such from his satchel. Oscar knelt down beside him, and watched carefully. Jackary then presented a small, wooden mortar and pestle, and nestled them in the gap between his crossed legs. He pulled out his small blade once more and carefully went about the business of shaving the mushrooms and trimming the weeds. He poured these shavings and trimmings into the mortar and mashed them furiously with the pestle. He didn't stop until the contents of the mortar had been ground into a fine powder, then rummaged in his coat pocket and revealed a vial of misty, green water. He emptied it into the mortar, and leaned back as it fizzed and popped when it mixed with the powder. He then poured this fizzing concoction into a small, glass bottle, and stuffed the Dancing Beetle in behind it. He quickly corked the bottle and gave it an aggressive shake. He stopped after a moment, sighing loudly, but the bottle still shook. Indeed, the bottle was shaking far more aggressively now than before. Jackary tried to get a firm grip on it, causing him to shake about wildly also. He looked at Lilly and laughed rather uncontrollably. Lilly offered him an alarmed expression, until finally the shaking and vibrating subsided, and Jackary held in his hand a bubbling, green potion.

'Done!' he announced, springing to his feet. 'Now for the tricky part: making Gombaroth drink it.'

'We will help you with that,' Oscar confirmed.

Jackary grinned, before dashing off into the forest. Lilly and Oscar followed, calling on Jackary to slow down. He led them to a narrow path that was cloaked in shadows. Through the thickness of the air and the gnarling of the trees, it was clear to Oscar and Lilly that the source of the forest's disease was at this paths end.

'Gombaroth is down this road,' Jackary coldly whispered, dread wavering in his voice.

Together, the three of them cautiously stepped onto the path. Lilly thought she heard strange whispers from behind her, and she wondered if it was the Seedlings watching them. She hoped that this encounter with Gombaroth would not be her quest's end, as these fairy-like creatures sounded fascinating. She also hoped that they actually existed. She couldn't make up her mind about Jackary, who seemed rather... twitchy. A lovely fellow perhaps, but certainly an odd one. Maybe he'd been drinking his own potions, quipped Lilly to herself.

An ominous growling breath echoed through the trees, which got louder as they edged further along the path. The shrouded road soon came to an end, and they found themselves standing in yet another opening, this one hideously tangled with twisted branches and dead trees. They walked to the middle of the opening, an uneasy feeling hanging heavy in the air. Lilly and Oscar drew their swords.

'He's watching us,' Jackary whispered. 'Come out Gombaroth! Show your wicked face, and lay claim to your wicked deeds!'

The trees ahead of them began to tremble with great vigour. Suddenly, the sound of crashing shook the ground, and from the shadows an entire tree trunk came flying towards Oscar, who dove out of the way just in time. It hit the ground with tremendous force and split in two as it collided with the trees behind them, knocking some of them down. Oscar got to his feet and at last found himself standing face-to-face with Gombaroth, who had emerged from behind a mound of torn tree stumps and lifeless grass. It hissed and wailed at Oscar, who contemplated how to take on this fearsome creature.

Gombaroth, after all, was rather enormous and unlike any toadstool either Oscar or Lilly could have imagined. It had six black, lidless eyes and a wide jaw with three rows of razor-sharp teeth. One of its smaller black eyes watched Lilly run over to Oscar.

'Any ideas?' she asked, shaking and more than a little frightened.

'None. You?'

'Nope, but I don't think vinegar is going to work this time.'

Oscar chuckled before instinctively charging at

Gombaroth. Lilly followed, her sword raised above her head, ready to strike. The monstrous toadstool roared, and the ground began to quake. From behind the creature, a dozen thick vines snaked out, barbed with needle-like thorns. They moved as if they were Gombaroth's tentacles, and they lashed out at Oscar and Lilly. They both ducked out the way, Oscar striking one of them as he did. He hit it well, and chopped the tip of it off. Gombaroth screeched in pain, and now Oscar knew how to hurt it.

'The vines!' Oscar screamed. 'Cut off its vines!'

With that, both he and Lilly started swinging frantically, while Jackary bobbed and weaved, dodging the vines and attempting to get close enough to Gombaroth's mouth to pour the potion in, an endeavour that was proving to be somewhat fruitless. Oscar moved quite fluidly with a sword, his lessons with the old sword master paying off at last. Lilly was a bit clumsier and lashed out at random, but still managed to pull off a few good strikes.

Gombaroth was growing frustrated with these bothersome children, with all their ducking and dodging and hacking and slashing. Jackary too was frustrated, as every time he got close to Gombaroth himself, the vines would lash out at him quite violently, forcing him to retreat. The vines seemed to be endless as well, more emerging with every one Oscar and Lilly chopped off.

The battle went on like this for a short while; Jackary, Lilly and Oscar edged ever closer to Gombaroth, before being forced back by more vines. They knew time was running out, as the shadows grew blacker and the forest grew sicker. Gombaroth would not be satisfied until it was the only living thing in the Golden Forest, and that meant killing these three pests too!

Gombaroth decided that it was time the tide of this fight turned, and a smaller, whip-like vine swung out from the side, heading right for Oscar. Oscar was blind to it, but Lilly saw it just in time and dove into him, sending them both to the ground. She had saved Oscar, but a thorn on the vine had caught her, tearing her coat and scratching her arm. She screamed as she rolled on the ground, before she suddenly fell silent.

Short on breath, Lilly's skin began to turn grey, and her yellowing eyes pleaded with Oscar for help. Oscar ran to her aid, but knew there was nothing he could do. Lilly used all of her strength to hand her sword to him, then gestured below Gombaroth's wide, cackling mouth. The soil beneath him was soft. If Oscar could get close enough, he could really hurt this monster by dealing with it the same way he'd deal with any weed: attacking it at the root.

Taking Lilly's sword, he fanned both blades and started charging towards Gombaroth. He dodged two slow swings from two large vines, and rolled forward into a sprint to take Gombaroth head on. Jackary intuitively clocked on to what Oscar's plan was, and ran as closely behind him as he could, being careful not to get hit by Oscar's swinging swords. Oscar could see more vines coming to block his attack, and so he threw Lilly's sword as hard and fast as he could. It flew between three vines that were forming a protective barrier around Gombaroth, and struck the beast right in its centre eye.

Gombaroth screamed an earth-shattering cry that chilled the entire forest. Its vines swung wildly, the creature now blind and in agony. Oscar lunged forward, driving his sword into the soft soil beneath Gombaroth's fungal chin. Its gaping jaws gaped even wider, and roared in protest. Without a moment's hesitation, Jackary uncorked the bottle and flung the potion right down Gombaroth's gullet.

The giant toadstool froze suddenly, a faint twitch here and there in its vines. Oscar stood up, picking up the swords and standing next to Jackary. From within the belly of Gombaroth, a deep gurgling sound was slowly brewing. It rose all the way to its mouth, before at last it belched out a disgusting cloud of purple wickedness. This odious burp was so powerful that it knocked Oscar and Jackary backwards, landing in a heap next to Lilly.

The soil Oscar pulled his sword from started to bulge and pulsate, until finally it cracked open and poured a dark yellow mist into the forest. Oscar panicked, thinking it was Gombaroth's poison, the same poison that was killing the forest. The mist flowed thick and fast throughout the woods, engulfing every tree, flower and creature in a golden blanket of fog. Straining his eyes, Oscar saw the fate of Gombaroth through the mist.

The foul beast slunk back defeated, its vines crashing to the ground and wilting into dust. A faint grin crossed Oscar's face, until at last the fog overwhelmed him, and he slipped out of consciousness.

-

Lilly's nose twitched. Something familiar smelling was tickling her nostrils.

Warm honey!

Her eyes opened, and she sat up to find that the Golden Forest was indeed golden once more. She beamed, before noticing both Oscar and Jackary were passed out next to her. She inspected them to make sure they were unharmed, but it seemed they were merely in a deep sleep. She stood up and stretched, before a shooting twinge attacked her arm. She looked at the tear on the sleeve of her jacket and the scar on her arm beneath it. She recalled Gombaroth striking her. She must've been poisoned. The cut still hurt, but she was sure the infection was gone, cured when Gombaroth was defeated. At least, it seemed he had been. The forest was clearly in a better state, and where the menacing toadstool had once stood before, there was now nothing.

Well, not quite nothing.

Lilly caught a glimpse of something twinkling and squirming in the soil. She approached with caution. As she knelt down to see what it was, she was startled by what she found. A tiny toadstool, with six eyes and a mouth - sans teeth, thankfully - was wriggling in the soil. It peered up at Lilly, and offered what seemed to be a smile.

'Is that...?' Lilly began.

'Yes,' Jackary answered, yawning and rubbing his eyes, before Lilly could finish her question. 'That is Gombaroth. For better or worse, he is a part of this forest, and like the forest he, too, has found new life. Something tells me that he might be a bit more agreeable this time round.'

Oscar wearily clambered to his feet. He looked over to Lilly and Jackary, who met him with warm smiles.

'I must thank both of you,' Jackary continued. 'But there is plenty of time for repayment. It will be nightfall soon and I am absolutely famished. I suggest we head back to my home to get some food and rest.'

Oscar and Lilly knew that there wasn't really plenty of time at all, and the sooner their questions were answered, the better. However, that being said, they were both very hungry and tired after facing such a ferocious villain, and so they agreed to go with Jackary. After all, Lilly thought, if they were going to ask questions, why not ask them over dinner?

Chapter Six
An Audience with Erdolet

'Well tug my pigtails!' Lilly exclaimed. 'You live here?'

'I do,' grinned Jackary.

He led them down an auburn path of rich soil that divided a large open space of pale red grass. Sporadically dotted around the grass, providing a kind of torchlight for the path, were brightly coloured flowers that glowed brighter as the night grew darker. It wasn't the illuminating flowers, the auburn path, or red grass that had caused Lilly's outburst, however. It was Jackary's *home* itself.

It was a wooden shack, hastily painted white and, by all intents and purposes, shouldn't have been standing. It leaned greatly to the right, defying many laws of science. It wasn't even the awkward looking shack that left Lilly aghast, though; it was the fact that it was somehow sitting on top of a tree.

'It's a treehouse,' Oscar confirmed to himself. 'You live in a treehouse.'

'I know I do...' Jackary replied, unsure as to why Oscar felt the need to inform him.

'I'm sorry. It's just I've never heard of anyone actually *living* in a treehouse.'

'Oh? And have you heard of squirrels?' Jackary gave a smug smile.

'Yes, but squirrels live *inside* trees. They don't build their houses on top of them.'

'But the tree is where their home is. They have a tree*home*. So, ipso facto, a treehouse! And then there are birds! Who do, in fact, build their homes on the branches of trees. And let's not forget about...'

'Does it matter?' Lilly interrupted. 'Can that thing hold all three of us?'

'Of course it can!' replied Jackary, offended.

'Then shall we go in? It's dark, there's a chill, and I'm starving!'

Oscar and Jackary looked at each other and nodded in agreement, and so they continued up the path to the foot of the enormous tree that housed Jackary's home.

For as rickety as the exterior looked, once inside both Lilly and Oscar felt very secure. Everything was a little slanted, of course, and walking across the floor made them feel a little seasick; however, it was sturdy and didn't threaten to plummet out of the tree, which was broad with strong branches that didn't move at all in the wind, as if they were made of stone.

The decor was clumsy, sporadic and scattered. Dozens of old rugs engulfed the floor, orbiting a small, grey, brick stove in the middle of the room. At the far end was something that resembled a bed, although there were so many books and scrolls and general tatter all over it, it didn't look like it was used much for sleeping. Large plump cushions and thick woollen sheets draped and littered the room without rhyme or reason, giving Jackary's guests the distinct impression that their host just slept wherever he fell. The wooden walls were dusty and cluttered with uneven shelves holding countless books. In fact, Lilly was quite astounded by just how many books were in this treehouse. Old books too, on a variety of subjects. She pondered quietly to herself that perhaps Jackary might know a thing or two about the mysterious book she had in her backpack.

Jackary beckoned them over towards the stove, where he had begun to make a fire. Oscar was halfway across the room when he stopped suddenly and rushed over to one of the awkwardly hanging shelves. He gasped excitedly as he pulled down a thin, green book.

'Something caught your eye there?' asked Jackary, knowing exactly which book Oscar had in his hands.

'*The Plights of Hendal Bowstalk,*' Oscar exclaimed. '*Volume One*! Oh boy, I never thought I'd see it for myself. I've read *Volumes Four, Five* and *Six*. But the first three are so hard to find. Well, they are for someone who lives in as remote a village as I do, at least.'

'Yes, I'm quite proud of my *Hendal Bowstalk* collection,' Jackary said smugly. 'I have *Two* and *Three* around here somewhere.'

'Would you mind...?' Oscar waved the book in his hand, gesturing to Jackary to let him read it.

'Please, there's no need to ask. Have a thumb through while I make supper.'

Oscar gleefully followed Jackary's order, sitting down on one of the enormous cushions and beginning to leaf enthusiastically through the pages of *The Plights of Hendal Bowstalk: Volume One.*

Lilly was already sitting near the stove, watching Jackary bring a pot of stew to boil.

'So, you're rather well read then?' Lilly quizzed.

'I am, for my part,' Jackary modestly replied. 'Knowledge is the centre of everything, and the best way to gain knowledge is from reading. My old mentor taught me that.'

'Your mentor in alchemy?' Lilly quizzed further, leaning forward on her cushion so that her face felt the warmth of the stoves fire.

'Yes. I forget his name now; he wasn't my mentor for very long. At least, it didn't seem like very long. It was a good while ago now, you see.'

'It couldn't have been so long that you'd forget his name. And if you really have, then he couldn't have been much of a mentor.'

'Oh, he was the best!' Jackary said assertively. 'Or at least, that's how I remember his reputation. I'm afraid I don't have a very good mind for memory. My brain has a constant thirst to know things, but it seems like every time I learn something new my mind erases something else to make room for it. The older the memory, the hazier it gets. Until it's gone. And like I said, the time I spent with my mentor was long ago, so most of my memories of him are all but gone.'

Jackary sighed as he said this, slowly stirring the pot of stew and concentrating on its bubbling and popping.

'With respect,' Lilly began, 'you don't seem old enough to be a fully qualified alchemist. The ones I've met have been old pedlars for the most part.'

'Well, I don't *pedal* that's for sure. But I am old. At least, I think I am. Again, I haven't got a good mind for memory, but I have got a lot of them, too many to fit into a youthful life.'

'You don't look very old,' Oscar stated, turning his attention away briefly from his book.

'No, I don't suppose I do...' admitted Jackary, pondering this for a moment. 'That's probably thanks to some potion I've made at some point. Who could say? Again, I don't have -'

'*A very good mind for memory,*' Lilly interrupted, mockingly.

'Erm... Yes.' Jackary nodded, chuckling slightly.

Oscar returned his attention to his book, and Jackary went about the business of dishing out the stew into small wooden bowls. Lilly had barely finished thanking Jackary before the first spoonful of the steaming stew entered her mouth. Oscar, though hungry, ate slowly and steadily, not turning his eyes away from the page he was reading. Jackary sat close to the fire and barely ate a drop. They chatted about this and that and nothing of importance while they ate, Lilly quite obviously avoiding a very specific topic of conversation.

At last, when the meal was done and Jackary was placing the bowls and spoons into a round wooden basin, Oscar put down his book and gave Lilly a slight nod. She opened her mouth to speak, but Jackary broke the silence first.

'So, you mentioned something about a book before,' he said, not turning to face Oscar or Lilly. 'And needing help translating it, yes?'

'Yes,' Lilly nodded, pulling the book from her backpack. 'It's an old book, from the Time of Mages, and is written in a language we don't understand. Roark Stoneheart told us to find you, as you can speak with the Seedlings. We were hoping you'd ask them to translate it for us.'

Jackary thought about this for a moment, before extending his hand.

'May I?'

Lilly reluctantly handed him the book. He flicked back and forth through the pages, seemingly just as fascinated by it as Lilly.

'This book is indeed old,' he began, 'and this writing is likely from the Time of Mages, as you say.'

He finally closed the book and handed it back to Lilly.

'I don't know if the Seedlings will be able to assist you, but I would be happy to ask them. Before that though, can I ask why you need this book translated? I'm guessing your interest in magic is more than academic?'

Lilly bowed her head as Oscar sat forward and told Jackary about the tragedy at Hylkoven, the curse that had ensnared Honeydale. He spared no detail, his hushed voice quivering as he spoke of his family. Jackary was aghast, and trembled as he listened to Oscar's story of sorrow. It sounded too terrible to be true, it had to have been some kind of horrible lie. But there was no falseness in Oscar's eyes, Jackary could see that, and so he sat quietly and listened in spite of himself.

'So, you see,' Oscar said finally, clearing his throat, 'magic was the source of the evil that struck Honeydale, and this book is our only link to that world. If there is something in there we can use to save the city, and my family, then we must know about it.'

Jackary gave only a moment's hesitation before rising to his feet. Without saying a word, he walked over to the open window on the far end of the room. He rummaged in his pocket and pulled out a small, yellow acorn, before placing it on the windowsill.

'Okay,' he whispered, 'I've summoned the Seedlings.'

'What?!' Lilly shouted, 'That's how you call them? By popping a seed by your window?'

'This isn't just any old seed. This acorn can only be grown in the Golden Forest, by the will of the Seedlings. The quickest and easiest way to get their attention is to offer them one of these special acorns.'

'What *are* the Seedlings?' Oscar asked.

'They're funny little things,' Jackary chuckled. 'They're as old as the Dales. Perhaps even older. They are the personal aides to the Guardian of the Forest.'

'And who, or what, is the Guardian of the Forest?' Lilly asked impatiently, frustrated that all of her questions of late were lacking in direct answers.

'Well, from what I've been told, when the world was created, powerful beings known as Guardian Spirits appeared to ensure the flow of life throughout the lands. They are both *of* and *for* the world. Everything from birds and insects to trees and grass, and even you and me, all exist because of the power of the Guardian Spirits. One resides in this forest, and is charged with maintaining the life of Vhirmaa.'

'And the Seedlings,' Oscar began slowly, 'they are this Guardian Spirit's aides?'

'Correct,' confirmed Jackary, giving Lilly a knowing look.

'That's all well and good,' Lilly sniffed, rolling her eyes at Jackary, 'but you still haven't told us what these Seedlings are, exactly.'

'Well perhaps you'd be best asking them yourselves,' Jackary grinned. Lilly and Oscar looked at each other, confused. Then Oscar noticed that the acorn had disappeared from the windowsill!

'The acorn!' he exclaimed.

'Well, if you could call it that,' said a stout, wispy voice, serious but light.

Lilly and Oscar turned sharply to look at the stew pot. Perched on top of the brass handle that dangled the pot over the stove was... well, as Jackary had described the Seedlings, a funny little thing. It was short, although the word short might suggest something slightly taller than what this critter was. It stood barely a foot tall in height, and its width wasn't far off that either. Belly, shoulders, legs, arms and head all contributed to this almost cube-shaped creature. Speaking of its head, Lilly couldn't stop staring at it. It was furry, like a mouse's fur, and its big, green eyes were doe-like and warm. It had short, cat-like ears on the side of its head where a person's ears would be, and a wide mouth full of small, white teeth. It was an oddity to be sure, and at once Lilly knew what it was.

'A Seedling...' she muttered. She turned to Jackary, grinning. 'You were right. It is a funny little thing.'

'Oh, funny, is it?' the Seedling grumbled, offended.

'Ah, come off it,' Jackary scoffed. 'Don't act all sensitive. And what exactly is wrong with that acorn?'

'Well, it's hardly going to grow into a mighty oak, is it Jack?'

'It might do. That depends on the gardener.'

'Having a pop at my gardening now, are you? Tell me, were insults the only business you had with me this evening?'

This back and forth bickering went on for a time, both Jackary and the Seedling exchanging snide remarks and criticisms. Oscar stood beside Lilly, both completely awestruck. They couldn't believe what they were seeing. At last, the bickering ended and Jackary went about the formality of introductions.

'Oscar, Lilly, may I introduce Chifu, a Seedling of the Golden Forest.'

'It's a real pleasure to meet you,' Lilly said, bowing slightly. Oscar followed.

'Yes,' he said, humbly. 'An unusual pleasure though, I have to admit.'

Chifu nodded to both Lilly and Oscar, smiling as he did.

'*The Champions of the Golden Forest.* That is what the other Seedlings are calling you. We owe you much. Gombaroth was an awful villain, I never did care for him or his wicked ways.'

'He wasn't always the most agreeable fungus, true,'

113

Jackary began, 'but how in blazes did he amass such power? How was he able to weaken the Guardian's hold over the forest so easily?'

'A combination of his nasty will and the diabolical magic that has plagued Hylkoven,' Chifu answered sternly, shaking his little head.

'You know what happened at Honeydale?!' Oscar coughed, stepping towards the Seedling.

'I do,' Chifu said mournfully. 'Although I wish I didn't.'

'Then you'll know how urgently we need your help,' Oscar continued, his determined eyes wide and wild. He took the book from Lilly and waved it in Chifu's face. 'We need help translating this. It's a book from the Time of Mages, and it might hold some clue as to how we can save Honeydale. We were told the Seedlings might be able to help us translate this... So please, help us translate this!'

Oscar panted as he squeezed out the final few words. He was breathless, and desperate.

'Whoever told you the Seedlings could help you translate this book were misinformed,' Chifu sighed. 'We're not big on reading. Probably down to us not being able to read. Yes, that would be it.'

Oscar and Lilly looked at each other, the wind knocked clean from both their sails. Even Jackary put his hands on his face, disappointed on behalf of his new companions.

'Now don't you all go huffy-puffy on me,' Chifu groaned. 'I didn't say your book couldn't be translated, did I? I said *I* can't translate it. The one who *can* translate it would be very keen to do so, and is patiently awaiting your company as we speak, in fact.'

'You mean we're expected?' Lilly asked, tilting her head. 'By whom?'

'By Erdolet, the Guardian Spirit of Vhirmaa.'

'What?!' Jackary barked. 'How does she know about Lilly and Oscar?'

'How does she know anything that goes on in Vhirmaa, Jack?' Chifu quipped. 'Spiritual intuition or something, how should I know? All I do know is that she is well aware of what happened to Hylkoven, and that these two young 'uns saved the forest. Now she would like to pay her gratitude, which I'm sure could take the form of translating some old book, if you asked her.'

At that, Chifu hopped off the pot handle and waddled across the floor to the window.

'Oh, and Jackary,' he added, 'bring a map of Adhera with you.'

'Why?' Jackary asked.

'I don't know. Erdolet asked me to ask you.'

Not keen to answer any more unanswerable questions, Chifu hopped out of the window. Oscar watched as the tiny fellow glided to the grass below. Jackary whispered some unpleasantry about Chifu under his breath while he started rummaging through a box full of old maps. At last, he pulled out a long scroll bound by a tatty old ribbon. He nodded to Lilly and Oscar, then made his way to the door.

'This is really quite the honour,' Lilly said, closing the door behind her. 'It's not every day you meet an ancient spirit. How do you greet a Guardian Spirit, anyway? Is it like meeting royalty?'

'I suppose you just have to mind your manners,' Oscar answered. 'Although perhaps it's best we don't say anything at all. They might not be very sociable, these Guardian Spirits.'

'I don't suppose they are,' Lilly agreed, looking to Jackary, who was unusually quiet as they climbed down the ladder and onto the soft grass.

Impatiently, Chifu hurried them out of the clearing and back into the thick of the woods. Night had well and truly fallen, and Lilly and Oscar could barely see 6 inches in front of them. Even Jackary was tripping every now and then as Chifu led them down unfamiliar paths. Finally, when the way back had become entirely lost, Chifu stopped them. He stood on a bulbous toadstool and eyed his followers up and down, including Jackary, who had turned a little pale.

'Well then, you all look appropriately nervous,' Chifu chuckled. 'Blimey, Jack! You've gone a funny colour!'

'Why are you so nervous, Jackary?' asked Oscar, concerned.

'It's just...' Jackary began. 'It's just, I've never met Erdolet before. I've heard a lot about her, and Chifu here never stops talking about her, but... Oh, I don't know. This is kind of a big deal for me. I've lived in her forest for so long.'

'That you have. And it is a big deal indeed,' Chifu whistled. 'But you'll be fine, lad. She's really rather pleasant. Now, if we are all ready...'

Chifu parted the bush he was standing in front of,

which in turn parted the branches that hung over it, creating an archway of sorts into another clearing. The light here wasn't nearly as dim: in fact, it was really quite bright. Dozens of fireflies danced here and there above a wide pool of water that sat before a small waterfall, pouring shimmering water like a white blanket over large, silver rocks. The light from the flies and the full moon in the sky were reflected in this water, which illuminated the entire pool. It was breath-taking, and the three children stood in awe for a moment at this blissful sight.

Chifu grinned as he waddled on. From the bushes and trees, lots of other little figures emerged. They looked similar to Chifu, but with individual differences; some were smaller, some fatter, and some furrier. All with different colours of fur too, ranging from blue to blonde. It seemed there was a whole community of Seedlings living in the Golden Forest. Chifu issued orders to his kinsfolk and they dutifully set about their business. They didn't even acknowledge Lilly, Oscar or Jackary as they approached. None but Chifu.

'Right-oh!' he cheerfully grinned, before turning to the pool. 'O Lady Erdolet, Guardian of this Forest and of all Vhirmaa, I present to you Miss Lilly, and Masters Oscar and Jackary.'

Silence.

The water lay still, save for the ripples caused by the gentle falling of the waterfall. Curiosity got the better of their nerves though, and Lilly and Oscar stepped to the edge of the pool and peered in. Jackary didn't move, and kept his eyes focused on the waterfall. It was changing.

The water was starting to fall faster, but not harder, and a strange mist was sweeping over the entire pool. A gentle wave danced across the water, followed by a light splash, as if someone was dipping in their toes. A few more splashes playfully bounced across the surface, before erupting into a spiralling typhoon that rose towards the sky. Little sprites of green and yellow lights orbited the tower of water, which slowly began to descend into the pool once more. As it did, it parted, and standing quite elegantly where the water had risen was a tall, pale-skinned woman, with long, emerald-coloured hair and wide eyes that shone with an unnatural green glow. She had an otherworldly beauty, and Oscar, Lilly and Jackary were nothing short of awestruck. She smiled at all three of them, and at once they were calm and quiet inside. An unnatural but welcome serenity fell upon them.

'I am Erdolet, Guardian of the Forest,' she sang. 'I owe you both a great debt, Lilly and Oscar. To you too, Jackary Stiltz, who has long lived in this forest, and been a friend to my aides. Tell me, young ones, how might I show my gratitude?'

Lilly took a short step forward and cleared her throat.

'Lady Erdolet,' she began, 'a terrible thing has happened in Honeydale.'

'Yes,' Erdolet hastily said, as if the horrors of what happened were fresh in her mind. 'I can feel the weight of the horrible curse that has engulfed the city. A dark magic that is indeed. The one who cast the spell upon Honeydale was also the one that cursed The Golden Forest.'

'But why?' Oscar asked sharply. 'Why is he doing this? Who is he?'

'The power he possesses leaves no question; he is undoubtedly a mage. He called himself Vardelem, and came here to offer me a threat; that his revenge would begin with the fall of my realm. He warned that not even I, a Guardian Spirit, would be able to stop him. To ensure this, he bestowed unto Gombaroth, an ill-tempered and jealous creature, the power to drain the life out of the forest, making him stronger and I weaker.

'This evil would not have stopped at the borders of the Forest, either. It would have spread throughout Vhirmaa like wildfire, until all that lived and flourished within its realm were no more.'

'I thought the mages were extinct,' mumbled Oscar, almost to himself.

'I have not felt the power of the mages in countless ages. There is something about Vardelem that I cannot place. He is a mage, most definitely, but he does not belong in this world. Something most unnatural has occurred to allow him to walk in this present. Indeed, I sense a great many things are out of place.'

She tossed Lilly a knowing look, who responded by sheepishly looking at the ground. The book in her bag became heavy in her mind, and she knew it was time to reveal it to Erdolet.

'Lady Erdolet,' Lilly began, pulling the book from her bag. 'I have this book. I believe it is from the Time of Mages, but it's written in a language I don't recognise.'

She handed Erdolet the book, whose delicate fingers

119

rummaged playfully through the pages, flicking in the breeze.

'Ah yes, I know this book,' Erdolet smiled. 'You have brought this to me in the hope that I might be able to translate some kind of cure to Honeydale's curse? Indeed, there might be such a cure within these pages, for this is the Magukon Codex, after all.'

Oscar and Jackary glanced at each other, a chill rushing through them both. There was something daunting in that title. It carried a weight of importance and intimidation, and seemed to be part of a larger world than either Oscar or Jackary knew. They both turned to share this expression with Lilly, but it was not returned.

Lilly was hanging on Erdolet's every word.

'It is, or was, the handbook of every apprentice mage,' Erdolet continued, 'and there were thousands of copies, once upon a time. Alas, the Purge happened, where the last resistance of men brought about the extinction of the mages, and as a final precaution all copies of this book were destroyed. All but one, it seems.'

Lilly once again looked sheepish. Quickly though, she straightened herself up and cleared her throat. She then began to tell the rather long tale of how she came to possess the Magukon Codex. How it all began with the encouragement of her grandfather, Dysan, who told her of the book and all she knew of magic.

'On the night before he died,' Lilly said quietly, 'Grandpa stressed to me how important it was that I completed the task he had charged me with, as if my life depended on it. The next morning, I found him sitting in his usual chair by the fireplace. He was...'

Lilly's voice trembled, and Oscar put a comforting hand on her shoulder.

'I left home that day, and followed my grandfather's scheme to enter the palace and uncover the secret library. Although, it seemed someone else had the same idea.'

'There was someone else in the library?' Erdolet asked, concern in her voice.

'There were two others. They were not men though, nor creature. They were veiled in an unnatural blackness, and seemed to be formed of shadows and dust.'

'Tell me Lilly, did the two you describe look like this?'

Erdolet held the Magukon Codex open at a page that had a crude ink sketch of one of the shadowy villains Lilly had seen in the secret library.

'Yes!' Lilly replied, somewhat startled. 'That's what I saw.'

'I thought so. The two you described were more than just in league with Vardelem; they were created by him. They were golems, mindless husks formed by the dark magic Vardelem wields.'

'Why would Vardelem want the Magukon Codex?' asked Oscar. 'Didn't you say that it was just an apprentice's handbook? Why would one who is already capable of powerful magic bother with it?'

'Vardelem is shrouded in darkness and mystery. I could not presume to guess what his intentions are.'

'Perhaps he wants it for sentimental reasons,' offered Jackary, who until now had remained completely silent. 'If this is the only copy of this book, and one of the few remaining relics of his time, then perhaps he feels that it is his by right.'

'Or maybe it's because of what we were hoping,' Lilly smirked, looking at Erdolet. 'There's something in there that can undo the spell he cast upon Honeydale, isn't there? And he's scared we'll find a way to undo what he did.'

'That would seem likely, little Lilly, as there are indeed pages within the Magukon Codex about the very magic Honeydale is at the mercy of. The spell is called Petrification.'

Erdolet revealed yet another page to Lilly, Oscar and Jackary, this one showing a man being turned to stone by the flames of a dragon, the same dragon that Vardelem had summoned.

'Petrification is no ordinary spell, however,' Erdolet continued. 'It cannot be wielded by any mage, but comes from the flames of the Pedrakon, an ancient dragon who terrorised the lands of old. It seems Vardelem has found a way to bring him into our world and control him to do his bidding. The effects of Petrification can be undone however, with a spell known as Deystona.'

'Deystona...?' Oscar muttered, a shade of optimism rising in his voice.

'Do you know where magic comes from? It is drawn from the planet itself. Mages had the power to bend the elements and forces of nature to their will. Without the planet and the power it possesses, there would be no magic for them to wield. So, you see children, as long as our planet exists and life thrives upon it, there will always be magic.'

Erdolet flipped the Magukon Codex open to another page, one with several sketches of rocks and crystals expertly painted in a variety of vibrant colours, now faded slightly due to the effects of time. She showed this page to the children, but looked only at Jackary.

'Do you recognise these stones, Jackary?' she asked.

'I do,' he replied, a little smugly. 'I saw them in a book I have called *What's Mine is Mine: A Step-by-Step Guide to Deep Cave Mining.* These stones are incredibly rare, and are found among vast clusters of crystals, way down underground. And I mean, *way* down, like a cave beneath a cave, beneath a cave. In spite of their value, they're so rare and difficult to mine that most miners don't bother.'

'What about their colours?' Erdolet asked, glancing to the bemused faces of Lilly and Oscar.

'Well, they are usually determined by their environment. Red and orange stones tend to be found in hotter, dryer locations, while greens and blues are in damper, earthier places. So that book says, anyway.'

'So, if I were to ask you where you would likely find a red stone like the one in this book, where would you suggest?'

'As bright a red as that? I'd say somewhere hot. Like a desert.'

Jackary suddenly remembered he had been instructed by Chifu to bring with him a map of Adhera, the desert region to the east. He pulled it out from his coat pocket and unravelled it.

'That's why you need this!' he exclaimed.

'Yes, Jackary,' laughed Erdolet. 'These crystals are

infused with the properties of magic. Mages would mine for these clusters of power and absorb their magic, like drawing water from a well. These stones still exist, deep beneath the ground. This red stone here, that Jackary correctly said would be found in a desert, holds the power to reverse the effects of Petrification. It holds the power of Deystona.'

'The Adheran Desert is pretty big,' Lilly said, scoffing. 'Where are we supposed to start looking?'

'An ancient Elvish city once stood in the Northern Region of Adhera, before sandstorms and age consumed it. There was a temple in this city, built atop a vast network of underground tunnels. Mines created to unearth these stones. If you find that temple, you will find the path to the Deystona infused stone.'

'There's no mention of a temple on this map,' Jackary said. 'Or a city.'

'Great,' Lilly mocked. She looked down at Jackary, who was kneeling by the map, studying the Northern Regions of the desert. Oscar, meanwhile, wore a concerned expression.

'Deystona...' he muttered.

'I know your concerns,' Erdolet said to him, her voice suddenly resembling his mother's. 'Yes, it is true; only a mage would be able to draw the power of Deystona from the stone. But it seems it is also the only way to save Hylkoven. In your journey to find the rock, you might also find a way to use it. So, do not be disheartened Master Grubb. You are on a path headed in the right direction.'

Oscar said nothing. Hope didn't swell inside him like

it did when he first met Erdolet, but it hadn't gone completely. Indeed, what little hope he had now was still a great deal more than what he had standing at the gates of Honeydale.

'That being said,' Erdolet added, 'it will be a path full of peril, and it is with a heavy heart that I send you down it alone.'

'Lady Erdolet,' Oscar began, 'I have no intentions of sitting idly by while the fate of the people I care about stands on a knife's edge. Even if no one had offered any help thus far, I would still have endeavoured to do something. I know that this path will be perilous, but I decided to walk down it long before I found my way into these woods.'

'He's right,' agreed Lilly, standing beside him. 'It doesn't matter how big or small you are, or how old or young, all that matters is that Vardelem is stopped. We will do all we can to see that he is, with or without the help of others.'

'But others *will* help,' Jackary added. 'Lady Erdolet, with your blessing, I would like to accompany Lilly and Oscar on their journey. They helped me in dealing with Gombaroth; without them, I fear we would have lost the Golden Forest. Now I wish to show them my gratitude. Besides, it's always handy to have an alchemist on hand when you're going on a quest where the word *peril* is bandied about. We're experts in peril. Also, I'm none too shabby with a bow and arrow, so I can take care of myself.'

'You're an archer?' Lilly chuckled, raising an eyebrow.

'I wouldn't go that far. But the juiciest apples in this forest grow on the tallest trees, and it's easier to shoot them down with an arrow than climb up to get them. And less perilous. See! What did I tell you? Peril averted!'

Erdolet laughed, which warmed the children.

'Yes, Jackary, you have my blessing. Such courage from three so young is to be applauded, and I do not doubt the skill of each of you. Besting Gombaroth in battle was no small feat, and for doing that, I too would like to show my gratitude.'

Lilly turned to the sound of hurried footsteps scurrying across the grass. Three small Seedlings, youthful yet reserved, presented Lilly, Oscar and Jackary with a leaf-wrapped parcel each. Oscar's parcel was broad, thin and heavy, Lilly's was long and narrow, and Jackary's was small and tightly wrapped, with almost no weight to it at all.

'I hope these gifts will help you on your quest,' Erdolet said, her voice buoyant, almost singing. The three children behaved exactly as such, and hastily unwrapped their parcels. Oscar split the large leaf open, and it flapped apart to reveal a shiny metal shield, elaborate engravings quite spectacularly decorating its face.

Just as enthusiastically, Lilly made short work of her parcel, and found herself holding a long, gnarled stick. A walking stick perhaps, or maybe even a club. It was weighty and disjointed, like a thick branch, and was only a few inches short of Lilly's height. Its tip was spiralled and crooked, and all in all, was something of an oddity.

Lilly glanced to her right, and saw that Jackary was still having trouble unwrapping his gift. She rolled her eyes before once again returning her attention to her own.

'This shield, Oscar,' began Erdolet, 'was left here by a knight thousands of years ago. He fought in the war against the mages, and this shield is said to be strong enough to defend against magic.'

'Thank you! Thank you ever so much!' Oscar sang gleefully, bowing his head.

'For you Lilly, I also present a relic from the Time of Mages. This is a mage's staff. From its size, it seems it would have been an apprentice's staff, and is an appropriate accompaniment to the Magukon Codex. It is true that a mage's staff is not much use to a non-mage, but that wood is infused with enchantment and is not easily broken. It will serve you well as a club if need be, and in a quest to seek out the secrets of magic, an item such as this may have its uses.'

'Thank you, Lady Erdolet,' Lilly replied, humbly.

'And finally, for you Jackary -' Erdolet began, before stopping and giggling.

Oscar and Lilly turned to see Jackary frantically pulling and tearing at the leaf wrapping his gift. At last, with one final tear, the leaf cracked open. Jackary caught its contents before it fell to the ground, and finally he had his present in his hand. It was a weed: bright green, with long roots and twisted leaves.

'A Hyan Root!' Jackary exclaimed.

'Yes, Jackary,' Erdolet nodded. 'I don't need to tell you how rare this weed is, or how potent. This one sprouted quite miraculously in the forest one day, and I knew a skilled alchemist such as yourself would appreciate its quality. It will serve you well before your journey's end, of that I am sure.'

'Oh yes, Lady Erdolet. Thank you! A thousand times, thank you!' Jackary yelled, giggling while he spoke.

Lilly and Oscar looked at each other, quite bemused.

'And now little ones, I would suggest getting some rest. The hour grows late, and at first light you must make your way to the deserts of Adhera.'

'If we make our way to Market Town, we can get the train to Adhera City,' Jackary informed the others. 'We can head to the Northern Regions from there.'

Erdolet confirmed that this was a good plan, but it was with hesitance that she bid the three children goodnight. Such perilous responsibilities should not fall to ones so young, and yet it was these brave children who stood before her, destined to take on these tasks. In as spectacular a fashion as she appeared, the great Guardian Spirit of the Forest faded once more into the pool of glowing water, and the three young companions followed Chifu back into the thick of the forest.

It was not long before they found themselves standing beneath the looming tree Jackary's house sat upon. Chifu didn't hang around long, quick to waddle off back into the bushes after seeing the children climb the ladder and get to Jackary's front door.

'Sleep well, little 'uns!' he called out to them. 'I'll be back in the morning to see you off!'

Jackary, closing the door behind him, stood and

sighed. It had been a long and testing day. His new friends, Lilly and Oscar, obviously shared his feelings, as they had both found themselves the biggest and plumpest cushions in the house and were readying themselves for sleep.

'Before you get too comfy,' Jackary began, rather seriously, 'I've been thinking. This is a pretty big adventure we're about to embark on. Probably too big for three children.'

'Are you getting cold feet, Jack?' Oscar asked, sitting up straight.

'No, no, no. I know we're all more than capable, but in the end, it *is* what we are – children. And that's all people will see. Never mind mages and monsters, our biggest obstacle is going to be convincing people to let us get on with our quest.'

'He's right,' agreed Lilly, 'Pah'lin wasn't happy until he left us with a babysitter.'

'True,' Oscar nodded. 'The last thing we need is to be *looked after.*'

'Well, I think we'll be getting a lot of that, so I've come up with a solution.'

Jackary disappeared into a messy corner of the room, clinking bottles and shuffling papers as he rummaged about in the clutter. He emerged at last with a perfume bottle.

'This should help us,' he said, spraying the contents of the perfume on his chin.

'What is it?' asked Oscar.

'Something that will help,' Jackary replied, wafting Oscar with a hefty dose.

'Ugh! That smells awful!'

'Yes, it does sadly,' agreed Jackary, finally spraying Lilly with the remains of the bottle.

'Yuck! You weren't kidding!' she yelled.

'Yeah, sorry about that. Unfortunately, it isn't the only side effect, either.'

'You still haven't told us what you've sprayed us with!' Oscar insisted.

'I know, but first the side effects. People always rush to potions without consulting the labels, and almost all alchemy-related mishaps happen because of too much gung-hoeyness and not enough carefulness.'

'Okay, fine,' Lilly relented. 'But hurry up. I want to know what on earth you just sprayed me with.'

'Okay dokey. Well, there's nothing to be concerned about, it's really just your usual run of the mill side effect type stuff: minor headaches, some light nausea, mild itchiness – but that's to be expected given the nature of the potion…'

'Itchiness? What is it?!' Oscar yelled impatiently.

'Oh, and occasional drows-' Jackary began, but never finished.

He fell forward, landing face first onto a large pillow. He was sound asleep.

'Oh great,' mumbled Lilly, meeting the eyes of a very concerned Oscar.

Barely a moment went by before they both fell and joined Jackary on the floor, all three of them in a long, dreamless sleep.

Chapter Seven
A Hairy Situation

'Aaaaaaaaagh!'

Oscar rose with a start. Lilly was screaming!

'I'm... I'm...' Lilly was yelling wildly.

Oscar stood up, still a little drowsy, trying his best to focus. He took a few stumbling steps before he saw Lilly, and when he did, he nearly started screaming too.

'I'm... I'm hairy!' Lilly finally finished.

And so she was. Her cheeks and chin had grown a quite spectacular blonde beard, long and bushy. She was staring at her reflection in a small round mirror, her eyes wild with panic.

'Lilly,' Oscar began, 'you have a beard.'

'Yes, Oscar, thank you. I can see that. Why don't you...' Lilly turned to give him a thorough scolding, but found herself speechless at the sight of him.

'Oscar,' she began, 'you have a beard, too.'

'What?!' Oscar yelled, thrusting his hands to his face. Lilly wasn't lying. Oscar also had a beard, his one shorter, but bushier and more tangled.

'I have a beard!'

'Yes, yes, we all have beards,' announced Jackary, not at all fazed, and quite beardy himself. 'The potion I sprayed us with is an instant hair grower. I call it *The Miraculous Hair-Come-Backer.* I planned on selling it to bald people, should I ever find my way to a market.'

'And why have you decided to dowse our faces in it?!' Lilly asked, furious.

'Because of what we talked about. At every turn on our quest we're going to be treated like children. If we have beards, people won't think we're youths, they'll think we're small, beardy men. Dwarves, even.'

'Not a bad idea, actually' Oscar thought aloud. Lilly glared at him.

'Not a bad idea?!' she yelled, flabbergasted. 'And what happens once we're finished questing and don't want to be *small, beardy men* anymore? What happens when I want to be a little girl again?'

'Oh, it's not permanent Lilly,' Jackary chuckled. 'That's why I've been hesitant to rush off to the markets. I can't get it to last very long.'

'So how long will this last?' Oscar asked, quite on board with Jackary's plan.

'Who could say? A day or two. Maybe a week. I once got it to last for almost an entire month. The moulting process starts almost immediately though, and actually the hairs can be pulled out with a good hard tug. I wouldn't recommend doing that, though.'

'This is just great...' Lilly sighed.

'Lilly,' Oscar began, 'I know you're upset, but this is

actually quite a good idea. It'll at least get us as far as Adhera City without hassle.'

'I suppose,' conceded Lilly, who marched over to her things and began readying herself to leave.

Oscar and Jackary also gathered their things. Jackary packed a bag filled with all kinds of bizarre potions, weeds and fungi, varying in smelliness and stickiness. It was not long before they were packed and ready, and the three very dwarfy-looking children left the treehouse and descended onto the grass below. Chifu emerged from the thick of the woods, but stopped in his tracks when he saw them.

'Well weed my garden!' Chifu guffawed. 'What in the name of the Good Lady herself have you done, Jack?'

'Not you as well,' sighed Jackary. 'We've already hashed this out. We're travelling under the guise of being dwarves, okay?'

'If you say so.'

Chifu chuckled as he led the children through the forest. Lilly was still huffing and said very little. Nothing, in fact, despite Oscar trying to draw her attention to some quite spectacular flowers the Golden Forest was boasting. Jackary, too, was now huffing, disappointed that no one seemed to appreciate the rather brilliant plan he had come up with for allowing them to travel hassle-free. A potion that allowed hair growth was no small thing to brew, and he thought his efforts were to be marvelled at, not moaned about.

After an hour or so, Chifu finally stopped and revealed to the children a path leading out into the open fields of the Dales.

'Here we are,' he said. 'The northern borders of the Golden Forest, and the final stretch of Vhirmaa before the Narrow Canyon.'

'The Narrow Canyon?' Oscar asked.

'It's the only way through the wall of mountains that divide the *Dales and the Dunes*,' Lilly answered, stepping out of her huff for a moment to reprise her *matter-of-fact* tone.

Oscar looked upon the mountains in question. A wall was right, the lofty peaks stretching for as long as the mist permitted the eye to see. He could see no canyon, but by squinting just so, he could see a small settlement of buildings at the foot of one of the mountains.

'That's Market Town,' Jackary informed Oscar. 'The train leaves from there and passes through the Narrow Canyon and on to Adhera City.'

'In that case, we'd better get going.'

Oscar, Lilly and Jackary bid Chifu a fond farewell, and then set forth for Market Town. They were clearly still a long way away. The fields of the eastern regions of Vhirmaa were flat, but gradually sloped downward towards the shadow of the mountains. Oscar eagerly led the party, marching across the grass in wide strides. Lilly was using her newly acquired staff as a walking stick. Her eyes fell to Oscar's shield, which was clearly made for someone of adult stature, as it covered his entire back, and nearly the rest of him too.

'Isn't your shield heavy?' she asked.

'You have no idea,' he winced. 'But I'll cope. I've always wanted a sword and shield. Real ones, not toys.

And now that I have them, I'm not about to start grumbling about their astronomical weight!'

'It's very pretty,' Lilly added, admiring the design.

'Thanks,' mumbled Oscar, not keen on his battle-ready gear being described as *pretty*.

'Your stick is pretty great, too,' Jackary said, attempting to get back in Lilly's good graces.

'Stick?' she replied, almost offended. 'Weren't you listening? This is a mage's staff. This thing is ancient, and filled with magical potential.'

'But you're not a mage,' Jackary sniffed, 'so really, it's just a stick. A swell stick though, I grant you.'

Lilly groaned, cursing Jackary under her breath. 'Well, what about your "*gift*"?' she asked sarcastically. 'What's so special about that weed?'

'Weren't *you* listening?' Jackary replied, completely offended. 'This is a Hyan Root, one of the rarest growths to sprout from the earth. One tiny clipping from it will make any potion a billion times more potent. Mix it with the ingredients for a poison antidote, you'll be immune to the poison for life. Making a potion of levitation? A shaving of Hyan Root will have you flying to the heavens and back. A minor wound-healing potion? Boom! Now you're back from the dead. Although, how you're supposed to take the potion when you're dead, I don't know. There are some corners you just can't cut, I suppose. Perhaps if you had the potion in a jar strapped to your head, with a straw...' Jackary began mumbling to himself, trying to figure out how a dead person would drink a potion.

Lilly and Oscar just looked at each other and shook

their heads.

The march across the fields went by fairly uneventfully, the three companions chatting and whistling and doing anything to pass the time. The closer they got to the mountains, the clearer the Narrow Canyon became, as well as the small settlement lying before it, known as Market Town.

Market Town had been named such by someone with not a great deal of imagination. When the two mighty cities of Hylkoven and Adhera were established, and in rather contrasting environments, it seemed only right that there should be a trade route between them. The Narrow Canyon was crafted by the finest miners and masons the two nations had to offer, and at last an easy and safe way to cross the border had been created. Although any traveller could pass through the Narrow Canyon, the train line was mostly used by traders, looking to peddle their wares from one nation to another. The rather small train station on the Vhirmaa side of the canyon soon became a hotspot for traders to trade, and word spread of a great market growing there. The rather humble train station became a not-so-humble town. With a market. And thus, it became known as "Market Town", although its original name was "The Train Station and Market Town", then "Town With a Market and Train Station". Thankfully, the dullard charged with naming the town had been revealed to be quite useless at it, and was made redundant before the simpler "Market Town" was settled upon.

Just before the sun peaked at noon and the looming shadow of the mountains made its switch to the Adheran

136

side, Oscar, Lilly and Jackary walked onto the main - and only - street in Market Town. There were three or four shack-like buildings on either side of the road, inns mostly, and a general store. At the end of the street was a larger brick building, with a large clock towering above the roof and a faded sign below it reading "Station". The street was busy and cluttered with stalls that had been put up hastily by chancing merchants. Pedlars of all types were hollering at the three children, referring to them as "Master Dwarf!" and complimenting their beards, much to Lilly's chagrin. Neither Oscar, Lilly or Jackary paid them any heed, however, and marched onward to the train station.

The station platform was busy with would-be travellers resting upon their luggage. They'd obviously been waiting a good long while. Oscar approached the desk marked *Tickets* and peered over the counter. A moustachioed, rosy-cheeked conductor peered back at him, and beamed a gracious smile.

'Good day, Master Dwarf,' he said cheerfully. 'A ticket to Adhera, is it? For you and your companions?'

'Yes, please,' replied Oscar, who suddenly realised something awful. His voice! Lilly, Jackary and himself might have the appearance of dwarves, but they still had the voices of children. The conductor gave him a curious look. Oscar cleared his throat.

'I mean... Aye!' he said, doing the best impersonation he could of his father, who wasn't a dwarf, but was a harsh-voiced, rough-and-ready sort. Indeed, if it weren't for the four extra feet in height he had, Old Grubb would've made quite a spectacular dwarf.

'I see,' the conductor said, dismissing the high-pitched voice as being a dwarvish joke, a brand of humour he'd never understood. 'That'll be 75 panz each.'

After some pooling of resources between Oscar, Lilly and Jackary, they paid the fare and took their tickets. The conductor informed them the train was due to arrive in just over an hour, and so they had a little time to kill. They quickly agreed that they were hungry and could use some refreshment after their long hike. They made their way to one of the smaller inns, and ordered what little food they could afford after the lofty cost of the tickets. They sat in silence for the most part, enjoying the scones, jam and honey they had ordered.

'Bleugh!' exclaimed Jackary suddenly. 'No meat! No ale! Nothing but namby-pamby scones!'

Lilly and Oscar looked at each other and shrugged - a mannerism that was becoming the norm since travelling with Jackary.

Jackary chuckled and leaned in to whisper.

'Just keeping up appearances,' he grinned. 'Scones and the like aren't really a dwarf's cup of tea, you know.'

A few moments later, after the attention of the other patrons had wavered away from the "noisy, fussy dwarves", Lilly froze mid-bite, and bowed her head as low as she could.

'What are you doing?' asked Oscar.

'Look who just walked in!' she replied, in a loud whisper. Oscar turned to look at the door, and standing there surveying the room was Pah'lin and the two guards he had left Roark's hut with.

'Oh no...' Oscar grimaced, although he was secretly pleased to see Pah'lin.

'What is it? Who is that?' Jackary asked impatiently.

'That's Pah'lin. Captain of the Honeydale City Guard,' Oscar informed him.

'And he left us to be babysat by Roark,' Lilly added. 'He won't be pleased to see us here.'

'I see,' Jackary nodded. He pondered for a moment. 'So, what exactly is the problem?'

'Well, he'll stop us from going to Adhera for one thing!' Lilly snapped.

'But he won't recognise you. You're dwarves now, remember?'

Pah'lin approached the table, Lilly and Jackary too busy bickering to notice. Oscar noticed though, and discreetly kicked the table leg to alert them. They hushed themselves instantly and lowered their gaze. Pah'lin was now right by the table, looming over Lilly.

'Over here,' he called to his guards.

That's it, Lilly thought. *We've been rumbled.*

His guards walked over to the table and now each child had a guard standing behind them. Oscar was about burst out with a string of excuses he was hastily preparing in his head, when finally, Pah'lin turned and sat at an empty table nearby. His guards followed suit. Both Lilly and Oscar let out a long sigh of relief.

'Eat up,' Oscar ordered. 'We'll go and wait on the platform.'

The train arrived before long, right on schedule in

fact. Dozens of passengers poured out of the carriages, all complaining about being back in the cold after their trips to Adhera. Oscar shook his head at them. Why would they wear shorts and vests to travel back to Vhirmaa? It could be mild here, and indeed this was a warm summer's day, but for as mild and warm as Vhirmaa could be, it was downright chilly compared to the blistering heat of the desert.

Lilly was hopping impatiently by the door of one of the carriages. She had never been on a train before and was positively excited. So was Oscar for that matter, when he was done grumbling about the grumbling passengers. Jackary was mumbling to himself, trying to remember whether or not he had been on a train before. He thought he had, but he couldn't be sure. All the while, Oscar and Lilly were acutely aware of Pah'lin and his men standing not far from them along the platform. So far, he hadn't noticed them, but they feared it was only a matter of time. They had serious reservations about their disguises.

When the train was finally ready for new passengers to board, signalled by a whistle blown by the conductor, the three children clambered on and found seats in the carriage furthest from Pah'lin. They sat in a private compartment and settled themselves by the window, watching the station workers running here and there, ushering passengers onto the train and trying to return stray luggage to their owners. It seemed like an eternity before the conductor blew his whistle again.

The train shuddered at the whistle's command, gears and wheels began to grind into motion, and slowly the train started to pull away from the station. Quickly, shadow surrounded them, and the view changed from the shacks and huts of Market Town to the black carved rock of the Narrow Canyon.

'Well, that's us on our way then,' Jackary smiled.

'Finally,' Lilly sighed, sitting back in her seat, watching the walls of the canyon whiz by as the train picked up speed.

'Can I see that map of the desert again, Jack?' Oscar asked.

Jackary nodded and pulled the map from his bag. Together they examined it.

'Erdolet said there used to be a temple in the Northern Regions...' Oscar said, half aloud, half to himself. 'That's a long way from Adhera City.'

'The Northern Regions are pretty big, too,' added Jackary. 'We could scour the desert for days and not come up with a crumb.'

'Perhaps someone in Adhera will know where it is,' Lilly offered, her tired eyes closed.

'Maybe,' nodded Oscar, reservedly. 'We should be careful about announcing our destination though.'

Agreeing with this, Lilly returned to her rest. Jackary continued to pour over the map with Oscar, attempting to find some clue or landmark that would guide them to the temples location.

Time didn't pass for very long before the train braked suddenly, tossing the startled children across the compartment. The sound of commotion and brew-ha-ha coming from neighbouring compartments filled the carriage, and suddenly the whole train was in a puzzled uproar. Lilly scrambled to her feet, rubbing her head, while Jackary straightened his beard and observed as Oscar opened the compartment door and walked into the hall of the carriage.

'I'm going to go see what the trouble is,' he informed the others, resting his hand on the helm of his sword and pulling his shield tight against his back. Jackary and Lilly didn't hesitate to follow.

They pushed their way from carriage to carriage, squeezing past the crowds of people who were murmuring to each other in confused tones. Some of them were hanging out the windows in an attempt to see what the hold-up was. At last, Oscar emerged from the crowd at the front carriage, where he saw Pah'lin and his men talking to the train driver. After some hushed conversation, the driver led Pah'lin onto the locomotive. Oscar, Lilly and Jackary slowly followed, and lingered by the furnace.

'You see? There!' the driver exclaimed to Pah'lin, panicked. The curious children, acting as curious dwarves, allowed themselves to etch closer to Pah'lin and the driver. They peered out the side door window, and could see what the cause for concern was; a wagon, battered and smashed, lying dormant on the track.

'I dunno what in blazes a wagon would be doing out there,' the driver said. 'Must've fallen off a path up in the mountains.'

'There are no paths bordering the Narrow Canyon,' Pah'lin said, sternly. 'Certainly none big enough for a wagon to pass through, or fall from.'

'Well, what's it doing there then?' the driver pressed.

'I don't know. It might've been put there.'

'Put there?!' laughed the driver. 'Funny place to park your wagon! Who would put a wagon there?'

'Bandits, maybe.'

'Bandits?' the no-longer-laughing driver asked.

'Or worse. You know what resides in these mountains. Either way, I smell a trap.'

Pah'lin turned to his men, ordering one of them to calm the passengers and make sure no one left the train. The other guard was to accompany Pah'lin outside to try and move the blocking wagon.

'I want you to have this train ready to move the second I give the order,' Pah'lin instructed the driver. 'And you there, Master Dwarves,' he said, turning to the not-actual-dwarves.

Lilly and Oscar turned their gaze away, not wanting to meet Pah'lin's eyes. Pah'lin went silent for a moment, squinting his eyes as he examined them.

'Well, laddie?' barked Jackary, in his best dwarvish voice. 'Speak quickly!'

'Oh, um...' Pah'lin quickly found his thoughts again. 'Will you assist me in trying to move that wagon? It looks pretty weighty, I could use the famed upper body strength of the dwarves right now.'

Jackary nodded and led his companions out of the train after Pah'lin. The wagon did look plenty weighty, and the famed upper body strength of dwarves would be as non-existent in Jackary, Lilly and Oscar as their claim to being actual dwarves. Still, not wanting to give up the ruse, they would give it their best shot.

They walked along the tracks cautiously, with

143

Pah'lin leading the way. His eyes darted around, waiting for the trap to spring. They hesitated for a moment before attempting to move the wagon, but when at last all seemed safe, Pah'lin instructed everyone to grab a section of the wagon and to push. It was covered in a strange dust, black and rough. Jackary quickly recoiled.

'This is firedust...' he mumbled to himself, taking several steps back and pulling his bow from his back. 'It's firedust! Run!'

Taking Jackary's advice, everyone backed away from the wagon, and not before time. The sound of something whistling through the air cut through the silent canyon. An arrow, a bright flame burning on its tip, flew from a crack in the canyon wall and stuck into the wagon's side. The firedust sparked as the flame spread, and within moments the entire wagon was engulfed in flame. The crackling of the burning firedust became ferocious, erupting in an explosion, sending debris and flaming shards of wood flying in every direction. There was a sudden unsettling howl from the shadows, followed by responding barks and growls. Now standing in front of the train, Pah'lin turned uneasily towards the harrowing sounds.

'Gnolls,' he said, drawing his sword. 'Everyone onto the train!'

No one hesitated, and quickly they barricaded themselves inside the train. There are few creatures in the world as vicious or foul as gnolls. Their ratty faces snarl from their dog-eared heads, bobbing atop patchy haired bodies, all twisted and gnarled. They bite and claw and always attack in packs. Roads, paths, and now train tracks, are prime targets for gnolls, who are, if anything, a breed of natural born bandits. Unlike goblins or orcs, they will not cower away in caves during the day, meaning they are a constant threat to travellers.

Oscar had never seen one in the flesh, only knowing of them by reputation. But in the few short seconds they had been back on the train, he had counted half a dozen. They were pouring out of cracks in canyon walls, abseiling down on long ropes. The driver had gotten the train moving, but it was clear that its slow start up speed wouldn't get them out of dodge quick enough. Pah'lin and his men readied their weapons as the claws of the coming gnolls landed on the roofs of the carriages. Oscar, Lilly and Jackary also drew their weapons, before darting into the first carriage.

With an almighty smash, every window gave way to a dozen gnolls. Jackary didn't hesitate, and loosed an arrow into the pack. They responded with fierce, quick movements, teeth bared and swords unsheathed. Pah'lin met them first, slashing and swinging expertly. His men coordinated around him, making the already narrow path even narrower, meaning neither Oscar, Lilly or Jackary could join in the fight.

'We have to move,' Oscar informed his companions. 'We need to get into the other carriages.'

'The roof!' Jackary exclaimed. 'If we take the roof, we can cover more carriages, as well as sort out any gnolls landing up there.'

They all nodded in agreement and climbed up onto a row of seats. Carefully, they clambered out of the window, pulling themselves up onto the roof of the train, the speed of which was gradually increasing.

Oscar was the first to find his feet, and was instantly attacked by three gnolls. He hastily parried each of their attacks, hopping from foot to foot, trying to throw his opponents off balance. Lilly swung her staff into the back of one of the gnolls' knees, tripping it up and sending it tumbling off the train. Jackary similarly hooked his bow round the neck of another, and burled it round until it flew from the train and crashed into the wall of the canyon.

Oscar was in the midst of a sword fight with the last gnoll, trying his best to stay focused and remember the lessons of the old sword master in his village. Jackary wasted no time in shooting off another arrow, which stuck into the left cheek of the gnoll's bottom. It howled in agony and whimpered in embarrassment, and almost of its own accord, dove off the train in a stumbled leap.

'I had that situation under control, you know,' Oscar said in a disappointed tone.

'I do apologise, but you needn't worry; there are still plenty more to fight.'

He was not wrong. Dozens of gnolls had bombarded the train, with more pouring out of the cracks in the canyon.

'Get down there and fight!' Jackary ordered. 'I'll pick some of these buggers off from up here.'

Oscar didn't give him a chance to finish his sentence, and was already climbing down the side of the train. He glanced to Lilly, who was a little hesitant, but dutifully followed regardless. The train was starting to pick up speed, and the air rushing along the side was hard to fight against, especially when dangling outside a window like a sheet in the wind. Oscar helped Lilly through the window and into an empty cabin, before leading them both out into the corridor.

They crossed over to the next car, and were pounced upon by three gnolls. The fight started quickly, with Oscar crossing swords almost as soon as their foes appeared. His swordsmanship was impressive; even Lilly admired it. It wasn't the most fluid or elegant of styles, but he had confidence, and was more competent than the clumsily hacking gnolls.

Lilly was less confident, nervously clutching her sword. She had never had much call to use a blade before, despite Dysan having attempted to give her lessons. As such, she wasn't a stranger to a sword, but she felt a lot more comfortable clobbering the gnolls with her staff. That required no style, nor lessons. Just swing and hit.

Using both their unique styles and weapons, they felled their opponents, save for one. It hissed and wailed in fear, before scurrying off into the next carriage. Oscar grinned; amidst all this mayhem, he was actually having fun. He gave chase, barrelling through the door after the gnoll. Lilly began to follow, when suddenly another one smashed through the window. It snarled as it crashed into her path, mouth foaming with excited drool.

Lilly was cornered, cut off from the all too eager Oscar. The gnoll growled at her, teeth bared, yellow and misshapen. It took three slow steps forward, and then sprung on the fourth, slashing its sword downward. Instinctively, Lilly raised her staff above her head, dropping her sword to grip it with both hands. She blocked the attack, but the blow was heavy and forced her to stumble backwards. The gnoll swung down its sword once more. Lilly rolled to the side, causing the sword to crack against the hard, wooden floor.

She fell into the wall as she scrambled to her feet. The gnoll advanced once more, swiping its blade across from the right. Without thought, Lilly parried the strike and thrust her staff forwards towards its chest. As it struck, there was a bright flash of white light, accompanied by a tremendous force that blew Lilly and the gnoll away from each other. Lilly hit the wall hard once more, and fell to the floor. The gnoll flew backwards, too quick to allow for a petrified wail, and disappeared out the window it smashed through.

Lilly opened her eyes to see long strands of hair glide gently to the floor. She put her hands to her cheeks. Smooth. Her faux beard had been obliterated with the force of the blast. Lilly was puzzled. What in blazes had just happened?

She didn't have time to ponder it though, as the door opposite suddenly swung open. Pah'lin came charging in, but stopped suddenly when he saw her. He looked around at the falling hair, and shook his head. He marched over to Lilly and opened his mouth to undoubtedly deliver a stern lecture, when more gnolls came flooding through the door behind him. He grabbed Lilly and held her tight against him. With his free hand, Pah'lin took care of the attacking gnolls. He did not let her go as they advanced up the train, his firm grip hurting her arm, though she didn't dare complain.

The train was pretty much now at full speed, charging steadily towards the other end of the Narrow Canyon. Jackary had been picking off as many landing gnolls as he could. The train was now moving too quickly for him to stay up on the roof though, and so he jumped down into the carriage below. He found himself standing with the huddled group of passengers in the rear car. A heavy hand fell on his shoulder. He turned and saw Pah'lin standing there. Behind him, looking very sheepish, were Lilly and Oscar, sans beards.

'If you really are a dwarf, then I apologise profusely for this,' said Pah'lin, before grabbing Jackary's beard and giving it a hard tug. It came off in a single motion, stinging his face slightly. 'What a surprise…'

One of Pah'lin's men came through the door, a relieved expression on his face.

'Sir, the last of the gnolls are off the train. We'll be out of the canyon in minutes.'

'Good,' sighed Pah'lin. 'Take these three to one of the cabins and stand guard on their door. I'll be along to deal with them shortly.'

Both Lilly and Oscar thought to argue with him, but his tone and expression was filled with frustration. The last thing they both wanted was to be sent back to Vhirmaa again, or kept under lock and key. And so, with heads bowed, they heeded his words and left the carriage, conceding to follow his orders. For now.

Chapter Eight
In the Court of Lord Eirron

The train emerged on the other side of the Narrow Canyon, riddled with arrows and burn marks. The rolling hills of green in Vhirmaa had been replaced by the endless Adheran desert. They passed across the vast white sands of the Dunes, free from danger and threat. Free from anything at all, in fact; the desert seemed to be precisely that – deserted.

The three children sat in their own carriage, alone and quiet. Lilly made eye contact with neither Oscar or Jackary, thinking about the incident with the gnoll. What had happened? Was it magic? She decided pretty quickly not to mention it to anyone. At least not until she had decided what *it* was.

After almost an hour of the creaking train trudging along the dusty tracks, the door to the compartment opened and in walked Pah'lin, with a face that looked like a thunderstorm. He said nothing at first, silently eyeing the now beardless children. He almost wanted to laugh, the farce of their disguise was worthy of that. However, his concern, anger and frustration outweighed any levity he held within. He leaned against the window, arms crossed. Oscar, Lilly and Jackary stirred uneasily in their seats.

'Well,' Pah'lin began, sitting up straight, 'where do we begin? Roark Stoneheart? Did you run away from his care the second I had my back turned?'

'I suppose you could put it like that,' Oscar admitted. 'Although we didn't run. He sent us on our way.'

Pah'lin cursed under his breath.

'It's a good thing he did,' Jackary chimed in.

'Oh, is it now? And who are you exactly?'

'My name's Jackary Stiltz, and I'd thank you to make your tone more respectful. For all any of us know, I'm older than all of you put together. And it *is* a good thing that Roark sent Oscar and Lilly on their way, as they just might've stumbled upon a way to save Honeydale!'

Pah'lin said nothing. Without invitation, Oscar and Jackary began to tell Pah'lin all of what had happened, from their leaving Roark's hut, to meeting the Guardian of the Forest, Erdolet. They even explained their sudden beard growth.

Lilly shot a cold glance at Oscar, who shrugged back at her.

'There's no point keeping the truth from him. He's got us locked in here, and he's not going to let us out of his sight in Adhera. He'll listen to reason though. He'll see the importance of our quest.'

Lilly turned her eyes back to the vastness of the

151

desert.

Pah'lin sat in silence for a time. This tale Jackary and Oscar were spinning was fantastical. However, recent events made Pah'lin a bit more receptive to the fantastic. Uncertainty ruled him. The only thing he could be sure of was his annoyance at Roark. How could he be so foolish?

But then there's this story, with the Magukon whatsit. Did Lilly really break into the palace? He knew the palace guards were soft, but did they really get outwitted by a nine-year-old girl? Was this curative crystal business true too?

Even if it was, how could he in all good conscience let Oscar and Lilly, and now a third one, Jackary, go wandering off into the desert? No, he would decide what to do with this magical rock affair later. His first order of business would be to take care of the children, whether they were willing or not.

They sat in silence for the remainder of their journey, all of them exhausted. Jackary even nodded off, while Lilly stared intently out the window at the passing sands, her thoughts deep and ponderous. She kept her hands tucked under her coat sleeves in an effort to hide the fact that they were trembling. The magic pulse that emanated from the staff, if indeed that's what it was, spooked her far more than the magic she witnessed in Honeydale.

It wasn't long before the train arrived in Adhera station.

Crowds gathered around the carriages as it came to a stop. All the passengers disembarking the train received concerned glances and whispers. Some official looking men anxiously asked the driver about what had happened. Pah'lin found himself roped into the conversation, keeping the children close to him. He tried to steer the topic away from them; however, the driver couldn't help himself.

'And these children!' he announced, pointing his shaking hand at Oscar, Lilly and Jackary. 'These children fought the gnolls! Fought as hard as these Honeydale guards! Saved my neck, they did! Saved all of us!'

He prattled on and on, and it was hard for Oscar to hide his smile. Not smugness as such, but he was brimming with pride. Jackary gloatingly grinned, welcoming the praise. Lilly smiled politely, but really, she was terrified that he had seen the staff incident, worried that he was about to yell 'And this one does magic!'

He didn't however, and as quickly as he could, Pah'lin rushed them out of Adhera station and into the hot city.

It was busy, even though it was well after dusk. Busier than Honeydale, by Oscar's estimations. The streets were cramped and narrow, with people hollering and clambering over each other. At last they came to an inn, and Pah'lin marched them through the door. He paid for a room for the three of them, and one for himself.

He ordered them some dinner; chicken and rice, and ate with them for a while. They didn't say much at all, beyond remarking on the heat – Jackary's attempt to strike up conversation. Lilly was the first to finish, and immediately left the table to go lie in her bed. Pah'lin watched her carefully; it was obvious something was on her mind.

Jackary and Oscar soon followed suit, and once all three were fast asleep, Pah'lin sneaked out the door, making sure to lock it behind him.

-

The familiar dream.

A swirl of blue light, moving faster than her eyes could focus. Lilly concentrated on the face behind the light. The woman she had always dreamt of. Holding her hand out, reaching for Lilly, eyes bloodshot with tears, beckoning to her. There was a yearning from both the mysterious woman and Lilly herself. The light brightened, she closed her eyes, the woman disappeared...

Lilly's eyes opened. Bright sunlight was pouring in through the balcony door. Jackary was standing out there alone, marvelling at the city. Sitting on his bed and pulling on his boots was Oscar. He smiled when he saw Lilly wake up.

'How are you feeling?' he asked.

'What do you mean?'

'You were awfully quiet yesterday, after the ruckus on the train, I was just worried...'

'Oh, I'm fine. Just never been in a fight with gnolls before.'

'Yeah. Creepy buggers they were!' announced Jackary from the balcony.

'Pah'lin just popped his head in two minutes ago,' Oscar informed her. 'We've to meet him downstairs in an hour. We're going somewhere important.'

Lilly nodded and got out of bed. She got washed and dressed and headed downstairs with Oscar and Jackary. Waiting for them in the lobby was Pah'lin, his Hylkoven branded armour buffed and polished after its scrapes from the day before. He greeted the children in his usual stoic manner, and then announced something rather surprising.

'The Sultan of Adhera, Lord Eirron, has requested your company,' he told them, quizzical concern on his face.

'Why?' Lilly asked, making no attempt to hide her suspicion.

'To thank us for helping out on the train, no doubt!' Jackary exclaimed.

'Something like that,' nodded Pah'lin, still not looking comfortable. 'He's also concerned about what he's heard of Honeydale, and given you are some of the few witnesses who managed to escape the city, your presence in his court has been deemed urgent.'

With this, Pah'lin turned and led the children out onto the street. A dorataur-drawn carriage awaited them. Dorataurs were bizarre creatures that fell somewhere between a reptile and a bird. Descended from dragons, according to the old legends, they were about the size of an ostrich, with long, scaly necks and round, fat heads. Their snouts hooked into a leathery beak, and their eyes were wide and unblinking. They were fast creatures and natural inhabitants of the desert, making them a far better means of transport in Adhera than horses.

The children followed Pah'lin and clambered aboard the carriage. The driver made a strange yelping sound, ordering the dorataurs to march forward. They yelped back in obedience and the carriage began to roll.

Adhera seemed even bigger by daylight. Markets, street vendors, and performers dominated every inch of the dusty streets. People pushed and dodged around one another, all trying to grab a bargain or do a shady deal. It was lively and jovial. Painted on almost every wall was some sort of tribute to Pyriona, the Goddess of the Desert and the Sun, worshipped and loved by all Adherans. Their day-to-day lives always involved a sermon at midday, when the sun was at its highest point in the sky. They would all congregate at one of the many temples dedicated to Pyriona in the city, all of which had the common feature of a circular hole in the ceiling that would baptise the worshippers in a beam of sunlight.

The Adheran Desert, and its capital city, had enjoyed much of the same peace as Vhirmaa. They had spent centuries wanting for nothing, enduring very little conflict, and overcoming what little turmoil the wind ever did blow their way. Adherans were a content people with a renowned, laid-back attitude towards life.

Their Sultan, Lord Eirron, shared that mentality. As his much more brittle northern name would suggest, Lord Eirron wasn't a native of Adhera. He hailed from Cragnarr, a vast, snow covered land northward of the Clashing Sea. His family had been the governing body of Adhera for generations, but Eirron was the first of his kin to migrate there. He had never been overly fond of the cold, despite being born and raised in it. So, when at last the title of Sultan was passed on to him, he took the chance to move himself and his wife, Ilga, to the much hotter climate of Adhera.

His palace was a giant dome, shaped rather ironically like an igloo. It stood proudly in the shadow of Pyriona's Altar, an enormous mountain of yellow rock, the ridges of which swooped round the side of the walls of the city like a protective horseshoe-shaped barrier. The palace seemed to be carved of the same yellow rock as the mountain, which made it glow in the sunlight. Atop the centre of the dome was an elaborate statue of a bird made of fire.

'The Phoenix,' marvelled Lilly.

'Yes, Lilly,' confirmed Pah'lin. 'Adherans believe the Phoenix is the protector of this desert, and of the city.'

The statue speared towards the sky, casting a jarring shadow on the path leading up to the wide-open doors of the palace. The dorataurs brought the carriage to a halt when they reached them, and they were greeted by one of the palace's stewards.

'This way, please. The Sultan is awaiting your company,' said the steward, before bowing respectfully and leading them all inside. The palace was a maze of pillars, intertwined with a labyrinth of staircases. Ahead of them was a set of double doors as big as the palace's yawning entrance. The steward opened them and gestured for Pah'lin and the children to enter.

It was the throne room, a hall dimly lit and sparsely occupied. Three or four advisers sat on cushions in the centre of the room, while maidens went about their serving duties, offering fruit and wine. A youthful-looking man, with an angelic face and wavy blond hair, gently plucked on a harp. The atmosphere was tranquil, and everyone seemed at ease.

Upon a raised platform at the far end of the hall was a large, rotund man, strewn in light fabric robes. He was tall, even while sitting down, and had a dome shaped head, similar to the palace, with precious little hair upon it. His pose was relaxed, lying on his side and resting his head on his hand, his pinkie tickling the wisp of white hair on his chin. He seemed to be lying on a cushion, so large and elaborately stitched that it must've been the subject of many a bard's tale.

By his side was a middle-aged woman with short, blueish-white hair and equally light robes. She smiled humbly as Pah'lin and the children approached, and rose out of her smaller, yet equally elaborate cushion.

'Captain Pah'lin, so nice to see you again,' she said warmly, her accent spiked with a northern tenor.

'And you, Lady Ilga. May I present Oscar Grubb, Lilly Rachert, and Jackary Stiltz: the three who defended against the gnolls' attack in the Narrow Canyon.'

'Ah, our young heroes,' she grinned. She touched the large gentleman sat next to her on the leg. 'My love, may I present Miss Rachert, and Masters Grubb and Sti-'

'Bawk!' cried the giant impatiently. 'Why must we always be so formal?! I heard the Hylkoven Captain, my love, I know who they are. They're the youngsters who gave those manky cretins a bloody good hiding! Tell me, young 'uns, how many did you kill?'

'Well, it was pretty hard to keep track of what was going on,' Oscar replied humbly.

'Bawk! Too many to count, eh? Wonderful!

158

Gnolls... Bawk! Bawk! Disgusting creatures! Vicious buggers, too. Would eat a horse while riding it!'

'Darling,' Ilga interjected, 'must we talk so morbidly? Horse eating is hardly appropriate conversation in the court of Sultans. You haven't even introduced yourself yet.'

'Double Bawk and Boomtickle! Have it your way... Young Master Gnoll-Slayers, I am Lord Eirron, Sultan of Adhera. There, happy now?'

'Ecstatic,' grinned Ilga.

'Those bloody gnolls have been a growing pain for me,' continued the Sultan. 'Outposts raided, traders ambushed... They've been terrorising these parts for months! Perhaps now, though, they'll simmer down a bit. You will be rewarded, of course; gold, jewels, we're not short of that in Adhera.'

'Thank you, Lord Eirron,' Oscar said, stepping forward, Lilly dreading the words that would follow, 'but gold and jewels aren't of much use to us. We're on a quest to save Honeydale, which I'm sure you know all about. We need your help to cross the desert and search the Northern Regions for an ancient temple.'

'To what end?' said a voice from the back of the room.

Oscar turned to see a tall man clad in military attire, striding briskly towards them.

'Allow me to introduce myself. I am General Nubar, leader of the Adheran army. What has happened to Honeydale is a tragedy, no doubt, but the only thing we can do now is protect ourselves, protect Adhera. We must fortify, strengthen our defences, not go on a wild goose chase around the desert.'

'And this spell can only be reversed by magic,' said another voice, belonging to an elderly gentleman in scholarly garb. 'Captain Pah'lin informed me of your so-called *quest*. Hardly inspiring...'

'Ah, Maester Dillon, you've been studying that old tome. What conclusions have you drawn?' Lord Eirron mused. In Dillon's hands was the Magukon Codex. Lilly's eyes became wide with concern.

'I have but two conclusions, my Lord,' Dillon replied. 'One, that I cannot read a damned word of this infernal thing. And two, finding that temple and this whatever-you-call-it rock is pointless. We'd need a mage to absorb the power from it, and the only mage we know of is the one we're trying to fight.'

'But it might force his hand,' Oscar argued. 'Panic him, push him to make a mistake. If he thinks we know how to reverse his spell, he may become desperate and expose a weakness. Vardelem won't just waltz into town and risk an arrow in the back. He'll come here on the back of his dragon, with all his magic and power.'

'And if nothing else, it's a step headed in the right direction,' Lilly added, mimicking Erdolet's words. 'We might not be able to use the Deystona rock the same way a mage would, but the secret to reversing Petrification lies within it. We'd be foolish to ignore it.'

Lord Eirron sat up from his relaxed pose and exchanged a glance with his wife. He then surveyed the room, observing his advisers' movements and gestures.

'It seems that my council considers your approach folly,' he said in a curious tone.

'My Lord, we cannot risk Adhera's defences for the sake of a fool's errand,' General Nubar insisted. Lord Eirron sat in thought for a minute.

'So be it,' he finally said. 'While I am not blind to the logic in your pleas, little 'uns, I can't afford to lose a single man from my city.'

'Then let us go on our own,' Jackary pleaded. 'We've done okay so far. You lot would probably get in our way, anyhow.'

'Bawk! Such gusto! I do admire you three… But letting you go on your own would go against the requests of Captain Pah'lin here.'

Pah'lin looked to the ground, daring not to meet the eyes the children. He knew they would be unhappy with him, especially Oscar. He'd feel betrayed, and he would be justified in doing so. But in his heart, he knew he was doing the right thing by them.

'I'm sorry,' he told them, 'but I've requested that you are kept here in the city tonight. In the morning, you'll be on the first train back to Vhirmaa. It's too dangerous for children to traverse the desert alone. Or anywhere in the world, for that matter. These are dangerous times. You'll understand one day…'

'Pah'lin! You know how important our quest is! It's the only way to save Honeydale!' Oscar yelled in a strained voice.

'I'm sorry Oscar. I believe everything you have told me, about Vardelem and the Pedrakon, the curse and its cure… and it is for that reason, I fear I can do nothing for Honeydale. All these things are beyond me, beyond anybody. Honeydale is lost, but I can still help defend

Adhera and keep you safe.'

'Keep us safe?' snorted Lilly. 'You're an idiot if you truly believe that. And you can't keep us prisoner here.'

'Actually, we can, although we'd prefer it if you were all on board with the idea,' hissed Nubar, before turning to two of his men. 'Take the children back to the inn and stand guard at every exit. Do not let them leave without first consulting myself. Understood?'

His men saluted in unison, grabbed Oscar, Lilly and Jackary by the shoulders, and dragged them across the hall. Oscar pleaded for Pah'lin's help, who still couldn't bring himself to look at them. Lilly called them all fools, and doomed fools at that. Jackary argued that he was probably older than everyone in the room, and should therefore get a little more respect.

They were dragged from the throne room and into the corridor. The doors slammed shut behind them, their cries echoing through the halls of the palace.

Chapter Nine
Royalty of a Different Ilk

It was night, and the sky was a black sheet speckled with diamond stars. Oscar sat sullenly on the balcony of the room at the inn. Lilly and Jackary expressed similar deflation.

'We should never have trusted him,' Lilly muttered. 'We should never have told him anything.'

Nobody argued with her. Oscar least of all, who kept much of the blame for himself. He was the one who trusted Pah'lin, who was eager to tell him about their quest. He idolized him and now he had paid the price for it. He recalled some of his father's world weary advice.

"Don't trust every twitch your line makes. Half the time it's just the maggot fidgeting."

A tear crept down Oscar's cheek as he heard his father's voice in his head. Would he never be able to help his family? Perhaps it would've been folly to look for the Deystona crystal, but at least it was something. Sitting in a room doing nothing but waiting for doom seemed more folly than that.

He glanced down at the street. Two guards stood watching the entrance of the inn. In the hallway outside their room door stood another two guards. There were probably more as well, strategically placed so that every angle of the inn was being watched. Escaping their room, let alone the city, seemed an impossible task.

Then suddenly, there was a knock.

Jackary hopped up from his bed and opened the room door. Standing in the hallway, rather unsurprisingly, were two guards, who looked at him curiously.

'Yes? Anything the matter?' one of them asked.

'Um, yes, I suppose. I thought I heard a knock at the door.'

'Nope, no knock here,' said the other guard.

'Must've been dreaming…' Jackary mumbled, slowly closing the door again. He turned to Lilly and Oscar. 'Did you hear a knocking too?'

They both nodded. Jackary shrugged and lay back down.

Another knock.

'There it is again,' said Lilly.

'It's not coming from the door…' Jackary added.

They all stood up and moved to the centre of the room. They waited a few moments, trying their best to not even breathe too loudly. Then, at last, a third knock.

'The cupboard!' they all shouted, and rushed over to the wardrobe, tripping over themselves. They swung the doors open and found the inside of it to be quite unremarkable.

'Nothing here,' Jackary said, disappointed.

'Wait, there's a draught…' Oscar whispered, holding out his hand to the back of the wardrobe. Cool air tingled the tips of his fingers. He felt around the edges and corners, trying to find a grip. He pushed his fingernails into a faint opening and pulled on the wooden backing. It slid open with ease, revealing a narrow opening in the wall. Standing there was the steward who had greeted them outside the palace, shrouded in an inconspicuous hood, a dim lantern dangling in his hand.

'Please follow me. The Sultan is awaiting your company,' he whispered, and Lilly wondered if that was the only thing he could say.

They all stepped into the narrow opening. The steward slid the false back of the wardrobe closed and pulled on a small lever on the wall. The ground shuddered, and after a moment's noise of gears turning, they began to descend through a secret shaft.

'Incredible,' Jackary observed.

'Being a Sultan means having to keep lots of secret appointments. Most buildings in Adhera have shafts like these,' informed the Steward, answering Lilly's earlier curiosity.

They eventually ground to a halt in what seemed to be a basement beneath a basement. They stepped out of the shaft and onto the sandy ground. Looking around, they could see an elaborate network of tunnels that must've spanned the entire city. Without wasting time or words, the steward led them down one of these tunnels.

They walked through the labyrinth for quite a while before emerging finally at what seemed like an exit, containing two surprising sights: Lord Eirron, and a giant pig.

'Bawk! There you are!' Lord Eirron guffawed.

'What's going on here?' Oscar asked cautiously.

'Well, firstly, I will never have it be said that I do not repay a debt. You fended off those filthy gnolls and I owe you for that. So, in repayment, I offer you Urug.'

He slapped the hide of the giant pig and it squealed wildly.

'A pig?' Lilly scoffed.

'Bawk! This is no mere pig! This is Urug, the High Lord of All Swine!'

'The High Lord of... huh?' Jackary was utterly confused.

'Think of him as a royal pig. These beasts are faster and harder riding than any dorataur, stronger than any bull. They need very little water or food, so can travel long distances without rest. Very few of them exist in the world, making them the Lords of All Swine. Urug here is the best, and therefore, the highest of Lords.'

'You're helping us now?' Oscar asked, remaining cautious. 'Why?'

'I agreed with my council, Master Grubb, but only to a point. Adhera is in danger and I cannot spare any men to leave the city defenceless. I do not, however, agree with locking you up like prisoners. I was half your age when I skewered my first boar, and only marginally older when I rode into my first battle. If there's a magical rock to be found out there, I reckon you three are the ones to find it, regardless of age. You're a lot braver, stronger, and smarter than my court was prepared to recognise, but what is a Sultan if he's not wiser than his court?

'So, take Urug and ride to the Northern Regions of the desert. I've never seen it myself, but I've heard more than once that there is an obelisk somewhere out there. Nobody knows what it is, or does, or who made it, but considering you're hunting old and mysterious things, it might not be a bad place to start.'

'Does Pah'lin know?'

'No, Master Grubb, he does not. And believe me when I tell you that it was with a heavy heart that he requested you be kept in the city. He is an honourable man, and is just doing what he thinks is right.'

Oscar did not reply, and went over to inspect Urug. There was a saddle on the pig's back with two large saddlebags attached on either side.

'I'm riding him!' Jackary yelled, and hopped up onto the saddle. He took the reins and shook with excitement.

'I guess we're in the saddlebags then,' Lilly said, rolling her eyes.

She clambered into one of the saddlebags, which was spacious enough for her to stretch out her legs. Oscar walked round to the other and climbed in. They all turned to face Lord Eirron.

'Thank you,' Oscar said, bowing his head.

'Bawk! Enough of that, young 'un! We're going to need to be prepared for all outcomes against this mage, so go find us that stone and make the bugger nervous, all right?'

With that encouragement, Urug let out a long grunting wail, and dug his trotters into the sand. He pushed off with great momentum and, at quite a miraculous speed, rode off into the desert, the stars guiding them northward.

Chapter Ten
The Elven Temple

Urug was every bit as fast and strong as Lord Eirron had promised. They made short work of distancing themselves from the city. Just before dawn, they were halfway across the Adhera desert, only a day's ride away from the Northern Regions.

The dunes were becoming steeper, turning into deep valleys of sand. The sun was burning them before it had even fully risen. Cacti and palm trees were becoming scarce as the desert became dryer and emptier. It seemed the Adheran desert would test the young companions to their limits.

They passed an occasional outpost, most of them just a few tents put up by some traders. They stopped at one of them around midday to find some shade under a marquee and buy some fruit from a travelling merchant. Urug snoozed, snoring as loudly as a pig his size would suggest it would.

Once they'd eaten, Jackary rummaged in his bag

until he found his map of Adhera. He laid it flat before Oscar and Lilly.

'So, by my estimation, we are... here,' he said, pointing to a completely blank section of the map.

'How can you tell?' asked Oscar with genuine interest.

'Well, if Adhera city is here, and we've been travelling at about double the speed of a dorataur, and it's after midday now, I reckon this is a fair guess of the distance we've travelled. Once we see this well, which I reckon we'll come across within the hour, we'll be on the fringes of the Northern Regions.'

'Jackary, with all respect,' Lilly groaned, disrespectfully, 'that map of yours is utterly pointless. It's just a big, yellow shape. It all looks the same. I mean, where the heck are you seeing a well on there?'

'That dot, there.'

'Dot? How does a dot equal a well?'

'Well, this is a map of the whole desert.'

'Yes?'

'So, in the grand scale of the desert, a well is only very small. So... a dot.'

'You've got to be kidding me. It's probably just an ink spill.'

'It's a well!'

'Jackary, for as *un*confident as I am in your estimations of where we are, I'm equally confident of that dot definitely not being a well!'

'Well, we'll find out who's right when we leave, won't we!'

'Jackary, I promise you, there will be no well!'

—

It was just shy of an hour later when they came across the well.

Isolated in the vastness of the desert, with no landmarks or anything at all nearby, it was bizarre that a well should exist on its own in the middle of nowhere. This made Lilly nervous, but not before being frustrated at losing an argument.

'Told you!' Jackary announced, as smug as could be.

'You got lucky,' Lilly snipped. 'It is odd, though, that a well should be way out here on its own.'

'Maybe there used to be settlements out here. Or outposts.'

'Maybe it's just for people to get a last drink of water before heading into the Northern Regions.'

Oscar walked past the well and looked off into the north.

'A city used to be here,' he said quietly.

'What? How do you know?' asked Jackary.

'See there, how that dune juts down suddenly? And that whitish mark at its base - that's brick. There's a building buried beneath the sand. There are buildings all over here, look!'

He was right. The sand was misshapen. The sweeping elegance of the desert before them had become an uneven sheet of gold, and sporadic intrusions of a ruined city clawed out from beneath the surface.

'This must be the city Erdolet told us about. The Elven ruins!' Jackary excitedly yelled.

'So, we're here, then? This is the Northern Regions?' asked Lilly.

She got no reply as both her companions ventured forward. Urug trudged along behind them, grunting and wheezing. Lilly followed too, and soon they were all standing at the white brick wall peering from the sand.

'This is just great,' Lilly groaned. 'So, the ruins are buried underneath the sand. How are we supposed to find this temple?'

'The obelisk Lord Eirron told us about,' Oscar replied. 'That must be in this region somewhere. We should try and find it.'

'But surely we would see it? Obelisks are generally pretty tall.'

'It could be concealed behind a dune,' Jackary added. 'The sand here is pretty wonky. We should explore a little, see what the desert's hiding.'

They all agreed to split up and search in different directions of the Northern Regions, whilst still remaining in earshot of one another. The hours burned away while they did this, the sun growing hotter and hotter as the day progressed. The heat was agonizing, nipping any exposed skin. The sweat on their faces grew irritating, constantly invading and stinging their eyes. To make matters worse, their searches were proving fruitless.

As dusk loomed and a faint wind eased the heat of the desert, Jackary's voice echoed across the dunes, calling to his friends. They rushed north in the direction of his cries.

In a flatter area, a vast valley hidden behind a giant ridge, Jackary was standing next to a strange yellow rock cone that was piercing out of the sand. It came up to his waist and was clearly the tip of a spire, attached to a

172

building far beneath the sand.

'I think this is it!' Jackary informed them. 'This is the obelisk!'

'It's a bit small, isn't it?' asked Oscar.

'It is. But think of how many centuries and millennia this obelisk must've been here. At one point, it probably was a giant tower, dominating the horizon. Now though, after thousands of years' worth of sandstorms, it's all but engulfed.'

'Makes sense, I suppose,' Lilly groaned. 'But what now? Are we even sure the obelisk has anything to do with this temple?'

'Temples traditionally have spires,' replied Jackary. 'I reckon the spire of a temple buried beneath the sand would appear rather obelisk-esque.'

They all pondered this for a moment, and even Jackary would admit that this was clutching at straws. But what had their whole quest been if not a massive straw clutch? Frustration, irritation and exhaustion informed their decision to get behind this hypothesis, as at this moment, there was nought else to get behind.

'Okay, I can go with that,' Oscar said, kneeling down and running his fingers down the obelisk, examining it, 'but that would mean we are standing above the temple; way above it, in fact. How are we supposed to get in?'

'Well, I hope you're not expecting me to dig,' scoffed Lilly.

Jackary knelt down also, and examined the obelisk carefully. Then he lay down on the sand and pressed his ear to where the sand met it. He cupped some of the sand

173

and pulled it back, pushing his ear in closer and tighter.

'It's hollow,' he mumbled, before shooting back up onto his feet and summoning Urug. The High Lord of All Swine lazily waddled over to Jackary.

'Okay, Lord Urug,' Jackary said in a respectable manner, 'kick the obelisk as hard as you ruddy well can.'

The giant pig tilted his head and offered a confused grunt. Jackary just smiled and nodded. Urug shrugged, about as much as a pig can shrug, and turned his back to the obelisk. He leaned forward onto his front legs, pushed back, and cracked the yellow stone right in its centre with his hind legs. The crack grew, splitting up the middle of the cone-shaped obelisk. Jackary leaned in once more, and smiled.

'Just as I thought,' he grinned. 'Wind. There's a breeze coming from inside; it's hollow from about a quarter of the way down. Kick it again, Urug. As close to the bottom as possible.'

Urug obliged and struck the lowest point above the surface. Its side caved in, and a small hole was revealed in a cloud of dust. Jackary started scooping back the sand around it, joined quickly by Oscar and Lilly. Before long they had dug a shallow ditch around the hole.

'If we make the hole a little bigger, we can get in,' Oscar instructed.

'Are you sure we want to do that? We still don't know if this is the temple,' warned Lilly.

'No, but we do know the temple is underground, and this is our only way down.'

Lilly conceded, and proceeded to help Oscar and Jackary in pulling apart the hole. The sun had almost completely set by the time they had made a gap big enough to enter. Jackary stuck his head in without a thought for caution. It was dark, as was to be expected, but for a faint orange light way down below them.

'There's some light down there,' he said. 'It must be coming from a chamber beneath the spire.'

Oscar fetched some rope and, with one end in Urug's sizeable jaws, he fished it through the hole. Jackary took a deep breath and mounted the rope, squeezing through the hole.

'I'll give you a shout if I see anything.'

With that, he zipped down into the darkness. Lilly and Oscar exchanged surprised glances.

'He certainly doesn't spare much thought for caution, does he?' Oscar said.

'I don't think he spares much thought for anything. Still, it's handy having someone around who will leap wildly into danger.'

'I've leapt...' Oscar began, sounding more than a little offended.

'Oh, you have,' Lilly fumbled to reply, in an attempt to back pedal. 'But it's different. You're brave; I doubt you'd ever shy away from a fight. But you're cautious, and do things practically. Which is great, you need that. But you also need someone who'll toss themselves into situations without thinking.'

Oscar didn't say anything.

'It's better that you are the way you are, Oscar. If we had two Jackary's, we'd be in real trouble.'

Despite Lilly's efforts, Oscar couldn't help but feel offended. An awkward silence hung uneasily in the air.

Finally, the faint call of Jackary's voice cut the tension.

'Get down here! Both of you! Hurry!'

Lilly moved forward to take the rope, but Oscar brashly cut in front.

'Coming, Jack!' he yelled, grabbing the rope. Stepping into the hole, he looked at Lilly and smiled sarcastically, before loosening his grip and zipping down the rope. He instantly regretted this decision, and nervously wailed all the way down. Lilly took a moment to herself.

'This could become a problem...'

—

She was close to the glowing light now, and could see the rope dangling out of a wide hole. She emerged on the other side to see that she was hanging from the ceiling of a great hall. A great hall filled with sand. Golden hills sloped from the high corners all the way to floor, where it had poured in through cracks in the walls. She lowered herself down onto one of the slopes and slid to the bottom, where Jackary and Oscar were excitedly waiting.

'Look, Lilly,' Jackary said, grabbing her arm. 'Up there! Look at the runes!'

Lilly looked at the wall. On it were carvings, elegant and highly detailed. It was lettering of some kind, though she did not recognise it.

'It's Elvish,' Jackary whispered. 'It has to be.'

'Well, Erdolet did say that an Elvish city once stood here,' Oscar said, in his business-as-usual voice. 'Now we need to figure out if this is the temple or not.'

'Agreed,' Lilly nodded.

'This has to be the place,' Jackary mumbled. 'Look at the size of it!'

The hall was huge, and even Oscar and Lilly had a strong feeling that this was indeed the place they were looking for. Vast pillars bordered the room, mostly consumed by sand now. Open doorways, also clogged by sand, hid quietly in the shadows.

Speaking of shadows, the most curious thing about the hall was how it was lit. Or rather, that it was lit at all. Torches burned all around, mounted on the walls and pillars. Their flames were long and unusual. They seemed to be of the same fire the sun burned with.

'How long have these been burning down here?' asked Oscar, examining one closely.

'We must be the first people down here in centuries, maybe longer,' Lilly joined in. 'How is this possible?'

'Really?' Jackary laughed. 'Isn't it obvious? It's magic. Has to be.'

Lilly and Oscar looked at each other, excitement and trepidation behind their eyes. Without saying anything, the three children split up to search the hall.

What little of the room that hadn't been concealed behind walls of sand was broken and scattered. Smashed urns and pots, withered fabrics and broken furniture littered the floors. All around, cracked statuettes of graceful figures, slender and long, in poses depicting kindness and strength, lay under ancient sheets of sand and dust. Lilly examined one in her hand. The ears she noticed instantly. They were pointed. Not jagged like a goblin's though, but more gentle and clean. There was no doubt about it, Lilly thought, they were definitely

Elves.

Elves were the first people, and that's about as much as anyone knew about them. They had been extinct far longer than the mages, and any historical evidence that might explain their disappearance had long since been wiped away with the passing of centuries. Occasionally, an old ruin or artefact from their time would be unearthed, heralded as priceless and sacred, but offer no insight to the race themselves.

The legends say they were powerful, akin to Gods walking upon the mortal world. With their power, they gifted Men with wisdom, taught them the structure of a civilised world. For thousands of years, Elves and Men lived side by side, so the old songs go. And, perhaps the most popular legend of Elves, they were immortal. Old age would never claim them; they would still stand as empires rose and fell around them. It was all the more curious then, that they should vanish almost without a trace.

Historians hypothesised that a great war brought about their demise; however, there was very little evidence to back this claim up, and would a single war really claim the life of every Elf in existence? And a war with whom? Men? Not very likely. Men were the inferior species, in every aspect. Elves were not only wiser and more powerful, but it was said that their immortality granted them resilience to pain and death by conventional means. That is to say, a mortal wound to a human would not necessarily be as devastating to an Elf. So, in a battle between Men and Elves, Men would most certainly fall.

An internal war then. Elves fighting Elves. Again, not very likely. Their greatest gift was their immense intelligence. They could out think a war, settle disputes democratically. And even if they did fight, would it again result in every single Elf's death?

The only strong fact the world had on the Elves was that their disappearance was mysterious.

Lilly, putting the statuette back down, turned to see Jackary and Oscar hastily sweeping the floor with their feet.

'Should I ask?' Lilly mocked.

'No, you shouldn't,' shrugged Oscar. 'Just help us sweep this sand away.'

Rolling her eyes, she began assisting them, and quickly realised why. Beneath the layer of sand was an image, a picture crafted in the tiles. After a few minutes, they swept enough sand away to reveal mosaic depiction of a bird, orange and red with wings of fire. Its beak was golden, and the eye shown was bright blue.

'Erdolet said the temple was built in tribute to Pyriona, the Goddess of Fire,' Oscar announced. 'And in Adhera, there were paintings of Pyriona astride a giant bird of flames. Pyriona's Aide, the Phoenix.'

'And this is definitely a picture of the Phoenix,' confirmed Jackary.

'Well, that settles it then, we're definitely in the right temple,' Lilly added gleefully, sharing a satisfied smile with her companions. 'So, now what?'

Their smiles fell away. They needed to explore the temple further, go deeper. But all the doorways were blocked by walls of sand. The furthest any of the doors permitted them to go was about a quarter way down a staircase, through an arch hidden in the corner. After a few steps, however, the sand blocked the way once more. This gave Jackary an idea, though. He figured that if the stairs led down, there must be a floor beneath the hall, a basement at the very least. He returned to the mosaic floor and pulled out his short alchemy knife. He began chiselling away the tiles. Within moments, he had knocked away half a dozen tiles, revealing a layer of solid concrete beneath. He sighed. It would take forever to break down the concrete with his knife.

'What were you expecting?' Lilly said sympathetically. 'We're going to need something a lot heavier than our weapons to crack that. Or some firedust.'

'Firedust...' Jackary mumbled, repeating Lilly's words.

'Yes, *firedust*. To blast a hole in it.'

Jackary grinned and dove into his bag. He pulled out a small hip flask and a clear bottle of red salt rocks. He opened the flask, and dropped a single rock in. Almost immediately, there was a fizzing sound, and a thin streak of red smoke seeped from the brim.

'What are you doing, Jack?' Oscar asked.

'Well, I don't have firedust, but I do have Ember Salt, which on its own won't do much more than make your chips extra spicy. Mixed with fresh water, though, it begins dissolving.'

'And how does that help us?' Lilly asked, unimpressed.

'Well, it basically dissolves and forms again into a

sort of solid bubble. A quaking ball of volatile air, would be more accurate...'

He placed the flask very carefully on the concrete surface, and slowly stepped back. Nervously, Oscar and Lilly did the same. Jackary felt around in his quiver, and found a short, thin arrow.

'Now, the bubble is harmless undisturbed, it'll eventually fizz out on its own. But if it is suddenly popped...'

Jackary rushed forward, his bow in hand, arrow readied. He took a bounding step before the flask and flipped over it, letting loose the thin arrow, shooting it with haste into mouth of the flask. Before Jackary's feet touched the ground, the flask ballooned for a second before exploding with a loud crack. It split the concrete floor, cracking it into four pieces that crumbled and fell beneath the surface. Jackary landed and turned to the gawking Oscar and Lilly.

'...it makes a bloody big hole in the floor!'

'Wow,' Lilly said, slowly. 'I'm impressed.'

'Yeah, Jack, that was really something,' Oscar laughed, patting him on the back.

There was a sudden shudder all around the hall. The sand mounds shifted slightly. Then a tremor began to rumble, shaking the whole ceiling. Suddenly, from the hole where they had entered, bits of rock and debris began to fall through. Their rope became loose and fell in also, bringing with it a ton of flooding sand. It was all over in seconds, their way out now completely sealed.

'Jackary, you idiot!' exclaimed Lilly.

'How are we supposed to get out now?' cried Oscar.

'Oops,' Jackary coyly replied, before clearing his throat. 'Shall we go down then?'

Oscar fetched the now fallen rope, tied it off around a pillar, and tossed it down the hole in the floor. They all took a burning torch, as there seemed to be little light in the room below, and lowered themselves down into the darkness.

They were now standing in a room far shorter and narrower than the great hall above. Long tables took centre place, with benches at their sides. Familiar relics, urns and ornaments, adorned the mostly bare shelves, and a bookcase held little more than cobwebs and dust. A wooden door, slightly ajar, opened out into a long corridor.

Oscar led the way, with Lilly and Jackary close behind. They followed the path, passing empty rooms similar to the one they had just been in. The walls were decorated with Elvish markings, which Lilly had a hard time ignoring.

'This must've been quite a place to see in its heyday,' she whispered.

They continued on, descending a spiralling staircase at the end of the corridor. They seemed to go down for quite some time, their torches illuminating the stairs in orange and creating misshapen shadows on the wall. Jackary, who was at the back, thought he saw something shudder and move out the corner of his eye, but by the time he had turned, he saw nothing. Jumping at his own shadow, he thought nervously.

When they finally stepped out of the darkness and off the last step, they found themselves standing on a narrow walkway, a bridge crossing over... other bridges! Oscar leaned and peered over the edge, and beneath them, going in all directions from doors and passageways sporadically dotted around the stone walls, were narrow bridges, much like the one they were standing on. Looking down on them, Oscar was reminded of a cobweb, a thought that chilled him for a moment. The orange glowing, much like the light in the main hall, had returned, but seemed to emit from nowhere in particular, illuminating the labyrinth of walkways with an otherworldly, almost haunting, ambience.

Oscar, Lilly and Jackary continued along the walkway, their footsteps echoing in the silence. At the end of the bridge, they found themselves walking through another doorway and descending yet more stairs. These stairs were narrower, so narrow, in fact, that they almost had to sidestep to get down them. They re-emerged on the bridge directly below the first one, cautiously walking along in short strides. These bridges were old, ancient in fact, and Oscar didn't trust their stability. They continued down the labyrinth in this fashion, crossing over six or seven more bridges, when Jackary finally stopped.

'Listen. I'm not sure we're alone down here,' he warned.

'Don't be ridiculous, this place is buried a hundred feet underground,' Lilly replied. 'We're the first people to set foot in this place in more than a thousand years.'

'But I keep hearing things. Shuffling and the like.'

'It's probably more exits closing themselves to us

thanks to your wonderful bubble bomb.'

'It's not that, Lilly! It's... movement.'

'Jack,' began Oscar, his voice calm, 'don't worry. There's no way anyone else can be down here. You're jumping at shadows.'

'Yes, I literally am! I keep seeing shadows move, and not our own.'

'Let's just keep moving,' Lilly grumbled.

Truth be told, Lilly had noticed these signs also, but had chosen to ignore them. She was feeling apprehensive, but forced herself to focus solely on her goal. The Deystona rock, the crystal with the potential to save Honeydale. No point in getting slowed down by noises and shadows.

They carried on across the bridge once more, all of them a little more nervous now than they already were. They descended another spiral staircase, as was now routine, but this time came to a dead end. The stairs ended at a black stone wall that resembled the side of a mountain.

'There are more bridges beneath us,' said Oscar, puzzled. 'This can't be the end of the path.'

'So, what now?' Lilly sighed, sitting on a step.

'I guess we'll have to go back up, maybe all the way to the hall, and start again.'

'I don't think we'll be able to do that,' Jackary croaked, his voice wavering.

'Why not?'

'Because we're not alone.'

'Oh, Jackary, for the last time, we're...' Lilly began, but could not finish. Her eyes widened as she looked up at the black stone wall. The rocks began to move, arching and twisting, making a creaking sound that irritated her ears. The rocks stepped away from the wall to reveal a tall figure with dark blue skin, stones and crystals protruding out of its body. No… they were a part of its body! As it straightened itself, its head lifted to reveal a face, a disgusting blend of rock and flesh. It struggled to open its mouth, even to growl as it did. One eye was open wide, grey and tragic. A shard of black crystal grew from where its other eye should be. It took a shuffled step forward, and growled once more.

It was terrifying, and all three children were frozen with fear. It took another step, the sound of joints waking from a long sleep cracked and creaked.

'Run!' Oscar yelled, and led Lilly and Jackary back up the stairs.

The creature called out after them, screeching loudly in a language they did not understand.

They came out onto the bridge once more, but were halted in their steps. The walls all around were moving, and looking closely they could see that hundreds of these rock beasts were crawling up the walls and leaping down onto the bridges above. In a matter of seconds, they would be sharing the same bridge.

'I guess going up isn't an option,' Lilly groaned.

'Then we go down!' Oscar announced, before running to the edge of the bridge and leaping off. There was another bridge not too far down, and he landed with a forward roll. He stopped himself at its edge and got to his feet. He looked up at Lilly and Oscar.

'Come on!' he roared.

Jackary and Lilly threw themselves from the bridge and landed in a heap beside Oscar.

'I think you took my *leaping* talk a bit too literally, Oscar,' Lilly sighed, climbing to her feet.

They barrelled on with a slight limp towards another doorway, and another staircase. The rock creatures were leaping from bridge to bridge, making short work of the distance between them and their prey, and howled like hyenas, coughing out chants in their own foreign tongue.

Oscar continued, leading Lilly and Jackary down the stairs and bridges much like they had done before. When they had passed the final crossing, and found themselves at the lowest point of this labyrinth, they gave themselves a moment. Their pursuers were close behind, but their legs were aching, and feet even more so. Jackary was panting loudly, and Lilly had begun wheezing rhythmically. They were now on sandy ground once again. Thick sand as well, like a vast pit. A wide, arched opening in the wall threatened a dark tunnel with more shadows and perils.

'Okay,' Oscar began, 'let's get mov-'

He was cut short by the sudden cry of one of the rock monsters leaping down from the bridge above. It landed next to them, its face and body the same twisted form of stone and skin. It stumbled towards Lilly, grabbing her by the shoulders. Oscar ran to her aid, sword drawn. He swiped at the beast, the blade sparking as it struck the rocky skin. The creature hissed as it rolled back, dropping Lilly to the sand.

Suddenly, more of its kind came leaping down by the dozen. The gap had been closed, and now they circled the three young intruders. The path to the opening had been blocked. Oscar cursed under his breath. They should never have stopped, even if it was only for a moment.

Jackary shot an arrow out into the crowd of hissing rock creatures. It splintered against the hard skin, and in reply he received a ramble of strange, bitter words. Lilly clutched her sword and staff, wondering if another incident like the one on the train would occur. Would the staff emit some tremendous power? As she thought this, the ground began to shake. She looked at her staff… *What have I done this time?* Quickly though, she realised the trembling wasn't coming from her.

From beneath the depths of the sand pit arose a long, snake-like creature. A stone serpent! Rare creatures that inhabited the deserts and depths of the world. It was enormous, scaleless and fleshless, unnaturally formed of nothing more than sand and stone. Its gaping jaws snapped shut with an echo, consuming more than half a dozen of the stone monsters.

The crowd screeched and growled, scrambling over one another to flee the giant snake. Oscar nodded to Lilly and Jackary, and they all bolted towards the opening in the wall. They were chased by many of the rock creatures who had not yet been devoured, led by their blood lust in spite of the mayhem the stone serpent was causing. The sand was deep though, and difficult to run in, their feet sinking under their weight. The serpent started picking off the creatures one by one, from the back all the way to the front of the line. Some stragglers were spared and carried on towards the opening, while the snake eyed its next prize.

Lilly.

She had started falling behind, her legs pulsating in agony. Oscar and Jackary crossed the threshold of the opening and turned to see her flail. Jackary quickly shot a string of arrows at the serpent, but it didn't seem to deter it any. Its jaws widened around Lilly, and so, in a last ditched effort to not be eaten, she turned and struck the snake with her staff. It ricocheted off its snout and… did nothing.

No flash of blinding light, no incredible force. Lilly did go flying backwards, however, as she bounced off the stone serpent's snout and went hurtling into the opening. The serpent snapped its jaws shut, catching nothing but air. It hissed and turned its attention once more to the other stone creatures, some of whom were also about to cross the threshold of the opening. Oscar and Jackary helped Lilly to her feet, and carried on running.

At the end of the tunnel was a large set of heavy double doors. With all their might, they forced the doors open and squeezed through to the other side. They slammed them shut again, and as quickly as she could, Lilly rammed her sword between the handles. The force of the chasing creatures crashing against the locked doors rocked them on their hinges. They scratched and yelled in their bizarre language.

'We're safe,' Jackary panted, hunched over, his hands on his knees.

'For now, but they'll break it down eventually,' Oscar said sullenly. 'Besides, we don't know what's on this side yet, do we?'

They turned and looked down yet another ominous looking corridor. Jackary wondered how deep underground they were now. Lilly wondered if they would ever make it back up.

Chapter Eleven
A Sea of Crystals

The corridor led them to a wide circular room, with not much in it save for a few remnants of old bedding and blankets. In the middle of the room was a hole built like a well, with a ladder poking out from it.

'Can we stop for a second? I'm in agony here,' Lilly said, taking a seat on the floor.

'Yes, let's catch our breath for a minute,' agreed Oscar, who was equally flummoxed.

Jackary joined them on the floor, and nervously darted his eyes around the room.

'So,' he began, 'what do you reckon those things were, then? I've read a great many things about a great many monsters, but those things are new on me.'

'Likewise,' nodded Oscar. 'Although I don't have as much experience in the world as both of you. I only encountered my first putridon a few days ago. Lilly, any thoughts?'

'Beats me.' She thought for a moment. 'Although,

there was something about their eyes… They looked…'

'Almost human,' Oscar nodded. 'I think that's what made them so scary. Were they human once?'

'I hope not…' Jackary said with a shudder. 'They were too tall, I think. Nearly seven foot.'

They all thought about the rock creatures for a moment, all thinking the same thing, though none of them would say it aloud. Was there a chance that they, being stuck down here as they were, could turn into one of them? They tried to block out the persistent battering at the door further down the corridor, but their fear finally outgrew their aching legs. They pulled themselves up, shook off the sand and dust, and started climbing down the ladder.

It led them into a cavern, with a dozen caves and tunnels that webbed away from the wider path. The walls were black stone, reflecting the shimmering light that, like everywhere else in this unusual locale, came from nowhere. It was dimmer down here though, and had a trace of blue. It was colder than in the hall of bridges, or the temple itself. Amidst the black stones were crystals, glinting like white starlight against the night sky.

'Crystals…' Lilly muttered to herself. 'We're here! This must be where the mages mined! The Deystona spell, it's down here somewhere!'

With that, she ran off, her eyes wildly jumping from one crystal to the next, examining each one in hurried detail. Oscar and Jackary gave chase, following her into the web of caves.

She picked up a crystal now and then, inspecting it in

closer detail. She felt nothing from them. They were thin and white, and weighed hardly anything. Lifeless, like empty vases. She knew the stone they sought was red, Erdolet had told them as much, but she felt like it would feel different, also.

Occasionally, they would pass a cluster of crystals that seemed to have exploded out of the ground. Looking closely, they noticed that some of the individual crystals had been removed. Mined, most likely. It occurred to them then that the Deystona crystal might just be a tiny rock hidden in a mass of others.

They finally happened upon a crystal that wasn't white. But it wasn't red, either. It was orange. Bright orange too, glowing brightly on its own in a sea of black. Like a moth to the flame, Lilly was drawn to it, and clambered up onto the wall to pluck it out. It slipped out of its crook in the black stone with ease, warming her hand. Its orange light pulsated, brightening and dimming with every second.

'That's amazing…' gawked Jackary. 'Do you think there's magic in it?'

'Oh yes,' laughed Lilly, unable to pull her gaze away.

Finally, realising they still had to find a red one, they moved on, but not before Lilly pocketed the crystal.

They carried on for what seemed like hours. Oscar was fairly certain they were looping, going in one cave and coming out another, all on the same stretch of path. They never stopped, though. Finding this cavern, and the orange crystal, refuelled their determination. There was also the looming danger of those rock creatures breaking down the door. With haste and urgency, they worked their way around the caverns, until at last they came across an unusual crack in the wall.

It was narrow. Extremely narrow, in fact. Low down as well, easily missed, which Oscar argued they had, as he was positive they had walked down this tunnel before. Regardless, they saw it now, and on the other side of the wall they could see more crystals. White and faded like all the others, but still, they had to inspect.

Lilly went first, not giving anyone else much opportunity to argue otherwise. She got down on her hands and knees and scurried through at a surprising pace. Jackary followed, the crack a tighter fit for his size. A good job they were all children, he thought to himself, otherwise he'd have to make another Red Salt Bomb!

Oscar was last, casting one final cautious eye behind them before entering. More than anything else, he was concerned about the rock creatures, although they'd probably be too big to fit through this crack anyway. As he climbed in, he chuckled to himself. Lilly was right about him: he was a cautious fellow. In that moment, though, he was quite proud of the fact; it made him feel like his father. *The man who's hasty is the man who's tasty... to a bear.* Don't rush into things, basically. Be cautious. Oscar never understood what the bear had to do with anything. He missed his father's old sayings. He missed his family.

Oscar swallowed hard as he emerged on the other side. Instantly, he was struck by just how many crystals there were. It was a circular cave that stretched up high. They were standing on a narrow ridge that ended in a cliff edge, overlooking a drop into a void so deep and dark, there was no hint of a bottom beneath the shadows. Hanging over this drop was a small rock platform, which looked like a floating disc. It was attached to the cliff edge by a sort of bridge, a narrow stretch of stone. It looked like a rocky frying pan protruding from the cliff edge. The walls were almost entirely made up of crystals, clustered together like before, and shooting out in all directions. They were mostly white, as expected, but a few colours speckled in between; green, blue, yellow, and red. One red, in fact. It was nestled in the middle of a large cluster of white crystals, situated in the middle of the floating platform.

Lilly was standing at the cliff edge, about to step onto the bridge.

'Be careful,' Oscar warned. Lilly turned and raised her eyebrow.

'So, you're saying I *shouldn't* leap head first off the cliff?'

Oscar shook his head and smiled. She turned and carefully started edging across the bridge. It was short, thankfully, but she felt the weight of the platform shifting as she stepped on. It was precarious, to say the least, and Lilly didn't feel like lingering. She eased her hand out into the cluster of crystals, and grabbed the red one, gently sliding it out of its groove. She held it in her hand for a minute, the red glow igniting her eyes. She wasn't sure how, but the aura emitting from the crystal in her hand made her certain; at last, she had it.

The Deystona Spell!

She turned with a smile, looking at Oscar and

Jackary, who were watching her with nervous enthusiasm.

'I got it!' she told them. 'We did it!'

A slow clap echoed around the chamber, followed by a low, dark laugh. They all shuddered, and froze in instant fear.

'My congratulations,' a voice hissed. 'You're all very tenacious.'

'Who's there?!' roared Oscar, although he knew exactly who it was. He recognised the voice from the Grande Show. Its bitter tone. Its long droll.

It was Vardelem.

High above them, on the wall behind Oscar and Jackary, there was a small opening acting as a rudimentary balcony. Standing there, arms crossed, dressed in a long, black cloak and black robes, was Vardelem. This time, though, without the mask. Now they could see his face. A surprisingly young face, too. He looked to be in his early twenties. He had white blond, shoulder-length hair, greased back behind his ears. His eyes were dark holes against his pale skin. A wide, sinister smile contorted his face.

'Vardelem…' Lilly whispered.

'You know my name, girl? Interesting. One wonders what else you know...' Vardelem said, amused. 'I must applaud all of you. Your journey through this temple has been most amusing. I've not seen the Elves so active in a very long time.'

'Elves? Those *things* were Elves?' Jackary asked.

'Oh, you didn't know?' Vardelem chuckled as he said this, before drawing a long breath. 'Yes, the Elves are quite tragic creatures now, but a long time ago, they were the most powerful beings in the world. So powerful, in fact, that they created us. The mages. They taught humans how to use magic, how to draw magic from stones such as these, and thus a new species was born. Of course, they underestimated the power of the mages, and in the end, they paid for that.

'Not with their lives, you understand. Not exactly, anyway. It is incredibly hard to kill an Elf, even for a mage. Instead, the mages cursed them. A curse that grew while much of their power vanished, and they became the pitiful creatures you see now.'

'That's horrible...' Lilly muttered.

'Yes, it is. But it's also evolution. The powerful outlive the weak; this is a fact of life. A fact of life humans have been defying for too long. The mages should be the dominant species of this world; we should rule you pathetic creatures, your lives should be in our hands...'

'But you don't,' Oscar interrupted, a smirk on his face. 'You didn't rule us then, and you don't rule us now. And one mage on his own? You never will.'

'Alone, am I?' Vardelem grinned, but also seemed to look genuinely confused by Oscar's words. He glanced at Lilly, holding her gaze for a moment. 'Then who was to draw the power from that crystal?'

Lilly remained silent. As did Oscar and Jackary. Vardelem watched them for a moment, before exploding into hideous laughter, which filled Oscar with frustration.

'Only half a plan, eh?' he continued, turning to face

Lilly once again. 'Tell me then, girl, what business do you have with the Magukon Codex?'

Lilly didn't respond. There was something about Vardelem, more than his obvious wickedness, which oozed from him with minimal effort. It was the way he kept addressing her, looking at her. He knew more than he was letting on, and these questions he was asking... he was toying with them.

'It's a good thing I didn't incinerate you on that stage. I would've set the Codex alight also. Now, I'll take it back, if you please.'

'That's why you're here? That's why you followed us all the way down into this pit?'

'Yes. For the most part.' He glanced at Lilly once again. 'I was also curious. But for now, the Codex.'

'For the so-called ruler of the planet, you're not very observant,' Jackary snorted. 'We don't have it.'

'Lying is a fruitless endeavour. I...'

'He's not lying,' Lilly interrupted. 'We don't have it. It was taken from us.'

Vardelem stirred, his grin fading. He growled something under his breath. 'Adhera...'

'No!' Oscar cried, stepping forward. His panic caused Vardelem's grin to return.

'I was planning on dealing with those Adheran fools anyway, deliver them the same fate as Hylkoven. But now that the book's in the city... I'll have some fun with them first.'

'Why do you care about the Codex? It's just a handbook, right? Are you not already an experienced mage?'

'As I understand it, it's the only known Magukon Codex left in this world, and it should be in the hands of a mage, not a lesser being. I can also assure you that there is a whole lot more in the Codex than you realise, or could ever understand. And I'm sorry to say, you never will.'

Vardelem waved his hand, and the crystal in Lilly's hand began to vibrate. Lilly screamed in agony, but try as she might, she could not release the crystal from her hand. The red glow turned into a blinding light. Oscar ran towards her, calling out her name. And then... flash!

The light of the crystal filled the whole room, and with it, an explosion of red, glittering dust. The crystal had shattered in Lilly's hand, the force of the explosion knocking Oscar backwards, sending him off the walkway and into Jackary, who was running behind him. As he was being knocked back, he cried out in horror. Not for himself, but for Lilly. The crystal had exploded in her hand, and the force against her was far greater. She, too, was knocked backwards, in the opposite direction. Oscar was powerless to help as Lilly fell from the platform's edge and down into the blackness of the abyss below them.

'Lilly!' Oscar screamed, dashing to the edge of the path. Jackary grabbed him, keeping him from falling off himself. Oscar, blinded by his tears, turned to face Vardelem, who, surprisingly, wasn't grinning.

'Before you say anything,' he told Oscar, 'I'm not interested in your grief. I'm not interested in your sorrow. The pain you feel barely scratches the surface of the horror my people had to endure at the hands of your kind.'

As he spat the last of his words out, a familiar howl echoed through the caverns. Vardelem's smirk returned.

'Ah, your Elvish friends. My cue to leave. I have a city to destroy. And you... have to die.'

He laughed sinisterly as he stepped back into the shadows, his cackle stinging the ears of Oscar and Jackary. It faded, and his presence felt all at once gone, as if he had disappeared in a breeze. His words, his actions, all of his being, filled Oscar with a rage he couldn't quite grasp. His heart hung heavy, like a cannonball in his chest. He hunched over on his knees, staring into the blackness Lilly had fallen into.

This horror clogged their senses, denied Oscar and Jackary the awareness of the twisted Elves gaining ever closer. At last, Oscar shook his head, turned off his mind, and rose to his feet. He put his hand on Jackary's shoulder and, without saying a word, commanded him to rise. Another horrifying cry from the shadows. The Elves were close. Jackary silently nodded to Oscar, communicating almost telepathically. They had to escape, and they had to do it now. Sorrow and grief would have to wait.

The cold truth would have to wait.

They crawled through the crack once more, returning to the familiar tunnels of the cavern. Without putting any logic to their actions, they began running in the opposite direction of the Elves' blood lusting screams. They had to find an exit, a way out of the depths of the desert.

They let their legs do the thinking. They ran through the cavern, trying to find new paths. It wasn't long, though, before one of those paths crossed with the hunting Elves. Their excited yelling erupted at the sight of Oscar and Jackary, and their scrambled march hastened.

The chase lasted for what felt like the length of the night. Oscar and Jackary became covered in cuts and bruises as they exhaustedly fell into the sharp rocks. Their situation was bleak, and barely a slither of hope existed between them. This buried cavern, beneath a buried temple, would seemingly be their graves.

That was until they stumbled upon a dead end, but an entirely different dead end than the others they'd encountered in the dark caves. The wall was curved and made of different stone. It was brick, and looking up, Oscar could see that the curved wall became a circular tube that shot up for quite a distance. At the end of the tube, a welcome sight. A slate of the darkest black, with specks of sparkling white glowing upon it. The sky! They were looking at the night sky.

'Oscar!' Jackary gasped, grabbing his friend's arm.

Oscar reluctantly turned his gaze from the sky to see the scattered shadows of the Elves upon the wall. They were just around the corner. They had to get out, but climbing the rocks would be difficult. The bricks were small and smooth, so getting footing upon them would be near impossible. Keeping their footing all the way to the top would be even more so.

Jackary pushed Oscar aside as he suddenly pulled his bow from his back. He grabbed a handful of arrows from his quiver and began shooting them into the cracks between the bricks at seemingly random points on the curved wall. He did not stop until he aimed his final arrow, shooting it into the wall just below the exit.

'Right,' he said assuredly. 'Follow me.'

With that, he leapt onto the first arrow, placing his foot as close to the wall as possible, and sprung onto the next arrow. He did this again, and again, hopping from arrow to arrow. He had constructed a makeshift staircase.

Oscar was impressed for a moment, until the horde of Elves came pouring around the corner. They snarled in almost gnoll-like fashion as they stormed towards him. He drew a long breath, and followed Jackary onto his staircase.

Jackary was at the top, pulling himself up over the edge. Oscar followed as fast as he could, slowly rising to the cylinder's peak. A sudden rush of cool air filled his lungs. He was close. He was almost out.

Beneath him, though he dared not look, the Elves were attempting to scale the walls. Trying but failing, thankfully. That was until one of them had the sense of mind to mimic Jackary and Oscar, and began bounding up the arrow staircase, its long legs making short work of the spaced steps.

As Oscar stepped onto the second to last arrow, it shifted under his weight, breaking out of the wall altogether. He fell forward, his hands raised, and just barely managed to grab the final arrow. It shook, threatening to give way also, and the eager Elves waited with baited breath on this eventuality. The Elf advancing up the wall opened its sizeable jaws as it got closer, like a fish nearing bait.

The arrow snapped, but Oscar did not fall. At the last second, Jackary had reached down, using his bow as an extension of his arm. Oscar grabbed one end of the weapon, the string cutting his hand as he did. Jackary pulled with all his might until, at last, Oscar's hands could find their grip on the wall's brim.

The Elf flung itself forward, its height advantageously keeping Oscar in its reach. Its prey pulled himself over the edge, however, and it crashed into the wall, its clawed hands scraping against the withered bricks. It fell spectacularly back to the bottom of the pit, taking out some of the arrows as it did. It crashed into the Elvish mob, knocking them all over like a row of dominoes.

Jackary and Oscar lay on the sand of the desert they had spent so long buried beneath. Jackary recognised their surroundings. They had emerged from the well he and Lilly had a disagreement over. He stood up, and took a few shaky steps. He scanned the horizon, confirming his location.

'We're out,' he croaked, his tired voice straining to speak.

Oscar didn't reply. The only sound was the disappointed cries of the Elves beneath the sand. What a hideous sound, what a nightmare they had endured. But Oscar…

Jackary turned to see his friend, eyes red and cheeks glistened with dried tears. Oscar took one shuffled step forward before, finally, his legs buckled under their own exhaustion, and he collapsed onto the desert ground.

Chapter Twelve
A New Dawn

When Oscar eventually awoke, the sky was the sunrise's orange shadow. His head was throbbing and every inch of his body ached. He stiffly sat up to see he was lying on a blanket, cushioned by soft, dense sand. He was sheltered in the shade of a palm tree, and seeing the tents and stalls around him, he realised he was back at the trading outpost he and his companions had previously stopped at the day before.

He didn't move for a while, just sitting there staring at the sky. Jackary soon appeared, holding a bowl of steaming stew. He didn't look Oscar in the eye as he sat next to him; he couldn't. He placed the bowl on Oscar's lap.

'I know you probably don't feel like it, but you should eat this,' Jackary instructed. 'You need to build your strength up.'

'I know,' Oscar rasped, his tone ominous. 'How did we get here?'

Jackary hesitated, shocked that Oscar had agreed to eat without argument.

'Urug found us,' he said at last. 'I was carrying you across the desert, and Urug sniffed us out. It wasn't long until we reached this place. There was a doctor, of a kind, that had a look at you. You had a fever. I made a tonic for you, too, and you drank it as best you could, although you probably don't remember. It cooled you down, rejuvenated your body. You'll feel back to normal in a day or two.'

'I feel fine,' Oscar lied.

'Once you've eaten that, we should set off again. I don't think we should risk the Narrow Canyon, not on foot, so we'll have to take a longer route around the mountains to get back to Vhirmaa…'

'Vhirmaa?' Oscar asked, midbite.

'Yes. I thought the best place for us to be is the Golden Forest. Lady Erdolet -'

'I'm not going back to Vhirmaa, Jack,' Oscar interrupted. His was tone calculated.

'What do you mean?'

'I mean I'm not going back there. What's the point? Once Vardelem's done with Adhera, he'll return to Vhirmaa and finish what he started with Honeydale. And he won't stop until the entire world is destroyed by his hand. Including the Golden Forest, and Lady Erdolet. I'm not returning to Vhirmaa, Jack. I'm going to Adhera City.'

'Adhera?! Are you mad? For what purpose?'

Oscar didn't answer straight away. His mind lingered on the word "purpose." What was his purpose? Since his journey's beginning, he had clung to any sense of purpose he could, any trace of hope. At the start, it was to unearth the secrets of the Magukon Codex, then it became finding the stone, then it would've become a quest to figure out how to use its power. All of this to save his family, to save Honeydale. Many purposes drove him, but all of them were now gone. Diminished by the will of Vardelem.

Vardelem.

The mere thought of his name filled Oscar with rage. First, he had robbed him of his family, and now his friend. Reduced Hylkoven – Honeydale – the vibrant, energetic capital of Vhirmaa, to nothing more than an empty void, a tragic sculpture. Adhera now faced that fate. Its people, its king, Pah'lin. All in the city would fall to Vardelem's evil. Just as Honeydale fell. Just as Lilly...

Oscar growled. He wouldn't allow it. Losing Lilly, and the Deystona-infused crystal in her hand, put an end to any hope he had of finding a cure for the petrified curse Honeydale and his family were under. And in this moment, he didn't care. All he cared about now was revenge. If he couldn't save those who Vardelem had made to suffer, then he would do all he could to stop him from doing it to anyone else.

'I'm going to take the fight to Vardelem,' he finally said.

'And get turned to stone in the process?' Jackary argued, his voice quivering with mounting disbelief.

'That's not his plan. Not for now anyway. He wants that book; think of how he spoke of it. He'll tear the city apart to find it, of course, but he won't use his dragon to curse it. Not yet. Which gives us time.'

'Time to do what?'

'To draw him out, use his desperation against him, and fight him head on. Yes, he has immense power, and I don't doubt that tackling him would be in vain, but I have to try. *We* have to try, Jack. Adhera has soldiers, an army willing to die for their city. And Pah'lin will fight until his last breath. United, we can overwhelm him, and so long as the Codex is not in his hands, we will have the advantage. We were using the book against him, but in completely the wrong way. It's not about reversing spells anymore. It's about stopping Vardelem himself. With the book in our possession, we can bait him.'

'And if it *is* all in vain? And Vardelem wins?'

'Then at least we can die knowing that he did not have an easy victory.'

Jackary examined Oscar's words, his motives. Oscar placed his hand on his shoulder.

'For Lilly, Jack.'

They exchanged a tearful glance, before Jackary finally cleared his throat.

'I'm going to need any gold you have on you,' he finally said, rising to his feet.

'What for?'

'If we're going into battle, I'm going to need to buy more arrows.'

Chapter Thirteen
Revelations of Time

For the first time in a long time, Lilly didn't dream. There was only a void: no thoughts or images, ideas or memories. Total silence. Total darkness.

She only became aware that she had been asleep, or unconscious at least, when it came time for her to wake up. Her eyes opened with some difficulty. It was sore to move, her body aching all over. At last, her heavy eyelids opened wide enough for her to see her surroundings, only to reveal a setting as dark as her sleep.

Cavern walls, black-stoned, jagged and narrow, surrounded her. She forced herself up from the damp grit on the cavern floor. Her clothes were moist, and she noticed the shore of a black lake nearby. The water must've broken her fall, she concluded. Just. Looking up, she could see nothing but dark shadows, giving no hint of a ceiling, no sign of the platform she had fallen from. She had fallen far, that's all she knew. And that's all she needed to be filled with dread.

Limping over to a wall, she rested her body. Her hand that had held the Deystona crystal was in agony, throbbing with pain. More than that, though, she was wrought with worry. Oscar and Jackary... Had they made it out? Lilly would blame herself if they hadn't. Lilly and that infernal book of hers, causing nothing but trouble, leading her friends to their deaths...

No, that's enough.

She forced herself to think of something else. Anything else. And after a moment or two of quiet pondering, her mind stumbled upon something worth thinking about.

The cavern was dark, no question about it, but not as dark as it ought to have been. Like the great hall in the temple, or chamber of bridges, there was an unnatural light illuminating it. There wasn't a crack or opening or even a suggestion of outside light anywhere, and yet the walls glowed blue as if absorbing moonlight. This same light shimmered on the surface of the dark water of the lake. Unlike the temple and caves above, there were no torches or crystals acting as the light's source. Scanning the room with her keen eyes, now less heavy and more alert, she spotted a cave not far from where she was standing, snaking off not into darkness, but more light.

She skirted the lake's edge, the sound of her wading through the cold water echoing around the cavern. She reached the mouth of the cave, yawning open ominously, and slowly entered. The cave took her deeper underground, tunnelling its way down, deeper and deeper. The mysterious light was becoming brighter the further into she travelled. She tried to quieten her footsteps, pricking her ears to try and hear anything or anyone. She heard nothing, which made her more nervous.

At last, Lilly reached the tunnel's end, which opened into a wider enclosure. A rock pool took centre place inside, with moss covered boulders rising from its centre. Atop these boulders was a figure, tall and dark, slender and somehow graceful. Lilly recognised instantly that it was an Elf, cursed just as the others were, a deformed creature of flesh and rock. Its hair was brittle and tangled, and it cascaded down a thin spine of blue stone. Its neck creaked with the sound of two rocks rubbing together as it turned its head to face Lilly. She froze with fear as her eyes met the black gems of the Elf's.

'You're frightened,' said the Elf, in a rasped voice.

'I am,' answered Lilly, edging backwards.

'That truly is a tragedy, that Elves have become something to be feared.'

'Well, they did attack me and my friends on sight.'

'Also, tragic. Do you think us evil, then?'

Lilly paused for a moment, considering her answer. 'No. I feel sorry for the Elves. Their story is, as you say, a tragedy.'

'So, you pity us?'

'In a sense. Still, I don't appreciate being attacked, so you could say I pity them to a point.'

'Do you pity me?'

'I suppose so, but that may just be because you haven't tried to kill me yet. You're not like the other

209

Elves, are you?'

'Not quite, no. It is true that my kin have fallen into a state of savagery. Most have abandoned their reason, adopted a more vengeful mentality. They have become twisted, broken under the weight of a curse older than history. I, on the other hand, have resisted the curse. While deformed physically, and robbed of much of my power, I have maintained my mind, held on to my identity.'

The Elf's expression changed, becoming more graceful and warm. Something resembling a smile crossed its face.

'My name is Milda,' she said, bowing slightly.

'And I am Lilly Rachert.'

'Rachert, you say? Ah, I see…'

'You know my name?'

'Curious you should ask me that…'

Lilly tilted her head in confusion. Milda shuffled on the boulder she was sat on, closing her eyes in ponder. Her smile returned after a moment of thinking.

'Now I understand,' she said, opening her eyes and looking at Lilly once more. 'Tell me Lilly, why do you think the Elves were so quick to attack you?'

'Because of the reasons you just stated. They're twisted and broken. They are cursed.'

'True. And it is also true that they attack most they encounter, but never to kill really. Just to warn off, to frighten. But the ones that attacked you, they most certainly wanted to kill you. Do you know why?'

Lilly shook her head, taking a seat on a rock by the pool, watching Milda like a student listening to their teacher.

'It is because, Lilly,' Milda continued, eyes widening, '*you* are a mage.'

Lilly remained silent. She could barely process Milda's words in her head. A mage? Ridiculous! Lilly did the only thing she thought was appropriate: she laughed. She laughed heartily, leaning back and kicking her legs. Milda remained still, observing Lilly's disbelief.

'In my time, before the curse, I was a Seer,' Milda said, ignoring Lilly's laughter.

'What's a Seer?' Lilly asked, trying to calm herself, coughing out the last of her guffaws.

'A Seer has the gift of Sight, and can see beyond the boundaries of time. A Seer can witness events occurring a million miles away, just by focusing their mind. They can know everything about a person from one conversation. They can see their life's history. Just as I've seen yours.'

'My life's history, Milda, for as short as it has been, consists of living in a hut with my grandfather. Until recently, I've lived a very normal, unmagical life with a very normal, unmagical old man. We were alone for the most part, with little dealings with the outside world, and in that entire time, not one remarkable thing happened. No spells, no adventures. Nothing remotely mage-like.'

'Dysan was not a mage, he was not magical, but he was far from normal, Lilly.'

'Dysan…' Lilly spoke her grandfather's name. Milda's s*ight* was clearly no lie, although there were street psychics who could pull a name seemingly out of thin air not dissimilarly. Lilly was still far from convinced.

'Yes. Dysan Ruhn. I also know that he was not your real grandfather. He was charged with raising you, being your guardian.'

'Charged by who?'

'Your mother.'

'My mother?! You know about my parents? Who they were?'

'Yes. Your mother's name was Chyrianna Rachert, wife of your father, Alric Rachert.'

In Lilly's head, she heard a soft voice whisper her name. This was no parlour trick; what Milda said was truth. Dysan had never told her the names of her parents, always avoided talking about them… yet she knew, she knew those names belonged to her mother and father.

'Your dreams, Lilly,' Milda continued, 'the dreams that have followed you your entire life. They are memories. You have always known who you are, who your parents were, but you have forgotten. Now you must remember.'

'But… I've already told you. The life I know, the life I remember, was with Dysan, in the hut in the forest.'

'You were raised by Dysan in the forest, yes. But you were born more than a thousand years ago, in the dying days of the War of Mages.'

'This is impossible…' Lilly's head began to spin; her mind was a battle between reason and the fantastic.

'Perhaps I can help you,' Milda said quizzically, rising from the rocks and striding over beside Lilly. 'I can use the Sight to show you, to help you remember, if you'll permit me.'

Lilly composed herself, fighting her instinct to run out of the cave. She stood up and faced Milda, taking a long, deep breath. She nodded quietly, and shuddered as Milda placed her cold hand on Lilly's shoulder.

'Close your eyes, and clear your mind of all thoughts. This could be a little disconcerting.'

—

'Open your eyes,' Milda ordered, her voice softer and quieter. Lilly did as instructed.

They were standing on a balcony carved out of the side of a mountain. Lilly turned and saw the oval room from her dreams. She recognised all of it. The sky was red with fire, and the dark land was stained with blood and littered with the bodies of one hundred thousand dead soldiers.

'What a terrible sight,' Milda said, who was standing beside Lilly.

'What is this?'

'The last battle of the War of Mages. It was a long time before the world could heal from this.'

'It's horrible. So much pain and death…'

Lilly's trail of thought was interrupted by the sudden bang of a door being swung open. She turned to see two very familiar people enter the oval room. The woman from her dreams was there, looking just as she should, with the same blood stains upon her robes. In her arms, though, was a bundled-up blanket, concealing something clearly precious to her. She was leaning against a man, clad in leather armour, with grey white hair and a rugged beard.

'Grandfather!' Lilly exclaimed.

He helped the woman into the centre of the room, where she stumbled and fell to her knees.

'Your Majesty!' he cried, kneeling beside her.

'Please, Dysan, I don't have much time. We must start the process…'

'My Lady, I'm not sure this plan is entirely sound.'

'We have no choice, Dysan! You know what they'll do to her if they find her. They will not be content to just kill me, they'll see her as a threat.'

'I know. But the magic you propose using is too unpredictable…'

'I will not argue this, Dysan! I am commanding you as your Queen. Will you listen to your Queen?'

'Of course, my Lady. I always have.'

'You have always served me well, Dysan, and are one of my oldest and dearest friends. I have always considered you one of my family. Please, look upon Lilly just the same.'

She handed Dysan the rolled-up blanket. It stirred as she did, and the faintest moan of a baby was heard. Dysan awkwardly took the child in his arms.

'How far will you send us?' he asked, rising to his feet.

'As far as I can, though my strength is failing me quickly.'

'Your Majesty, I…'

'No more words, Dysan, they will be here soon.'

The infant Lilly began to cry, and so did her mother. Chyrianna struggled to her feet and walked towards her child. She kissed her lightly on the forehead.

'Forgive me for abandoning you, sweet Lilly.'

'I will protect her with my life, my Lady. In whatever time we emerge, in whatever state of existence, I will keep the Princess safe.'

Chyrianna lifted her head and gave Dysan a tearful smile. She placed her delicate hand on his cheek.

'Alric was always proud to call you Brother.'

'And I was always proud to have him as my King. And you as my Queen.'

Chyrianna stepped back, her hand still raised. Her smile quivered, eyes watering wildly. She closed them, forcing a tear to roll down her cheek. Her fingers began to dance. Blue light formed between them, creating little sprites that glided toward Dysan like fireflies. They surrounded him, making him nervous. His clutch on the baby tightened. The sprites grew bigger, their glow more intense. Their revolving around him quickly became a hurricane, until he was standing within a wall of spinning blue light.

The light peaked, blinding Lilly and Milda for a second. When their sight returned, they could see Chyrianna standing alone in the middle of the room. Dysan and her infant daughter were gone. She let out a long, painful wail that exhausted the last of her strength. She fell to her knees once more and lowered her head to the floor. Her crying was forceful and agonising, but lasted only a few moments. All of a sudden, a silence suffocated the room. Then, the crouched pose of Chyrianna fell to the side. She rolled onto her back, and breathed her last breath.

'Your mother knew that sending you through time

was a risk,' Milda said quietly. 'She was one of the few mages who could use Time Altercation, and even then, it was unpredictable and dangerous. The future is always uncertain and impossible to predict. She knew not what fate she had sent you to. All she could be certain of was that you would not die in this room with her.'

'Where was my father?'

'Alric Rachert did his Kingly duty and led his army in the Last Battle. His body is out there, with his comrades.'

'They were Royalty?'

'Oh yes. King and Queen of Elrost, a once great and powerful nation. By birth right, Lilly, you are a Princess.'

'Princess of a country that no longer exists' Lilly's tone was bitter. She stepped towards the body of her mother. 'Why did they have to die? Why did so many die in the name of magic?'

'Questions to which answers cannot be found here. Needless to say, there were many things that motivated the War of Mages, as there always are with any war. Your Father died to protect his nation, your mother died to protect you. But do not burden yourself with the deaths of mages fallen before your time.

'Come, close your eyes and I will bring your mind back to your body. You have already seen past the point of your memories, and those who are not attuned should not spend too much time within the Sight. It can warp your mind and madden your brain with confusion.'

'Wait,' Lilly said, eyes fixed on the door. 'There's someone coming.'

From the shadows of the hallway emerged a figure, draped in a black cloak and instantly recognisable to Lilly.

Vardelem.

He stormed into the room and marched over to Chyrianna's body. Two more mages, similarly dressed, entered the room. One of them began to tear the room apart, hunting for something. The other stood by Vardelem, who was crouched next to Lilly's mother.

'Where is she?!' the hunting mage roared.

'She's gone,' Vardelem whispered. 'Chyrianna's sent her forward in time. Along with that knight of hers.'

The hunting mage stopped and let out a squawking laugh. 'Perfect! She's gone!'

'No, not perfect, you imbecile!' said the other mage, who crouched down beside Vardelem. 'We must know where she sent them. It would be a foolish risk to leave the girl unchecked. Can you sense how far she sent them, Vardelem?'

'No,' he answered with frustration. 'Not to an exact year, anyway. It's far though. Very far.'

Milda put her hand on Lilly's shoulder and squeezed it firmly.

'Lilly, you've seen enough now. Close your eyes.'

'Why do they need to know where I am? Why am I a risk to them?'

'Lilly!' Milda snapped, her voice becoming a devilish shrill. Even her face contorted into a terrifying form, far from the tragic grace of her true being. Lilly shuddered with fear and snapped her eyes closed.

—

217

As quick as a blink, Lilly's eyes opened again, and she was standing in the cave with Milda once more. She looked around, disorientated and short of breath.

'Take your time,' whispered Milda. 'Remember your surroundings. You're with your body once more.'

'Answer my questions,' Lilly rasped, panting and wheezing. Milda retook her seat on the boulders in the rock pool, and rested her head on her hand.

'Your mother was a very powerful mage, one of the most powerful to ever exist. It would be no stretch to imagine that her child would match, if not exceed, her power. Leaving you alive would mean risking your return. It is probably why Vardelem chose this time to travel to; he had probably hoped to find you and kill you.'

'Well he found me, anyway.'

'And thankfully, did not kill you.'

'*Thankfully*? I thought the Elves hated the mages. Wouldn't you rather I died?'

'As we have already established, I am not like the Elves you encountered before. I pity you, Lilly Rachert, as you pity me. Your tale is also tragic. An orphan of heritage and time. From one pitiful creature to another, I wish to help you.'

'Thank you, Milda. I'm still not sure what I… This is all very…'

'Revelations have a tendency to knock the wind out of one's sails, but you will have plenty of time to make sense of all that has been revealed to you later. First, you must consider your friends.'

'My friends? Oscar! Jackary! Are they okay?'

'They are still alive, though they are rushing wildly towards danger as we speak. A battle has begun in a city in the desert.'

'Adhera City! Vardelem has begun his attack.'

'And he will win unless you stop him. This battle cannot be won with swords, but with magic.'

'How am I supposed to help with that?'

'You are a mage, Lilly!'

'An untrained mage, a mage who has never been shown how to cast a spell in her life. I wouldn't know where to begin.'

'You can begin with that staff on your back.'

Lilly pulled the staff from its harness and held it out in front of her. It felt unusual. Like it did on the train in the Narrow Canyon.

'You can feel that, yes? The vibrations?'

'I can. I felt it once before…'

'Ah, so you lied about never having cast a spell.'

'It was cast by accident! I only meant to hit the gnoll on the head with the butt of this thing. I don't know how I did it!'

'You *did it* through instinct. The staff is little more than a stick. It merely has the power to harness magic, to be used to wield magic. The magic, however, comes from within you. Your powers are your own. The vibrations you feel are the staff reacting to that magic. Use the staff to channel it.'

'You make it sound so simple…'

'Then allow me to make it simpler,' Milda grinned. 'Blow a hole in that wall.'

'What?!'

219

'On the other side of that wall is a tunnel that leads to the heart of the desert. A literal heart: an eternal bonfire of ethereal flames that bathes the Phoenix, the guardian of the desert. I can commune with Pyriona's Aide, ask it to help you, speed you to the battle so you can confront Vardelem. But first, you have to get through that wall. So, blow a big hole in it.'

Lilly walked over to the wall and held up the staff. She squinted and focused hard, her face turning red.

Nothing happened.

'Think about your mother,' Milda said, turning on the rocks. 'Think about her power, how it has passed to you. Think about Dysan. Think about Oscar, and Jackary. Think about Vardelem. Think about all these things at once, and nothing else. Magic doesn't come from the mind, it comes from the heart. Think about all that has happened, and what will happen, and let your heart take care of the rest.'

Lilly took a deep breath and turned back to face the wall. She stared at it unblinkingly for a few moments. Then she raised her staff and closed her eyes. She filled her head with everything Milda had just said.

She thought about living with Dysan in their shabby little hut. She thought about finding the Magukon Codex in Hylkoven. She thought about meeting Oscar and Jackary, their adventures in the Golden Forest and the Narrow Canyon, and here in this ancient temple.

She thought about her mother and father, the sacrifices they made to save her, and Vardelem, standing over her mother's body a thousand years ago.

That image remained until it darkened, and all she

could see was Vardelem's face.

She thought about Vardelem, and nothing else.

Finally, the staff began to twitch in her hands...

Chapter Fourteen
The Battle for Adhera

Pah'lin led a small band of men, only a half dozen or so, through an abandoned shopping district. Echoes of skirmishes happening in other parts of the city haunted the streets, but for now, where he stood, it was quiet. They were trying to get a jump on their enemy, fight them any way they could, grasp any sort of advantage.

What even *was* their enemy?

Pah'lin had been in a panic, hunting frantically for the children. They had escaped, fled the city in some foolish notion of finding an ancient temple. Why couldn't they listen to him? Running around the desert isn't safe, regardless of age. He should have locked their doors, had even more guards posted at every possible exit from the inn. Such things filled his head when he first set out into the desert himself in the hopes of finding them. He hunted all day, from dawn till dusk and beyond. He travelled miles upon miles in every direction to find a trace of them.

It was a fruitless endeavour. He returned to the city to rest, planning to search for them again the following morn. He was failing them, he told himself. Just as he had failed his king, and his city. He slept restlessly, wrought with angst and worry. Before dawn, he readied himself for another search and made his way to the stables. Alas, his planned search would never begin.

The alarm bell signifying an attack shocked the city awake. Suddenly voices, yells and screams poured through the streets. Who would attack? Gnolls? Bandits? He ran to the city square, to the Ice Fountain. A myriad of people ran over one another, fleeing from a threat still hidden from Pah'lin. That was until he heard the blade cut the air behind him.

Quick as a flash, Pah'lin dropped to his knees and rolled forward, turning as he returned to his feet, unsheathing his own sword. His foe stood before him, tall, broad shouldered, and clad entirely in black armour. A strange metal, not steel or iron. It looked almost like coal. Behind the slit in the helmet's visor was nothing, just a black void offering no eyes, no soul. Its heavy gauntlets clutched a jagged, black blade, seemingly made of the same metal as the armour. Rhythmically, this villain marched toward Pah'lin, sword raised high. Pah'lin parried his attack. Once. Twice. On the third heavy swing, Pah'lin sidestepped and thrust his sword into the black breastplate. His assailant crumbled, falling to the ground and exploding into ash and dust. Pah'lin turned and saw more soldiers, identical to the one he faced, chasing down Adheran citizens, clashing with city guards, and burning buildings.

He rushed into another fight, helping some soldiers fend off a small horde of black-armoured attackers. A few soldiers fell, their opponents strong and quick. Pah'lin and the few remaining soldiers fought on, but it seemed for every foe they felled, two more would appear, as if from nowhere.

In fact, that wasn't far from the truth. Pah'lin watched as the pile of black ash that remained after one of these warriors died merged with the wind and dust, reforming into one, or sometimes two more soldiers. And then, from little more than the dust on the paved road, no black ash in sight, a similar pattern created new warriors. These things weren't human, not even beast. This was magic, no doubt about it.

This was Vardelem.

Evacuation was their first priority, and with the aid of the Adheran army, as small an army as it was, they set about getting the citizens out of Adhera City. Using themselves as bait, they escorted a great number of Adheran people out through the city gates. The black-armoured soldiers didn't seem to care much about the fleeing residents, nor leaving the city walls. Their numbers grew greater with each passing hour, however, and soon any hope of pushing an assault through the city gates in an attempt to flee seemed impossible.

The city troops, and Pah'lin too, pulled back into the city centre, and set about protecting what citizens remained in the city. The fight was relentless and unending. The numbers of their enemy were seemingly infinite, while the numbers of their own was falling fast. The black-armoured army broke the Adheran troops into smaller groups, dividing them across the city. They were spread thin, though each group did what they could for Adhera and its people.

Pah'lin's group was looking to secure the shopping district.

They slunk through ruined shops, stepping over debris and wreckage. They crouched behind a wall as they watched a patrol of black-armoured soldiers march down the street, unbeknownst to Pah'lin and his men's presence. They stopped outside a building, a residence largely untouched by the battle thus far, and smashed down the door. Two soldiers entered while the others stood guard outside. Through the window, he saw the two soldiers tossing furniture and hauling open cupboards and drawers. They were looking for something, and Pah'lin knew what.

The Codex!

Pah'lin remembered the children's story. That book Lilly had *borrowed* from some unknown library in Honeydale Palace called the Magukon Codex. She said that while she was there, two shadowy figures appeared also looking for it. She called them something too. Ghouls, was it? No…

Golems! They were golems, and these unnatural soldiers could only be the same. This was Vardelem's army, and they were looking for the Codex. It had been taken from Lilly by Lord Eirron's advisor, that old priest, Dillon. At last, Pah'lin felt like he had an advantage over his enemy. Vardelem's golems were looking for the Magukon Codex and he knew exactly where it was.

Pah'lin turned to his small band of soldiers and signalled for them to leave. A mere moment later, however, a black-shadowed fist latched onto one soldier's hair, and hurled him onto the street. Pah'lin's group were forced into the open, and both parties clashed hard, swords swinging and stabbing.

As was the case with every encounter in this battle, Pah'lin found himself surrounded with the bodies of fallen allies and the emotionless black mist of the golems' faces. His last comrade fell, and alone Pah'lin stood. He held his sword out in front of him, doing his best to watch his attackers, who were slowly moving in on him from all angles. He couldn't fight them all. Not alone. It seemed that, alas, this would be his last stand.

Or at least it would've been, if not for the arrow that suddenly speared through the helmet of the golem in front of him. It fell into a cloud of ash, as per the norm, and now before Pah'lin was an inspiring sight, if not an altogether unusual one.

A pig, larger than any boar he had ever seen, was galloping wildly down the street, grunting and squealing intimidatingly. On its back were two boys, one holding the reins, the other squatting, wielding a bow. It was Oscar and Jackary! A second arrow whistled through the air, making another direct hit in the head of a Golem. His assailants distracted, Pah'lin let loose with a flurry of stabs and slashes. The pig drew nearer and launched Oscar from his back, who now had his own sword in his hand.

Their skirmish didn't last long, between Oscar and Pah'lin's swordplay, Jackary's arrows, and Urug's hind trotters. Panting, they huddled together. Without saying a word, Pah'lin grabbed both Oscar and Jackary and hugged them tightly, to the point of backache.

'Thank goodness, you're okay!' he yelled, his voice breaking. 'Although this is the one time I wish you were both far from me. Why in blazes did you come back here? Did you not see the smoke? The ruins? And...' he stopped short, looking around. 'Where's Lilly?'

Silence. Jackary opened his mouth to speak, but could not find any words.

'Vardelem,' Oscar said, in a hushed voice. 'That is what happened to Lilly. And that is why we're here. Honeydale cannot be saved, but Adhera can. And that can only be done by stopping Vardelem.'

'Please, Pah'lin,' Jackary pleaded, 'where is the Magukon Codex? That is the one thing keeping Adhera from being turned to stone.'

'So, that *is* what they're after...' Pah'lin whispered, mostly to himself. 'Follow me.'

—

The Temple of Pyriona was the first building Pah'lin and the Adheran forces had aimed to fortify. When it became clear that escaping the city was no longer a possibility, they split up into groups to lure the Golem soldiers away, allowing the citizens to barricade themselves in the temple.

It was a modest size for a temple. Big, sure, but not impressively so. In fact, the building to its left was taller, even more so with the large reservoir tank looming on top of it. It was strong, however, thickly bricked and heavily tiled. It had no windows, just a solitary circular hole in the ceiling that let in sunlight. At noon, the sun would shine from directly above this point, and this was when the people would worship the Goddess of the Desert, Pyriona.

Noon had already passed, and light was dimming inside the temple. Soldiers barricaded the door behind Pah'lin, Oscar and Jackary after they entered, forcing furniture, statues, anything heavy in front of it. Urug, in his royal vastness, planted himself against the barricade, reinforcing it, and affording him a chance to get some well-earned rest. The temple hall was cluttered with people, old to young, male and female. Parents clutched at their children, praying to Pyriona for divine intervention. Temple attendants aided the wounded, most of which were soldiers. Painful moans and sorrowful cries scored a rather tragic picture.

Without hesitation, Jackary went about opening his alchemy case.

'I can help the wounded,' he announced. 'I can make some healing potions.'

Oscar followed Pah'lin further into the hall, and at the altar, amidst a small posse of soldiers, was Dillon. He was tearing through the pages of the Magukon Codex. Standing next to him was the ill-tempered General Nubar, the current circumstances making his temper even worse.

'Stop fiddling with that book!' he ordered. 'None of us can read it, and it's not doing diddley-squat to help us!'

'But those warriors we're fighting, they're depicted in these pages,' pleaded Dillon. 'There must be a way to kill them.'

'Oh, we can kill them. We can kill them over and over. The problem is, Priest, that they keep getting back up!'

'And they'll continue to do so,' Oscar interjected, receiving wide eyes and raised eyebrows from the gathering. 'They are golems, magical beings formed of little more than dust and shadow. Lilly told me of them before. They are being controlled by Vardelem, and they will not relent, and their number will not drop.'

'An inspired diagnosis, but ultimately unhelpful, boy. I thought I made clear in the halls of Lord Eirron's palace, we do not need the counsel of children.'

'He speaks the truth, General Nubar, and you would do well to listen to him,' said Pah'lin, sternly.

'All right then, boy, go on. What more can you offer us?' Nubar's tone was disinterested, and he had already turned his back to Oscar.

'The only reason Adhera hasn't fallen to the same fate as Honeydale is because of that book,' Oscar said with as much command as he could muster. 'Vardelem wants it with a fiery passion and will not risk losing it, and so he plans to slaughter everyone in Adhera and pluck the book from the cold, dead hands of whoever happens to be holding it.'

Dillon suddenly turned very pale.

'The slaughtering I was already privy to, boy. We've been getting slaughtered since dawn. We've been fighting all day and made no steps toward victory. We are losing this city.'

'What about the other parties? The other

strongholds?' asked Pah'lin.

'The Palace, as poorly guarded as it is, still keeps our Lord Eirron and Lady Ilga safe. For now, at least. But as far as *strongholds* go, you are standing in the last one. One with a bloody great hole in the roof, through which our enemy can come pouring in. These men you see here, Pah'lin, these fifty soldiers, are the last bastion of Adhera. There is no more army, there are no more parties. Soon, those ghoulish creatures will smash down that door, descend from that hole, and bring about our untimely demise. So, you see, boy,' Nubar turned once more to Oscar, 'that I'm not speaking down to you for no reason. I do it because you have done nothing more than describe the problem but offered no solutions.'

'The solution is to use the book against him. Draw him out. Bait him!'

'And again, another question of how? That book is as useless as your infantile wisdom.'

'That book is the only thing keeping you alive!' Oscar yelled. Pah'lin pulled him back, and crouched down beside him.

'Choose your battles, Oscar,' he whispered. 'General Nubar is headstrong and stubborn. He won't listen to you. I will talk to him, try to formulate a plan. Go and rest awhile. Don't worry, Oscar, I will not ignore the truth you have presented this time. Trust me.'

Oscar nodded, face beaming red with frustration. Pah'lin returned to the group, arguing relentlessly with General Nubar. Dillon still held the book, hands shaking, casting a nervous eye on the hole in the ceiling. Oscar left them, reluctantly. He stormed over to a bench not far from the altar and sat in silence. He looked around, watching the despair of the people.

Fifty soldiers… Oscar feared Nubar may be right. With each passing minute, hope was slipping. He looked at the hole in the ceiling. Scaffolding laddered down from it. The ceiling had been in the middle of being repainted. Oscar sniggered cynically; they had built a ladder for the golems.

Jackary hastily wandered over, frustration drawn on his face.

'They're out of water!' he exclaimed, sitting next to Oscar.

'What are you talking about now, Jack?'

'Water! They're out of it! I have all the ingredients to make potions to give everyone in this temple a boost of zeal and vigour, save for the most basic one: water. Stupid city… Who builds a city in the desert anyway?'

'They don't have tap water, then?'

'No. Just those stupid reservoirs dotted all over the place.'

'There's one on the roof next door, right? Why can't we get water from there?'

'Too dangerous, which I can't disagree with. But these men can't fight any longer. They've been at it all day. If Vardelem's golems attack the temple, which they most certainly will, and breach the entrance, which is very breachable, then this battle is over.'

'There's only one way to win this fight, and that's by going after Vardelem himself. We can't just sit here waiting for the inevitable.'

Right on cue, a familiar roar tore the air outside. It

echoed through the hole in the ceiling. It was long, and deep, and caused every man, woman and child in the temple to freeze.

'That'll be the inevitable then,' Jackary joked, nervously.

Deep waves of wind howling beneath heavy wings shook the city. Like a vulture circling a carcass, it was flying low over the temple roof.

After a moment of chilled silence, Oscar heard Pah'lin and Nubar return to their arguments.

'We need to seal that hole!' yelled Nubar, issuing orders to some exhausted men.

'That won't do any good,' Pah'lin calmly argued. 'That dragon doesn't breathe fire that burns. We'll be turned to stone, encased in this temple, whether you plug that hole or not.'

'What would you suggest then, Captain?'

'Get out and fight head on, like the boy said. The only way to win is to fight the mage.'

'You mean the mage who is currently flying on the back of a dragon? And how should we go about fighting him, oh wise leader? Get a rope and lasso the beast?'

Their bickering continued but Oscar was no longer listening. Inspiration flashed in his head. He slowly got to his feet, not saying a word.

'Jackary,' he whispered, his eyes fixed on Pah'lin and Nubar. 'They're distracted. Let's go.'

'Go? Go where?'

'Outside. It's time to go on the offensive.'

Jackary, without saying anything, stood up in agreement, and together they skirted the edge of the room, staying low and against the wall. They reached the beginning of the scaffolding and delicately clambered on. They ascended as quickly as they could, doing their best to remain unseen, successfully for the most part, until they mounted the last section nearest the hole. When they were about halfway up, they heard a voice from the crowd draw the room's attention to them. 'Up there! Those children!' the voice cried, alerting Pah'lin, Nubar and everyone else to Oscar and Jackary's goings on. They climbed the last ladder and, drawing his sword, Oscar turned and looked at Pah'lin. He tilted his head apologetically at him, then slashed at the rope linking the scaffolding to the roof. The first ladder fell away, and so too did the planks of wood beneath it. Then, like a house of cards, the entire network of poles, planks and ladders gave way, crashing to the ground section by section. Pah'lin sighed as Oscar and Jackary disappeared out of view.

'Not again…' he muttered.

He moved to start finding a way of getting to the roof to chase after them, but was halted all at once by screams coming from the door. He turned and, as the crowd parted, saw that a cloud of smoky dust that had slipped under the door was forming into Golem soldiers. He drew his sword, as did Nubar and any other soldier still able to fight, or at the very least stand, and charged to the front.

Chapter Fifteen
A Shift in Tides

Standing on the roof of the temple revealed to Oscar and Jackary the vastness of the devastation that had consumed Adhera. Not one building had gone untouched or undamaged. The whole city was aflame, smouldering in black smoke, debris and embers dancing like fireflies in the night. Looking down on the street below, they saw the black mist of the golems rush towards the temple door.

'They won't last ten minutes,' Jackary said, his voice cold. 'Half those soldiers in there could barely lift their swords. I hope you have a plan.'

Oscar didn't say anything. His eyes were fixed on the sky. On the Pedrakon, and Vardelem on its back.

'I'm going to try and get on the dragon, get in close to Vardelem,' Oscar finally answered. 'Hopefully it'll take less than ten minutes. Do you think you could attract him? Draw him near?'

'Hang about... Get on the dragon?! Oscar, you've

lost it!'

'Can you draw him near or not?'

'I can try.'

Jackary, arguing no further, pulled an arrow from his quiver and a small, yellow vial from his satchel. He removed the lid and fixed the vial onto the arrows head. He then struck a match and stuffed it in the vial. It began to vibrate, rattling the arrow wildly. He readied his bow and shot the arrow into the sky. It flew unpredictably, the vial causing it to spasm and jerk. When the arrow was finally high above them, the vial exploded, colouring the sky with a yellow cloud. As hoped, the Pedrakon roared, changed course, and began a sweeping descent towards Oscar and Jackary.

'Okay, Mr. Hero, now what?' asked Jackary, taking a few steps back.

'Something very stupid.'

Oscar sheathed his sword, and pulled the strap of his shield hard against his shoulder, tightening the slack it had on his back. Then, from its holster on the back of his belt, he revealed the fishing rod his father had given him. He twisted the handle, causing the rod to extend. The line dangled, the thick hook shining at its end. He whipped it back, extending the line with a hiss. He held this pose for a moment, until the dragon drew near.

It sped over them, roaring threateningly. Jackary hit the deck, while Oscar dropped to one knee. At the same time, he flicked the rod forward, sending the hook flying towards the dragon's wing. The Pedrakon's flight missed both children, its wing clipping the top of the reservoir tank on the neighbouring building, causing it to lean precariously to its side.

In a split second, Oscar felt the line snap tight. The hook had caught one of the Pedrakon's thick scales. A further split second later, Oscar was shooting across the roof of the temple, his grip firm on the rod's handle as the dragon turned and ascended into the sky.

The speed was unlike anything Oscar had ever experienced. Tears blinded his eyes and the wind slapped hard against his face. Going on instinct alone, his thumb found the switch on the rod attached to the reel. With a click, the line began to wind itself in automatically. It pulled Oscar in close to the body of the Pedrakon, and when he was finally close enough, he held out his hand and grabbed for one of the deep ridges between its scales. Finding his grip, he pulled and clambered and dragged himself up until, at last, in the centre of the dragon's back, Oscar was within a few feet of the mage.

Vardelem turned, his eye twitching in frustration with Oscar. He raised his hand and spread his fingers. Sparks flew from fingertip to fingertip, until they formed an orb of fire, which he shot from his palm towards Oscar. Fully prepared, Oscar spun on his heel, allowing the shield to slip from his back and onto his arm. The fireball smashed into it, disappearing in a flash, leaving not one trace or burn mark. Vardelem growled in anger.

Oscar wasted no time and moved as quickly as he could across the Pedrakon's back, its speed slowing with its master's distraction. Vardelem unleashed another fireball, which met Oscar's shield once again. The force behind this one was stronger, and knocked Oscar off balance a little. Seeing this, Vardelem leapt forward, drawing the thin bladed longsword from his side. He brought it down hard, but Oscar parried it, stumbling backwards. His own sword in his hand, and his feet finding themselves once again, he returned the attack, lunging and slashing at Vardelem, who deflected each blow expertly.

—

Several dozen feet below the duel on the dragon's back, Jackary had managed to get onto the roof of the building looming over the temple, by leaping across and landing through an open window, then climbing the stairwell up. The screams and cries and the losing battle being fought within the temple was haunting him, and he could not stand idly by while Oscar fought Vardelem. He had come up with a plan and it involved the reservoir.

He climbed to the top of it, forcing open a heavy metal hatch. Gallons of water splashed around inside, its waves echoing with a hum. He pulled his satchel and alchemy kit from his shoulder and opened every compartment and pocket. He began mashing and preparing various ingredients, muttering to himself several recipes. Four mounds of different coloured herbs lay neatly before him with shavings from two exotic roots stuffed into a cup. He grated something that looked like some sort of fungus into a bowl, and mixed in the dust of a strange blue stone he had ground down in just seconds.

He then began adding these ingredients one at a time into the tank of water. It began to bubble and tremble with slow momentum. At last, he pulled from a compartment in his bag the final ingredient: the Hyan Root. He looked at it for a moment, its glowing twisted leaves seemingly eager to be used.

'Just one clipping can make any potion a billion times more potent,' he said, reaffirming his plan. 'Let's see what happens when you stick the whole thing in.'

With that, he tossed the entire root into the tank. Within seconds of it sinking into the now foul-smelling water, the bubbling and trembling became more vigorous, until the trembling became a rumble and the bubbling became a typhoon. The root was dissolving, creating a foam on the water's surface. Jackary slammed the hatch down and jumped to his feet. The tank's support beams were giving way with each jolt; the knock the dragon had given it had all but broken them completely. It was about to give way, all it would need is a push in the right direction. Jackary's plan was to make sure that it fell in the direction of the temple's roof.

He hung from the side of the tank, and pushed and forced his weight toward the temple. The wood of the beams creaked and cracked, the potion forming within the tank becoming more zealous in its brewing. Finally, the wood split completely, and the tank tumbled off the roof and down onto the temple. It hit the flat roof hard, breaking the hole in the centre even wider. The hatch from the tank swung open, and the freshly brewed potion poured out and flooded into the temple.

Jackary rolled alongside it, and found himself dangling over the hole's edge. Somehow, he fought against the flow of the potion and pulled himself up. He saw for a moment Pah'lin and the others failing in their fight with the golems, their enemy surrounding them completely. A moment later, the entire temple hall was drenched in the downpour. The tidal wave that formed after it hit the ground knocked everyone, golems included, off their feet. The feeble structure of the golems' form caused some of them to crumble in the wave's force.

Silence.

Jackary's anxious eyes scanned the room. Already, more golems were forming, continuing their advance. Pah'lin was the first to rise to his feet, dripping from head to toe. Nubar quickly followed. Then another soldier. Then another. A dozen more. Then another dozen. Then every person, man, woman and child, stood and came together. Their eyes were unblinking, determination pumped through them. Their scars and bruises were washed away, replaced with an itch to fight back. Some of the soldiers bounced on their heels, eager to strike. The golems, mindless and soulless, paid no heed to any of this, and carried on in their usual fashion. Their advance was met with a surprise however.

The people fought back. Fast and hard. They barely gave the golems a chance to reform, smashing each gathering cloud down before it took shape. They pushed the golems back, and forced the fight through the door and onto the streets. The battle was not yet over. Adhera was taking control of its fate.

Jackary smiled, pleased with himself. He looked upward, towards the dragon and Vardelem. Towards Oscar. Flashes of fire-red light illuminated the

Pedrakon's back, showing the silhouettes of Oscar and Vardelem crossing swords.

Oscar and Vardelem's fight upon the back of the Pedrakon had moved further away from the city and closer to the mountainous Pyriona's Cradle. The unstable and moving location of their duel meant that neither swordsmen was fighting at his best, having to swing, block and keep footing in a routinely fashion. Interjecting this was the occasional attacking spell from the hand of Vardelem, which Oscar deflected with his shield.

'Once again, I credit your tenacity, child,' Vardelem hissed, 'but your courage is nothing more than misplaced foolishness. Fighting against a golem is one thing, but taking on a mage is something else entirely.'

Vardelem hopped suddenly onto the wing of the Pedrakon and allowed it to carry him up into the air. He landed eloquently behind Oscar, and in a streak of blue light, knocked him down with a thunderbolt fired from his fingertips. Oscar shuddered uncontrollably, twitching in electrocuted shock. Vardelem grinned.

'Still, it is interesting that after travelling across a thousand years in time, the greatest challenge presented to me has been the whims of children. An unexpected and amusing twist. But I fear now the joke has reached its end. Prepare to walk the afterlife alone, as you will not find your family there. They shall remain lifeless in the world of the living, trapped in their stone prisons for all eternity.'

He raised his hand above him, and in his palm a ball of blue lightning energy began to form. He was about to strike down Oscar with a killing spell, when he was suddenly distracted.

A light as bright as the sun was moving fast across the desert. It was large, almost the size of the Pedrakon. As it got closer to the city, the light became more blinding. Vardelem squinted, unable to even see Oscar, who was beginning to regain control of his body.

Suddenly, a screeching cry, like an eagle's call, pierced both their ears. Vardelem staggered, the lightning spell in his hand fizzing into nothingness. Then the light dimmed, going out in an instant. In its place was a feathered creature, wide-winged, sharp-beaked, the colour of fire and piercing eyes of burning gold. Long feathers swept along its back, creating a tail of flames. It was the immortal guardian of the desert, the Aide of Pyriona; the Phoenix.

Oscar barely noticed the bird, however. He was more concerned with who was riding on its back. Crouched on the Phoenix's neck, staff in hand, was Lilly, glowing with an unusual aura.

The Phoenix crashed into the side of the Pedrakon, scorching its hide with its ethereal fire. The force of the clash sent Oscar flying from the dragon's back. He hurtled toward the ground, as the Pedrakon, still carrying Vardelem, spiralled into the side of the mountain. Lilly guided the Phoenix downward, aligning with the falling Oscar, and turning upward just in time for him to land gently on its back. It darted skyward, with Lilly holding Oscar's arm. The bird halted above Adhera, hovering over the city.

'Are you okay?' Lilly asked.

'Me?! What about you? You fell into that pit! And now you're here! On a… what even is this?!'

'It's the Phoenix, the spirit of the desert. I know you've probably got a million and one questions for me, and I've got a million and one things to tell you, but right now we've got a chance to put an end to this once and for all.'

Oscar looked to the mountain. An avalanche of rocks and boulders had come down on the Pedrakon, and presumably Vardelem too. A cloud of stony mist formed around the motionless dragon on the widest flat over the cliff's edge.

'You mean he's still alive?' asked Oscar.

'I think it'll take more than a knock against a cliff to end him for good. But we've weakened him. We'll never have a better chance to beat him than now.'

Oscar nodded in agreement, and knelt down beside Lilly. The Phoenix cried once more, announcing its flight toward the cliff.

Towards the Pedrakon.

Towards Vardelem.

Chapter Sixteen
The Vengeance of Mages

The Phoenix hovered low over the cliff. Lilly and Oscar scanned the cloud of dust that hung in the air following the avalanche. The Pedrakon moved warily beneath the piles of rocks and boulders. Slowly, the dust cleared, and finally they saw Vardelem, hunched over on his knees, hands clutching at the earth. He was muttering, and fingering runes into the dirt.

He looked up, eyes red with frustration and rage. He raised a shaking hand and screamed something in an ancient language. Suddenly, the Pedrakon smashed free of the rocks, and unsteadily flapped itself into flight. It moved with difficulty, clearly hurt. Its neck and arms were red with scorch marks. When it finally had its bearings, it roared at the Phoenix and charged towards it.

'Fight it!' Lilly ordered Oscar. 'Keep it distracted!'

'Wait… Where are you going?!'

Without a word, Lilly leapt from the neck of the Phoenix and landed hard on the cliff's edge. Oscar didn't have time to react as the Pedrakon collided with the Phoenix, its horned head forcing the bird backwards. Effortlessly, the Phoenix swooped backwards, looping and skirting past the dragon. Oscar, clutching for dear life on the Phoenix's back, noticed something unusual about the dragon's burn marks as they passed it. Some of its scales had been burned away, revealing fleshy red skin. Thick, sure, but not on par with its scales. It could be pierced. And if the right scales on the right part of its body were burnt, the pierce could be deadly.

Without another thought, Oscar's hand found the hilt of his sword.

The ongoing battle between the two gargantuan creatures went by almost completely unnoticed by Lilly and Vardelem, who watched each other with an unblinking focus. Vardelem was shaking and panting wildly. Lilly kept her cool, gulping back the nerves ever snowballing inside her.

'I wondered if I would find you,' Vardelem at last muttered. 'I sensed the length of time you had travelled; the aura of your mother's spell lingered after your passage. Combining that aura with my own magic made the time altering process so much easier. But it did mean following your path. A path of a thousand years.

'And Dysan; how disappointed I am to not have had the chance to kill him myself. Did he age too quickly? Get old before his time? Time magic can be devastating to non-mages. Your mother was a fool to entrust him with your protection. In my dreams, I had hoped to find you and raise you as my own, awaken you to your powers immediately. You would've been my student, my partner, and together we would have destroyed this world. Fulfilled my revenge.

'Or, should I say, *our* revenge. All mages should be avenged, even the idiotic ones who sided with lesser beings, who chose mortals over their own kind. Like your family. So-called royalty. It was their kindness that betrayed them. Their compassion that wiped out our race. But now our revenge is at hand.

'Twisted fate sent you to stop me, the guardian spirits of the world knew only you could. But it was in vein. I don't care if you are the daughter of Chyrianna and Alric, the daughter of royalty. You are a princess no longer, that died with your parents…'

He grinned as he raised his hand, launching a stream of lightning bolts from his fingers. Lilly reacted quickly, thrusting her staff forward, producing a wall of white light. It shielded her, bouncing the lightning bolts away. Vardelem stepped closer, the bolts becoming thicker and more powerful. Lilly's barrier grew thicker in turn, but her spell was draining her. Vardelem's laugh became wild, enjoying the exhausting effort Lilly was putting herself through.

'This is impressive, considering you've only had your powers revealed to you for a few hours. Truly the daughter of Chyrianna. But do not think you will be joining her in the afterlife. You will suffer the fate of the mortals of this world. You will live eternal, encased in a veil of stone!'

Suddenly, the Pedrakon's roar split the air, shifting Lilly's focus for a moment. One of Vardelem's bolts scorched her shoulder. The dragon was hovering just over the cliff's edge, eyes fixed on Lilly. Where was Oscar? Where was the Phoenix? But Lilly could not think of their fates, she needed all her concentration.

With a nod from its master, the Pedrakon let loose a continuous jet of purple fire. Endless was its breath, the flames constant in their flow. Lilly thrust her staff into the ground, twisting her wrists. The wall of white light expanded into a ball, a spherical cocoon protecting her from both Vardelem's and the dragon's spells. Sweat formed on her brow, the focus needed to maintain the barrier was agonising. She began to scream, which amused Vardelem even further.

'Your spell is weakening. In seconds, I will have to but stand aside and watch as your shell crumbles and you are petrified by the flames. Just another fallen mage, another cause for our vengeance.'

'It is not *my* vengeance,' Lilly growled. 'I will not be burdened with the deaths of a thousand mages!'

Lilly loosened her grip on her staff, and turned her tearful eyes to meet Vardelem's.

'Today, I will concern myself with only one.'

She dove forward, towards Vardelem. He didn't see where she landed, however, nor have time to look. Lilly's barrier fell almost instantly. He let out only half a scream before disappearing into a wave of purple fire.

—

Moments earlier, the Phoenix and the Pedrakon had been fighting a deadly duel. The Phoenix, through the will of Oscar, had been charging at the dragon's chest in an effort to burn away the scales surrounding its heart. However, this meant getting in close to the Pedrakon's

246

claws and teeth, and the Phoenix, as powerful as it was, was getting hurt. The scales were burning away, though, and Oscar was determined that on this final charge, he would deliver his killing strike.

The Phoenix cut through the air with vigour, spiralling to make its descent. The dragon watched it, but behaved differently this time around. As the Phoenix drew near, it opened its jaws and shot a ball of purple flames at Oscar. The Phoenix leant back, taking the force of the fireball in the chest. It didn't turn to stone; however, it was hurt by this attack, and was sent flying backwards and down to the base of the mountain.

The Phoenix clawed at the mountainside to slow its fall. It stopped finally as the slope flattened out, far beneath the Pedrakon. It panted and wheezed. Oscar looked up and saw the dragon breathing its petrifying flames upon the cliff's surface, where Lilly and Vardelem were fighting. He shook with panic.

'Please!' he pleaded to the Phoenix. 'We have to help her!'

Finding its strength once more, the Phoenix straightened itself and cut the air with a ferocious screech. It pounced from the rocks and soared upwards at a blinding speed. Oscar had to grip so tightly to its feathers that his knuckles whitened and his hands began to ache.

The Phoenix smashed into the Pedrakon from beneath, stopping its onslaught of flames. It clamped onto the dragon's wing with its beak, and forced it down to the ground. With the Phoenix on top, the dragon's arm around its neck, Oscar leapt down and drew his sword.

He made three bounding steps across the chest of the Pedrakon, before lunging forward and ramming his sword into the soft, flame-scarred tissue of its breast. He buried the blade as deep as it would go, all the way to the hilt, twisting it like a corkscrew.

The Pedrakon squirmed, jerking violently and letting out terrifying cries. Oscar was tossed backwards onto the ground as the Phoenix pulled back and hovered above. The dragon's breath became lighter, quicker and shorter. Until at last, it was no more.

The Pedrakon was dead.

Returning to his feet, Oscar gave no time for victory, and ran as fast as he could towards the flickering purple embers that decorated a new statue. He slowed and approached with some hesitance as he saw, at last, the full detail of the Pedrakon's victim. Oscar sighed in relief.

The statue's arms thrust forward, a pointless attempt to shield the face from the flames. Eyes clamped shut, mouth wide in mid-cry. Robes frozen in motion, blasted backwards from the force of the dragon's breath. It was Vardelem, cursed by his own spell.

From behind the mage's lifeless form came a cough. The cough of a young mage. Oscar rushed round and saw Lilly lying on the ground. The fringes of her coat were grey and solid. The dragon's flames had missed her only by a hair.

'I used him as a shield,' she said, sitting up. 'Pretty gutsy if you ask me.'

Oscar nodded and sat down beside her. Their eyes

met and they began to laugh in exhaustion.

Chapter Seventeen
A Moment's Respite

Jackary walked around the streets surrounding the temple. Some fifty soldiers, Pah'lin and his new best friend, Nubar, among them, were sitting on the dusty pavement, laughing and nursing wounds. All around them, amidst the chaos and destruction, were mounds of black ash. All that remained of Vardelem's golems.

The battle in the streets had been ferocious. The Adheran troops had forced the golems out onto the street, fighting away from the temple doors, blocking passage to the women and children who were still sheltered within the great hall. They also blocked the golems' path to the Magukon Codex. Jackary, looking down on the battle from the roof of the temple, rained arrows upon the ashen warriors from on high. The tide had turned in their favour, but the fact remained: the golems' number was eternal. They continued to be reborn, and continued to relentlessly attack. The soldiers' last push from the temple was admirable, and encouraging, but alas, utterly in vain. Fatigue would catch up with them once again when Jackary's potion finally wore off, and the mage's husks would best them at last.

A glimmer of hope returned though, when the golem forces seemingly lost their power to regenerate.

There had been flashes of brilliant light coming from the mountains. A dragon and a Phoenix battled in the air. Such brilliant sights, thought Jackary. As Lilly and Oscar continued their fight with Vardelem, his power over his army was failing, and their collective focus was fading fast. When, at last, things seemed to reach a crescendo on the mountain and the dragon seemed to fall and roar its last, the golem army slowed to a halt, before dissolving into nothingness, little more than dust blowing in the wind.

Jackary returned to the street and lost himself among the crowds. The Adheran soldiers all praised the alchemist and his miracle potion, patting Jackary's back and wrangling him into hugs. He did not join them in their rejoice, however. Everything was too quiet. Where were his friends? Where were Lilly and Oscar?

Pah'lin found him in the crowd.

'I'm sure they're okay, son,' he said quietly.

'I know. If anyone can survive a bout with a dragon, it's Oscar. And Lilly's too stubborn to die.'

'Come, get a drink of water. Rest a while. We'll organise a search party to climb the mountain.'

'No need,' said Nubar, walking up beside them. 'That bloody big bird is bringing them down now.'

Jackary and Pah'lin turned to face the mountain.

251

Nubar was right. Soaring down towards the city was the flame-feathered Phoenix, and upon its back were Lilly and Oscar. It swooped in a circle, landing with a flourish outside the temple. Some of the soldiers cautiously rose to their feet, but Jackary pushed through the rabble and ran to his friends.

Dismounting the Phoenix, Lilly turned and touched the bird's beak.

'I will burden you no longer, Lord Phoenix,' she said humbly. 'You have done as Milda promised, you have protected Adhera and the desert, and now you must return. We shall all be eternally grateful.'

Lilly bowed, as did Oscar and Jackary. It squawked heroically, then with three enormous flaps of its wings, it rose high into the air and flew off into the desert. It soon became the colour of the sun, and disappeared in a burning light.

Jackary, remaining still for only a second, grabbed his friends by the scruff of their necks and hugged them tightly. The friends, once again reunited, savoured the embrace.

Pah'lin burst into tears, which received a few shocked looks from the surrounding crowd. Nubar raised a scoffing eyebrow. Then, building with a ripple, the crowd erupted into applause.

'You did it!' Pah'lin whimpered. 'You bloody well did it! All three of you!'

The cheering peaked when the Sultan, Lord Eirron, joined the crowd with his wife, Lady Ilga. He was his usual chuckling self, waving and winking at everyone he passed. He approached the children.

'You tried to warn us,' he said to them, making sure his counsellors could hear. 'About this mage and his dragon. We thought we could defend the city, ignored your warnings. And it nearly cost us everything. But you followed your wisdom, and thank Pyriona you did. Even the great Phoenix, the spirit of the desert, could see the wisdom of your words. To cut a long, grovelling speech of gratitude short: thank you. Adhera owes you a debt I could never hope to repay.'

'We are honoured by your praise,' said Lilly, bowing, 'however, our mission is far from over.'

'Honeydale…' Oscar said, turning to face her.

Lilly nodded. 'Lord Eirron, we need to return to Vhirmaa immediately. Is there a quicker way out of the desert than by the train?'

'There is, by cutting across the dunes on dorataurs. It's a hard ride over the uneven desert, but its more direct than the safer train route.'

A few short words later, Eirron had summoned his best riders to escort Lilly, Oscar and Jackary across the desert.

Jackary readied Urug's saddle as it slurped cheerfully from a puddle of his spilled miracle potion. Lilly had hastily filled Oscar and Pah'lin in about what she had learned from Milda, sparing some details for a more convenient time. Even now, as sure of the truth as she was, where she came from, her true self, it still seemed fantastical. She couldn't blame Oscar or Pah'lin then for their expressions of disbelief that grew as she spoke.

'A mage?' Pah'lin kept repeating.

'Yes, Captain,' answered Lilly. 'Which, above all else, means we might at last have a chance to save Honeydale.'

'You're sure?'

'I... I can't be sure of anything, truth be told. I barely understand it all myself. But the stone we found in the desert... I can still feel its power. I know only two things for certain: only magic can reverse magic, and no spell is irreversible. The dragon's curse *can* be undone, and I *am* a mage.'

'But... really?'

The conversation looped like this for a while, with a lot of repeating questions and increasingly cryptic answers. Oscar, despite all he had seen, still had his doubts. However, he was at this moment focused on only one thing: saving his family. And so, once his patience had run out and the riders were ready to leave, he ushered Lilly and Jackary onto Urug, and Pah'lin to a dorataur, and they left the city for the Narrow Canyon.

The Sultan, his wife, Nubar, and all the citizens of Adhera hailed praise at them as they rode off into the desert. It was hard for the children not to feel a little pleased with themselves after what they had endured. They had saved the city.

Now it was time to save another.

Chapter Eighteen
A Cure from the Clouds

They emerged on the greener side of the Narrow Canyon shortly after dawn. All of them were tired, in desperate need of food, drink and sleep. Lots of sleep. Not one of them would admit to being tired, though. Perhaps because none of them even noticed. Anxiety, giddiness, and equal doses of optimism and pessimism were driving the troupe.

Galloping ahead was Urug, carrying Jackary on his back, with Oscar and Lilly tucked into the makeshift saddlebag-seats on either side of the kingly pig. Pah'lin was bringing up the rear astride a dorataur that had proven to be every bit as sturdy and hard-riding as Lord Eirron had promised.

Their journey across the desert from Adhera hadn't taken as long as anticipated. They had departed well into the night, a blanket of stars in a clear black sky lighting their way. The convoy of Eirron's riders that guided them from the city gates had led them across quicker paths that snaked over and around the deeps and shallows of Adhera's sandy seas. It was a difficult ride, but a lot more direct, and a quicker route to the entrance of the Narrow Canyon than circumnavigating the flat sands the train tracks lay upon. After a few short hours, just as the sky was beginning to threaten the arrival of the sun, they arrived at the gaping jaws of the canyon, where their Adheran guides left them.

Thankfully, there were no appearances from the odious gnolls that had attacked them while travelling through the canyon before. Either it was too early for them to be going about the business of attacking travellers, or they were still licking their wounds from the hiding this particular party of heroes had given them just a few days prior. Whatever their reasons, they did not appear. And so, after an hour of following the tracks through the grey, rocky walls looming over them, they eventually stood on the green grasses of Vhirmaa once again.

They didn't bother to stop to get teary-eyed and nostalgic about being back, however; their mission was not yet over. Speed and urgency propelled them across the green fields and grassy meadows. The sky above them, an almost luminous blue, held the sun aloft, the only feature in the cloudless sky. By midday, they were already approaching the Golden Forest.

Jackary wondered if Lady Erdolet could sense his presence, could sense what was about to happen. They all did, in fact: Lilly and Oscar too. Oscar asked Erdolet, with a quiet thought, to bring speed to Urug's legs, for he knew that just beyond the hills ahead of them stood the petrified prison of Hylkoven. And his family. His mother, the ever loving Tryca. His father, Old Sea Grubb. Baby Amber, would she remember what had happened to her? Borris and Norris, heavens! He even missed them. Missed their teasing and joking. Yes, even their belching competitions. What horrible fates befell them. But now, Oscar was close once again, and with a means to save them. With the help of his friend, Lilly. A mage.

Urug grunted wearily as he ascended the hills and mounds of Vhirmaa. The High Lord of All Swine was he, and that title was truly being tested. Never had the pig been ridden so hard, and his trotters were unfamiliar with the grassy terrain of the dales to boot! He was bred to traverse the dunes, to endure blistering heats and biting sandstorms. Even in this sunny, summer Vhirmean day, that most would find more than pleasant, poor Urug was positively chilly. Still, sensing the urgency of his riders' charge, he pushed himself harder and further until, at last, he stood at the top of the hill, revealing the lifeless husk that was Hylkoven, devoid of the vibrancy and joy the city affectionately named Honeydale was famed for.

They all stopped for a moment, pitying this tragic sight. They were nervous, almost afraid to take another step closer. Oscar peered over Urug's head to look at Lilly. She didn't return the look, but instead climbed out of the saddlebag-seat and started to walk down the dirt path. Oscar and the others watched her for a moment, before slowly following behind, allowing Lilly to lead the way.

She could feel their eyes on her back, but she just stared ahead with unblinking determination. She had been struggling to push aside a splitting headache that had been burdening her since her battle with Vardelem upon the cliffs of Pyriona's Cradle. Great focus and concentration was what Milda had told her was needed to produce magic, to control it, and she most certainly gave all she had to shield herself from Vardelem's spells. She was drained, exhausted. Her magic-making was not yet over with, though. She swallowed back the mounting nerves within. She couldn't entertain the notion of failing. She had the Deystona spell, absorbed from the ancient crystal. Her staff would guide her, act as a conduit, allow her to unleash the power only she possessed. Only she could reverse the curse. Only she could save Honeydale. She could not fail.

She would not fail.

It wasn't long, although it seemed like an eternity, before she stood in front of the towering South Gate, the place where she had first spoken to Oscar. Where she had told him that everything would be okay. That they could fix this. Her eyes fell instantly to Oscar's father, the brave man who had tossed both children through the gate, saving them from their curse. A curse that he was victim to, standing in a mid-run pose, his arms arched forward. Close behind was Tryca, Oscar's mother, fear frozen upon her face, holding his baby sister close to her chest. Lilly turned and saw Oscar dismount from Urug's side. He took three short steps, and froze at the sight of his family. His eyes welled with tears, and his hands began to shake. He opened his mouth to speak, but his throat dried in an instant and stole any words before they could escape his mouth.

'Oscar,' Lilly said, forcing his eyes to meet hers. She said nothing more, but instead offered him a smile, faint and warm. Oscar nodded, bowing his head. With that cue, Lilly took the staff from her back.

She raised it high in front of her, closed her eyes, and for a few moments, there was nothing but an unnatural silence. No wind rustled the long grass, no birds sang or frogs croaked. Silence. Then, without warning, a flash of green blinded them all. It dimmed into an emerald orb that quivered and pulsated at the end of her staff. Slowly, the wind returned with mounting force, and blew from all directions towards Lilly. Her hair and clothes flew to and fro wildly in the strengthening gusts, yet the staff and her grip upon it remained steady and firm. Clouds formed out of nowhere in the sky above them, sculpted in shapes unusual to most clouds. As leaves and blades of grass formed a typhoon around her, the orb of green light grew bigger and bigger, brighter and brighter. Just when the light grew almost too bright to look at it, it shot from the staff like an emerald shooting star, beaming towards the sky and piercing the cluster of clouds that now spiralled in symmetry with the wind. The orb disappeared behind the blanket of pale grey they had created, and with a final flash of green, they slowed to a halt. As did the wind. And the grass and leaves. Again, there was silence.

But not for long.

A noise like thunder cracked the air, and from behind the veil of clouds, flashes of green lightning threatened a storm. Jackary felt the first drop. It landed hard on the crown of shaggy hair upon his head. He touched it, examined his fingers, and saw that it was rain. But unusual rain. It reflected the sun with a green tinge. Another drop fell a few feet in front of him. He was sure this time. It was definitely green. Within seconds, they had all seen the large tears of rain fall from the clouds. With a final roar of thunder, the clouds gave way to a downpour, shining brightly and lyrically, like stars falling from the heavens. It engulfed Hylkoven, drenching the city from spire to gutter. And what Oscar saw next made him fall to his knees.

The greyness of the stone shells trapping his family, all the citizens of Honeydale, and the city itself, began to fall away. But not like stone ought to, with chipping and sharding, but instead like wallpaper being stripped from an old wall. It peeled off in small pieces, flickering and turning to dust in the wind, revealing bit by bit, the familiar colours of the city. The magnolia walls of its towers, the vibrant greens, reds and yellows of the festival decorations. And then, the red hair of his mother. Her blue eyes. His father too, with his red, sunburned dome of a head. Amber's pink little hand, her chubby digits reaching out from her blanket. The identical brown hair of his twin cousins, Borris and Norris. He half expected to hear a belch from one of their mouths as the stone peeled away. Still motionless, the entire city had its colour returned to it, and the people no longer looked like fearful statues.

The clouds began to disappear into nothingness, and the rain slowed to only a few drops. Finally, the last drop fell, and as it hit the ground, a noise echoed around the city. Not the most pleasant of noises. Screaming, in fact. The recognisable screams from the night the city was cursed. And then, movement. The continued hurried steps that began too on that fateful night. But the screaming and the running ended as quickly it began, and was replaced by overwhelming confusion. Mutterings and chattering and many a 'What the...?' hopped from one mouth to another. 'Where's the bleedin' dragon?', 'Wasn't it just night a second ago?', 'Why have I got cramp?'

Questions piled upon questions reverberated around the walls of Hylkoven. But none of that was important. All that mattered, to Oscar, Lilly, Jackary and Pah'lin, was that the people they cared about, the people they loved, their friends, families, and neighbours, were once again themselves. Free from Petrification. The curse had been lifted.

The spell had been reversed.

Oscar stood by Lilly, completely speechless. She, too, was in a similar state. Only Jackary offered a word or two.

'Have they seen you yet?' he asked Oscar. 'Your family?'

'They haven't,' Oscar smiled.

'Then don't you think you should go to them?' Lilly smirked, putting her hand on his arm. He nodded, and took a step forward, but turned before running off.

'No words could ever stress this enough, but thank you. Both of you.'

With that he ran through the city gates. Jackary and

Lilly shared a knowing grin, and were joined a moment later by Pah'lin. He said nothing, as was his style, but bowed ever slightly in a gesture of humility.

'Not bad for a couple of feeble, snot-sniffing children, huh Pah'lin?' she said, scoffing.

'Yes, young Lilly, not bad at all.'

They slowly walked through the South Gate, and watched Oscar reunite with his family. His mother had him in an affectionate headlock, kissing his face and dripping tears on his head. His father, Old Grubb, was drying his eyes with his moustache, and Borris and Norris were doing likewise on his kilt. Oscar pulled himself away from his mother's grasp and held Amber in his arms, bouncing her about and pinching her cheeks.

Lilly and Jackary agreed it would be polite to introduce themselves, but thought it best not to interrupt this family reunion just yet. Pah'lin, forever duty bound, informed them he was going to find King Mallon, but told them not to stray far. He was sure the King would have questions for them.

The King, and everyone else in Honeydale.

Chapter Nineteen
A City Renewed

Hylkoven was in a state of riotous celebration. But not immediately so. In the hours following the curing rain, families and friends were reunited, waking from a terrible sleep at long last. Confusion and weariness clung to the people of the city, and more questions than answers filled their heads. Soon, the people rallied in the Royal Square, upon the ruins of the Grande Show that had been the source of their curse. They demanded answers, and it was presumed their king would have them.

Before long, the good King Mallon ascended the great balcony, took his place in the Royal Box and addressed his people.

'Good people of Hylkoven. Good, frightened, tired people of Honeydale. I feel your pains. I feel your fears. You have many questions, and I pray my answers satisfy them. Firstly, what of the dragon? What indeed. I have assurance from my Captain of the Royal Guard, the honourable Pah'lin, that the dragon was slain upon the mountains of Adhera. So, too, was the beast's vile master, the sorcerer who claimed to be a *mage*, also bested upon the mountainside, consumed by the flames of his own dragon, a victim to his own curse. A truer justice could surely not be had.

'This is what I know to be true. I have been advised by those most knowledgeable in these matters that this was indeed magic, but that with this so-called mage defeated, we have nothing more to fear. The ones responsible for his defeat - surprising individuals to say the least - will be commended, rewarded for their heroic deeds, and in the days to come you will learn their names and hail them from the rooftops. So please, as best you can, try not to fret and worry about what has already happened, and instead rejoice, and be merry at current circumstances. We have been saved from a curse, and, at last, my birthday celebrations can continue!'

Roars of laughter and applause met the King's jolly quip. Of course, many were unsatisfied with this all too brief address from their ruler. But what more could the King tell them? He omitted the fact that one of the individuals responsible for defeating Vardelem was, in fact, a mage herself. That she had cast her own spell upon the city. Magic had both cursed and saved Hylkoven alike. He concealed these facts after careful consideration, following a very secretive and intense council.

The King, upon awaking from his petrified state, did as all others did and grasped his family for dear life. As quickly as possible, he was returned to his palace and within a matter of hours, his responsibilities as ruler of Vhirmaa were thrust upon him. He summoned a council. All his chief advisers, scholars and generals alike were to be present. So, too, his Captain of the Guard, Pah'lin, and his three charges, Oscar, Lilly and Jackary.

Oscar was last to arrive, his mother more than reluctant to let him leave Mrs Gallow's Inn. Pah'lin stressed the importance of this meeting, and conceded to allow her to accompany her son to the palace, but told her she would have to wait outside the throne room while the council was in session. Some haggling later, it was agreed that the entire family would accompany Oscar, and that they would sit outside the throne room so long as the door was left open just a slither, as not to miss anything.

When, at last, Oscar did arrive, following Pah'lin into the throne room, Lilly was in the middle of being berated by an elderly, scholarly-looking man, who was foaming at the mouth as his screechy voice hit devastating tones.

'Not only did you break into the palace, rob us blindly of a most valued and treasured possession, a relic unbeknownst to most, but you are also in actual fact a mage yourself, capable of the same horrors that Vardellow wizard damn well nearly ruined us all with?!'

'No!' Lilly argued, 'that's not it at all. Yes, I took the Magukon Codex, but only when Vardelem's golems appeared looking for the book as well. Had I not taken it, it would've fallen into his hands, and who knows what further horrors he would've brought to you and the world.'

'Horrors you too are capable of!' the old scholar spat.

'No, I'm not! I am a mage, yes. A wielder of magic. But Vardelem was evil, whereas I am not. A little short tempered from time to time, I'll admit, but far from wicked. Magic in and of itself is not evil, so my being a mage should cause you no concern.'

'I will vouch for that,' Pah'lin interrupted. 'Lilly Rachert is a good and honourable sort, and whether you like or not, she is the saviour of Hylkoven. Together with this boy here, Oscar Grubb and…' Pah'lin searched the room. 'Where's Jackary?'

'I'm here,' Jackary said, leafing through the pages of a book in a dark corner of the room. He scrambled to his feet and sauntered over to stand next to Oscar and Lilly. 'They've been at each other's throats for ages. I got bored so thought I'd go have a sit down. Anyway, you were about to tell the good King how I'm a hero and such.'

'Yes,' Pah'lin chuckled. 'Jackary Stiltz. One of three. These three, your Highness. These noble children, the ones who had the intelligence to seek the aid of the Guardian Spirits, to use the book, and turn Vardelem's own magic against him. They defeated that monster and his dragon, and I would stake my reputation that all three of them are the furthest thing from evil in this room. Including Lilly Rachert, whose own magic lifted this curse.'

King Mallon sat back in his throne, scratching the edge of his beard. His scholarly advisor was shaking with rage, speechless that the Captain of the Royal

Guard would come to the aid of a magic wielding witch!

'Be that as it may,' he snarled, 'the people will not accept that, regardless of what you stake, honourable Pah'lin. Magic will raise nothing but fear in the people of Hylkoven, whether it brought them a curse or a cure. Rumour will spread of spells cast by a young witchlet, and they will fear your *noble* Lilly Rachert, and demand she be locked in a cell. Or worse.'

'Rumours started by you?' Pah'lin growled.

'Enough!' King Mallon yelled, standing up from his throne. 'I will not have this council turn into a brawl. I have half the city congregating on the Royal Square, demanding answers from their King. And I must deliver them, promptly. So kindly stop this bickering and assist me on reaching some conclusions.

Pah'lin and the scholar bowed apologetically.

'Now,' continued the king, 'when it comes to Lilly Rachert, I see it like this: I am willing to pardon your burglary of the secret library, whether it was accidental or not. Your leaving the palace with that book seems to have worked out best for all concerned, and so I will turn a blind eye to your giving my palace guard the merry run around.

'That being said, if you are indeed a mage, I fear I cannot go out there and tell the people of this city that they've had not one, but two spells cast upon them in little over a week. My learned friend here is correct, in a way, and therefore I will not be informing them of that truth. I would advise you to do likewise, and keep your being a magic wielder to yourself. Not only for your own safety, but to save my people from running around in a blind panic.

'The more fantastical elements of your tale will be attributed to the Goddess of Flame and Light, Pyriona, which wouldn't be an altogether lie.

'Unlike my esteemed council, however, I will not judge you for being a mage. There is no way of getting around it; your magic saved us. Saved us all. And for that, you shall be rewarded. Before we come to that, however, there is the matter of returning the Magukon Codex…'

'I'll stop you there,' Lilly shrugged, holding up her hands. The council members were aghast. 'I mean no disrespect, but I ask for only one thing as a reward. I ask that you permit me to keep the Codex. Try to understand; I have only just discovered these powers, discovered my true heritage. For every question your council has asked me, I have a thousand more. I beg of you, if I am to be rewarded, allow me to keep the one thing I have that links me to my past.'

The scholar scoffed, turning to his King with a smirk. His smirk quickly began to diminish, however. King Mallon was actually considering this proposal.

'Sire, you can't!'

'Oh, but I can,' King Mallon replied quietly. 'And indeed, I think I shall. Fine, a fair trade I feel. I consider you a friend to Vhirmaa, and I trust my friends not to do ill unto my realm, least of all my beloved Honeydale. It is important that we all know who we are, and where we fit in this world. It would be beyond me to keep you from discovering that. Take the book, and may it serve you well. I couldn't read the bloody thing anyhow.'

'Thank you, your Highness.' Lilly curtsied, surprisingly quite expertly too. Oscar and Jackary chuckled at her sudden ability to be courteous.

'And for yourself, brave Jackary Stiltz, what reward could the King of Vhirmaa offer you?'

'Well, your excellency, I won't ask for much. I'm a chap of simple pleasures. I am pretty keen to get a nosey around this secret library, though. I mean, beyond that Codex there, I bet there are a few interesting reads to be found. So, free reign in the *Not-So*-Secret Library, if you please.

'Also, I wouldn't mind having a sift through your pantries. As an alchemist, I'm always looking to get an ogle at some new ingredients. And lastly, a chunk o' change wouldn't go amiss either. Following this adventure, I've developed something of an appetite for exploration, and for a life on the road I'm going to need a little coin.'

'Hmmm, won't ask for much, eh?' the King giggled quietly. 'So be it! Not so tall an order, I suppose. But the Secret Library is named as such for a reason, so the books you read there will be kept there, as will their contents.' The scholarly aide took a seat, deflated and defeated.

'And lastly, young Master Grubb,' King Mallon began. 'What could I offer you?'

'Actually, your Highness,' Pah'lin interrupted once again, 'I have some thoughts on a fitting reward for Oscar, but I would have to discuss it with him and his family first.'

'Very interesting. So be it, return to me later after

269

your discussions.'

Oscar looked at Pah'lin curiously; he had no idea what this reward could be. Actually, he hadn't even considered a reward at all.

'Now, before I address the good people of Honeydale,' the King said, stepping down from the raised platform his throne sat upon and approaching the children, 'I would like to offer you my sincerest thanks. You will hereby be known to me as the Heroes of Hylkoven, and I shall never forget the great deeds you have done for my city. Nor will anyone else.'

Without another word, King Mallon bowed quite eloquently before the children, and his advisers and aides did likewise. Including Pah'lin, who was aware Oscar was still staring at him, trying to work out his reward. Pah'lin tilted his bowed head to Oscar's ear, and whispered something. A huge grin crossed Oscar's face, and his eyes became excited.

Soon after this meeting, King Mallon made his address, and eventually, the people of Hylkoven began to celebrate their liberation. Luckily, with the whole curse occurring on the night of the King's Birthday Celebrations, the city was already prepared for a party of epic proportions. Soon, the streets became rivers of ale and cider, and choruses of cheery songs bounced from wall to wall, from the palace walls to the South Gate, to the dockyard, where drunken show-offs leapt from piers completely in the nip into the cool sea water, turning baritones to sopranos in an instant.

Meanwhile, in one of many bed chambers in the palace, Lilly and Jackary were talking about this, that and everything that had occurred. Several hours had passed since their council with the King, and they hadn't seen Oscar since. Pah'lin had whisked him off with his family to discuss this mysterious reward.

'It's curious, isn't it?' Jackary said all of a sudden, lying on the bed, staring at the ceiling. 'How you and I would share in this adventure together, and both of us are sketchy at best when it comes to our families.'

'I suppose,' Lilly agreed, sitting back against the wall, the Magukon Codex open on her lap. 'The thought did occur to me. Who knows, perhaps you're a mage too?'

'No, I don't think so. I'm old, for sure. But not by a thousand years. I remember having a mother, and I remember being taught alchemy by... someone. And I remember a potion, a potion unlike any other. I'm certain that potion is what caused me to stop ageing and played havoc with my memory.'

'Does it bother you?'

'Not really. It can be frustrating at times, but my concern for that potion is much the same as your concern for that book. I'm just worried I've accidentally made myself immortal, and if the wrong person had that power, well...' He tailed off, his thoughts taking him places he didn't bother to share. 'Heck, perhaps we'll find out on our next world spanning quest!'

'Perhaps! Well, maybe the books in the Secret Library will tell you something.'

'Maybe. Maybe not. It'd help, but really, that's not why I've asked to snoop around in there. My main concern with that library is its name. You can't call something the *Secret* whatever, and not expect me to go in there. It's like handing me a cake and asking me not to eat it. Insanity!'

They both laughed, and after a moment of quieting down, the door opened and in walked a very pleased-with-himself looking Oscar. He rushed over to them, excited and bouncing like it was his birthday.

'Lilly! Jackary! You're not going to believe it!'

'What?!' Lilly gasped, caught by surprise.

'Your reward! What is it?' Jackary asked.

'Oh, my reward! Oh blazes! Are you ready for this? I'm going to join the Royal Guard!'

A stunned silence. Of the million and one things Lilly and Jackary had been hypothesising this reward could be, a *job* was not on the list.

'You're a bit young, aren't you?' asked Lilly, raising an eyebrow.

'Well, there are a few years of training, so I'll only be an apprentice for a while. But still! I'll be a noble knight, sworn protector of the realm! Just like…'

'Hendal Bowstalk!' Jackary screamed, before bouncing off the bed and grabbing Oscar by the arm. They skipped about the room, exclaiming over the exploits of Hendal Bowstalk.

'Hendal who?' Lilly asked, her nose wrinkling in unknowing.

'Bowstalk! The greatest knight that ever lived!' Oscar snapped.

'Oh, that stupid book you both like.'

'"*Ooh, look at me with my thousand-year-old magic book, I'm too hoity-toity to read silly adventures!*"'

Jackary sang, prodding his nose up with his thumb.

They all laughed, although Lilly was a little cheesed off at his impression. Eventually, Oscar and Jackary stopped gushing about Hendal Bowstalk, and all three of them sat on the floor as the hours grew later.

'It took some convincing,' Oscar explained. 'I didn't think my mother would go for it. She didn't let go of me for the entire conversation. My father was rather reluctant too, although he's always been that way. Trying to steer me off an adventurous path. Pah'lin talked them round, though. They've agreed to stay in Honeydale over the summer, until I start my guard training. Although I believe my father is currently adding some conditions to the contract.'

'What kind of conditions?' Lilly asked.

'Fishing conditions, mostly. He'll let me do my guard training so long as I keep up with fishing. Doesn't want me forgetting my roots.'

'Well, roots are important,' Lilly said cryptically, but with a smile.

'Yes, they are,' agreed Jackary.

'Well, with that in mind, what's your plan now Lilly? What's next in the life of a mage?'

'I'm going to head to the Golden Forest, leaving first thing tomorrow morning. I'm going to see if Erdolet can help me make sense of this book, and of everything else. Like before, I'll follow Dysan's wishes, and learn all there is to learn about magic, but now I know why it was so important to him. And to me.'

'Well I hope you come back to visit often,' Oscar nodded, smiling warmly at her. 'What about you Jack?

Life on the road, was it?'

'I'm going to accompany Lilly to the Golden Forest, just to check in. I have to let Lady Erdolet know that I'm all right, and make sure that Chifu hasn't eaten me out of house and home. But I'll be back again in a day or two to get started on taking that Secret Library apart.'

'Don't forget to keep an eye on that Gombaroth!' Oscar laughed.

'Oh, he better toe the line if I'm going to be there for a while,' added Lilly. Within seconds, all three children were hysterically recounting their encounter with the fungal menace, and how they came to be known as the *Champions of the Golden Forest.*

They talked the entire night, reminiscing on every aspect of their adventure. Finally, when the hour grew especially late, and Jackary had collapsed on the floor as if whacked on the head by sleep, Oscar said goodnight and exited out into the hall. Lilly stopped him, and kissed him on the cheek.

'I told you we'd fix it,' she smiled.

Oscar returned her smile. 'Thank you, Lilly. For everything.'

Chapter Twenty
A Familiar Road

The sky was burning red with the morning's new sun. Jackary was busy fiddling with the saddlebags strapped to Urug, who snorted and sniffed uncomfortably. Occasionally, he would pull a small watch from his pocket, and then assess the sun's position in the sky.

'She best be quick,' he said to the pig. 'Daylight's burning, and we want to hit the Golden Forest by dinner time.'

Right on cue, Lilly's footsteps clip-clawed up the cobblestone road, alerting Jackary to her coming. She appeared next to him, standing in the arch of the South Gate. Before them lay the dirt road that split the green of the fields and hills of the dales. The path that had begun their quest to lift the curse from Hylkoven, as well as seeing that quest's end.

Now the path promised the beginning of an all new adventure for Lilly. A quest with more questions than answers, about her family, Dysan, magic and the mages. It would also mean living a secret life. She could never share her newly discovered powers with anyone. Magic had all of a sudden shot from myth to reality, in a devastating way, and was currently a word to be feared around the world. She would heed the advice of King Mallon in this regard, and never tell anyone of her true heritage. She was a mage, and as it stood, the only one in existence. It would be easier to ignore her powers, pretend she wasn't one, but really, that wasn't an option. She had initially come to Hylkoven with a promise to her grandfather, that she would learn all there was to learn about magic, and now, with the Magukon Codex in hand, she would finally make good on that promise.

And so, she had quickly made up her mind to train; to learn the language of the mages, read the Codex cover to cover, and become the best possible mage she could be. She would start by asking the assistance of Erdolet, Guardian of the Golden Forest, with her infinite wisdom and knowledge of the world. She suspected that she would then return to the buried temple in Adhera, to speak once more with Milda. She wondered if she might lift the curse upon the Elves, too, one day. She knew not yet the limits of her powers, if indeed there were any, and this made her burst with anxious optimism.

'Ready to go then?' Jackary asked, climbing onto the back of Urug, breaking Lilly's train of thought.

'I am.' She packed a few things into the saddle bags, and fastened the strap on her shoulder, tightening her staff against her back. 'Let's hit the road.'

They stepped out onto the dirt road, crossing the

threshold of the South Gate. But were stopped in their tracks after only a few feet by the sound of their names being called from within the city. They turned to see Oscar running up the path, excitedly waving his arms.

Lilly, who had been walking alongside Urug, broke away and walked slowly towards Oscar. He ran out onto the dirt path, panting hard, but grinning wildly.

'I couldn't let you both leave without saying a proper goodbye,' he gasped.

'I thought we said our goodbyes last night?' Jackary mumbled, mostly to himself.

'Well, we did,' Oscar nodded, 'and we didn't. A quick "cheerio" is okay for you and I, Jack, as I'll see you again in a few days when you return. But Lilly…'

He broke off as his eyes met Lilly's. His words had once again escaped him. Lilly's expression was similar. Again, this road… Only days before, Oscar had stood where Lilly was standing, staring at the petrified city of Hylkoven and the motionless stone statues of his cursed family. He had been alone, scared, and lost.

But only for a moment.

Lilly had offered him a kindness, embraced him and given him hope. If not for that hug, if not for her words, Oscar would have crumbled, fallen apart right then and there on that dirt road. In an instant, his destiny had changed, and all because at that moment Lilly had made the choice not to walk away. She had chosen to be Oscar's friend. Oscar's family. Oscar's hope.

Oscar could now see the same fear he had felt in Lilly; her lip was quivering, suppressing the tears that were reddening her eyes, and so he did the only thing he could do.

He stepped forward, extended his arms, and hugged her.

'It's okay,' he whispered. 'Everything's going to be okay.'

Lilly returned the hug, and allowed herself a few tears, before backing away and straightening herself. She cleared her throat and smiled at Oscar.

'I'll be back soon enough,' she began. 'Back to see if you've made any impact on these guards. Breaking in and out of that palace was far too easy.'

'Making that Secret Library secure from burglars will be my first priority as a Royal Guard. Especially the *little girl* ones.'

'Careful who you're calling "little", Oscar. I'm All-Powerful now.'

'Indeed, you are. Just try and not blow the world up or anything.'

'At least not until he's graduated as a full-fledged Royal Guard,' Jackary jested.

They all laughed and joked and teased each other for a time, delaying the inevitable parting of ways. Soon, though, they all agreed that the morning wasn't getting any earlier, and as the city began to awaken, and the hustle and bustle of the market stalls opening up shop echoed around the city, Lilly and Jackary guided Urug down the dirt road, leaving Oscar standing by the city gate.

He watched them for a while, until the path steered them in the direction of the small cluttering of trees. Roark Stoneheart's house. He would pay him a visit soon, take his father to see him. They would get on like a house on fire, he thought.

Before long, Lilly, Jackary and Urug were little more than black dots against a green canvas, and so he turned back into the city. He looked ahead and saw his father debating the finer points of bait selection with a stout fishmonger.

Catching his eye, Oscar smiled. His mother wasn't far behind, holding baby Amber. And there, having yet another in a long series of belching competitions, were his cousins Borris and Norris.

As Oscar walked slowly towards them, he decided that first he would deliver the mother of all burps, reigning supreme over his cousins, becoming the only kind of hero they could ever respect. Then he would suggest a fishing trip in the afternoon, and tell his father of how he cast his line and caught a dragon.